SHERRI L. KING

RAYVEN'S Awakening

ELLORA'S CAVE
ROMANTICA PUBLISHING

An Ellora's Cave Romantica Publication

www.ellorascave.com

Rayven's Awakening

ISBN #141995315X

Edited by: Christina M. Brashear & Heather Osborn
Cover art by: Darrell King

Electronic book Publication: August, 2002
Trade paperback Publication: July, 2005

Warning:

The following material contains graphic sexual content meant for mature readers. *Rayven's Awakening* has been rated *S-ensuous* by a minimum of three independent reviewers.

Ellora's Cave Publishing offers three levels of Romantica™ reading entertainment: S (S-ensuous), E (E-rotic), and X (X-treme).

S-e*nsuous* love scenes are explicit and leave nothing to the imagination.

E-*rotic* love scenes are explicit, leave nothing to the imagination, and are high in volume per the overall word count. In addition, some E-rated titles might contain fantasy material that some readers find objectionable, such as bondage, submission, same sex encounters, forced seductions, etc. E-rated titles are the most graphic titles we carry; it is common, for instance, for an author to use words such as "fucking", "cock", "pussy", etc., within their work of literature.

X-*treme* titles differ from E-rated titles only in plot premise and storyline execution. Unlike E-rated titles, stories designated with the letter X tend to contain controversial subject matter not for the faint of heart.

Also by Sherri L. King:

Bachelorette
Beyond Illusion
Fetish
Manaconda (anthology)
Midnight Desires (anthology)
Moon Lust
Moon Lust: Bitten
Moon Lust: Mating Season
Moon Lust: Feral Heat
Sanctuary (Quickie)
Sin and Salvation
The Horde Wars: Ravenous
The Horde Wars: Wanton Fire
The Horde Wars: Razor's Edge
The Horde Wars: Lord of the Deep
The Jewel
Twisted Destiny (anthology)

Raven's Awakening
Chronicles of the Aware

Prologue

She was blinded by the iridescent colors glinting within his midnight feathers. He was by far the largest bird she had ever seen. He had the predatory features of a hawk, or falcon—a dangerous bird of prey, but he was even larger than the bald eagle she'd once seen housed in a zoo. His eyes were molten silver, their gaze full of dark promise and an intelligence that was belied by his bestial appearance. He was power and beauty in its purest form.

Warily she regarded the bird before her, shoving her long tresses away from her face. He sat perched upon the foot of her bed, calm and serene. He looked for all the world as if this was a common occurrence for him—as if he flew into many a sleeping fifteen-year-old's bedroom in the dark of night.

"How'd you get in here, fella?" she whispered.

He gazed back at her, a noticeable warmth and hunger entering his molten eyes. His sharp beak opened. *"Do not be afraid, you are only dreaming,"* he seemed to say.

Rayven clutched the comforter to her throat. His silky voice was pure sorcery—deep and textured like velvet. It echoed hauntingly, not aloud in the night air, but rather in her mind.

"I hope this *is* a dream," she said shakily, more to herself than to the giant bird, "or else I'm really losing it." Her genius's brain refused to believe in the existence of a telepathic bird actually dwelling beyond the plane of her dreams.

"You are dreaming," came his voice again in her mind, "but you need to wake up now. They are coming for you."

"What? Who's coming for me?"

"Our enemies. Yours, and therefore mine. They seek to destroy you. But I am here and I will keep you safe. Just do as I command and awaken now."

Rayven looked around the moonlit room, at the menace of light and shadow. "Man, this is a vivid dream. Even for me."

The bird flapped its wings ominously, ruffling her hair and the bedclothes. He came at her swiftly from his perch at her feet, and one of his razor-sharp talons struck out wildly, leaving a bleeding furrow down her arm. Crying out, she flailed at it, seeking to escape the confines of the bed. At her panicked actions, the bird immediately settled its bulk once again at her feet, looking calm and unaffected, not a feather out of place.

"You will awaken now." His voice echoed in dulcet tones within her mind. She felt compelled to obey its iron command despite her fear.

"Awaken!" he commanded again.

Rayven Smith gasped awake, shooting upright in her bed. She glanced down as pain lanced through her arm. She had scratched herself in her sleep. It was no wonder the bird's attack had felt so real. She had probably rolled onto something sharp in her covers. She was always finding stray pencils and notebooks floating in her bed after doing her homework there.

Outside, the night wind gently caressed her window lattice. She could sense a change in that wind. Something dangerous was out there, waiting for her. Searching for her. She had always known, always felt when her hunters were near. This time she would be unable to hide from them. This time the price for neglecting her destiny could well be her soul.

*****

Sometime later the smell of acrid smoke awakened fifteen-year-old Rayven Smith from yet another dream of the black hawk. As she surfaced from the last clinging remnants of the dream she could hear the screams of her foster mother down the hall. She jumped from her bed and rushed to the door. Sensing the handle would be hot, she grabbed the bottom of her nightgown and used it to grasp the knob and open her door.

"Melody!" Rayven called out, before she tripped over the discarded gas can in the hallway. She gasped aloud in her terror. Someone had deliberately set the house ablaze! "Melody, I'm coming. Hold on." Breathing raggedly in the suffocating haze of smoke Rayven hurried to the end of the hall where her foster parents' bedroom lay. A huge wall of fire stood between her and their door.

"Melody! Daniel! Can you guys hear me? There's fire everywhere," Rayven called above the roaring blaze. "Don't try to come out this way, go out your window! I'm going out the front way." She couldn't hear any noise coming from behind the door now. She hoped they'd jumped out the window to the ground below the second story. Any broken bones they might sustain from the fall would be a small price to pay for their lives.

Rayven turned back down the hallway and was almost crushed by a falling section of ceiling. Her pathway back through the house was blocked! She now had a wall of flames before and behind her, trapping her between them. She had no way out. She moaned in terror, her eyes going wide, their pale gold depths mirroring the brilliance of the flames.

Suddenly from the corner of her eye she saw the flash of iridescent feathers. It was the black hawk! She let loose a relieved cry. Maybe this was a dream and she would awaken, safe in her bed, just before she died in it.

"Rayven, this way," the bird called in her mind.

Rayven saw a break in the wall of flame before her and followed the bird's flying form through it. Now that she suspected this was a dream, she didn't fear the kiss of the fire. Her friend the hawk would get her safely back through this nightmare. She instinctively sensed that he would do everything in his power to keep her from harm. Blindly she followed him through the twisted, flaming wreck of the house, trusting him to guide her to safety. As they reached the stairs Rayven faltered when she saw that half of them were already ablaze. How quickly the fire burned!

The black hawk's silver gaze looked back at her steadily, as he hovered in the air before her. *"Rayven, you must gather your strength now. You have to pass through the flames. The fire cannot hurt you so long as you do not fear its power. I promise you will be safe. Put your faith in me and in yourself. You must come through the flames if you want to live."*

"Are you crazy? Even if this is a dream, I can't just walk through the fire without being scared of it. Maybe we should go back. If I can get back in my room I can jump from my window there." Rayven turned back from the flames.

"No, Rayven, the way is blocked there too. You must trust me. Take hold of the power that lies dormant within you and walk through the fire. I will be with you." The hawk's beautiful voice compelled her to obey.

Taking a deep breath Rayven stilled her mind, as she had been able to do since she could form conscious thought. Her terror and dread fled from her as dust on the wind. She breathed slowly, forcing her heart to calm and slow its wild beating.

Her body was still that of a fifteen-year-old girl, but her mind was well advanced, even by adult standards. Her counselors at school had sent her to specialists after her first revealing day in kindergarten. They had known from the beginning that she was gifted. A child prodigy, they had called her. Genius, they had called her.

"It doesn't take a genius to know that fire burns," she muttered to herself, her previous panic and terror now replaced by frustrated acceptance.

The orange flames before her blazed like the gaping maw of hell. Rayven's gold gaze wavered before its awesome heat. A shudder racked the house and her eyes shot up into the gaze of the hawk. Gold eyes met silver and held, and a preternatural understanding passed between them. The hawk nodded its sleek black head and flew through the flames.

"Come to me, Rayven. Your destiny unfolds." Whispered words that seemed to her in that moment more dangerous than the flames roaring before her. The moment stilled and all sound receded. Rayven closed her eyes, inhaled slowly, and stepped through the fire.

* * * * *

Rayven's tortured, weary gaze remained locked on the blazing inferno that used to be her foster home. Angry waves of heat beat at her bruised and ashen form. Uniformed figures swarmed around her in various degrees of professional purpose. Firefighters struggled to control the raging flames, like fierce warrior knights before a deadly dragon. Paramedics prepared for their war with pain and death, righteous in their cause. Policemen held back the chaos of confused souls, striving to protect their fellow heroes behind the scenes. All of these images bombarded Rayven's awareness, but still she could not look away from the flames.

Her flight through the now-towering inferno had taken on a dreamlike quality in her mind. As she'd walked through the fire, the flames had kissed her skin with no more than a pleasant whisper of heat. Her brain refused to compute the impossibility of this phenomenon. She listened to her heart and it bid her follow the hawk, and so she had. Her dream friend had sailed ahead of her, guiding her out of the roaring house and into the crisp night air.

After landing in a tree some yards away from the heated inferno he had spoken to her one last time. *"Our enemies have found you out. You are no longer safe here. You must flee from here, as far as you can, and as soon as you are able. Your hunters will be hot on your trail and our only hope is that you somehow evade them. I would take you with me, but it is not yet safe to do so. The danger for you here, though great, is safer than with me. Trust in yourself, and in your power. My heart is with you,* a grifa. *Now go."*

On a sigh of wind the great bird was gone, and with it the last of Rayven's childhood innocence. She felt the bird's departure with a rending deep within her soul, as if she had lost her best and only friend. She knew she would never be the same again. Her heart was gone, taken from her, with the flap of a wing and a breath of wind.

Now Rayven stood amidst the rubble of her youthful dreams and tried to hope for a miracle. Every time a spent and weary figure emerged from the flames Rayven prayed fervently that with them would come the unharmed forms of her foster parents. Her prayers went unanswered as from the smoke, emerged only weary firemen, searing heat and shattered hopes. Her eyes glazed with tears and her young woman's heart shuddered in sorrow.

Her dreams of belonging, at last, to a loving family were being burned away along with the lives of the only two people on earth whom she had loved. Melody and Daniel were to become her adoptive parents. They had loved her enough to make her their own. She had loved them more than she had ever loved anything. Now they were gone.

When she was only an infant she had been abandoned on the steps of a police station. Whatever parents she'd once had were gone from her memory, or perhaps had never been there. She had become a ward of the state, moving from place to place as space became available.

From the beginning she had been considered strange. Her eyes alone, bright gold with a disturbing propensity to shine like a cat's at night, were enough to ward away most potential adoptive parents. Her stillness as an infant had alarmed many foster parents. They had feared all sorts of birth defects at the beginning.

As she'd grown older other strange nuances about her had become apparent, and alarmed those in whose care she'd been temporarily placed. Her disturbing gaze had the ability to send the staunchest adult into a panic. She was unusually independent and disinclined to indulge in play with other children her own age. Her vocabulary was well advanced, and she had a fierce desire to learn anything and everything—surely an odd pastime for any child so young.

She had started school at age five like most other kids. However, her first day at school had been anything but normal. She'd already read the complete works of Shakespeare, lovely stories that had enchanted her enough to steal them from one foster parents' home; and she had learned from other books how to read Latin, French and Spanish. Not only could she read in these languages, but she could write in them as well. Her teacher had immediately sent her to a special school where her intelligence had been put to standardized tests.

She had scored higher than any other person tested before.

Her phenomenal intelligence at such a young age had, understandably, been newsworthy. As she was in between foster families, and staying at the state orphanage, she had been pushed at the press as a ploy to gain more public funding. It had worked. Money had come in by the droves to fund the orphanage's "revolutionary educating techniques". Many prospective parents had come to visit her, but none had been brave enough to take on such a brilliant and disturbing child.

As time wore on and more interesting news had surfaced in the media she had gone back to being a nobody, just another orphan, albeit an extremely intelligent orphan. One who at the age of nine had enrolled at MIT, but still just another orphan capable of slipping through the cracks of the system.

Rayven's intelligence grew by leaps and bounds. It became apparent to one and all that there was no real chance of her being adopted into a family. Not a child her age and not a child of her disposition. Every couple that came to the orphanage wanted to see the infants or the toddlers. The younger the better. Who wanted a child whose future life and personality had already been influenced by circumstances beyond anyone's control? Why take the chance on potentially damaged goods when they could adopt a young child who could still be molded into their image of the perfect addition to their family?

No one wanted to adopt a disturbing teenage girl, no matter how brilliant testing showed her to be. Her intelligence was, in fact, all the more reason to shun her. She was smart enough to deceive adults should she choose. They all realized this and were threatened by it. No matter how much a family wanted to give a poor orphan a chance, the stigma of distrust would always be between them. Since she was brilliant and advanced for her age, most potential parents felt they could not teach her any new qualities she didn't already possess through her own knowledge and experience. It frightened away most adoptive families.

All except Melody and Daniel had turned away from her. They had loved her on sight. The moment they had entered the orphanage they had seen her and wanted her for their own. When told her history they had, unbelievably, desired to adopt her even more. They had wanted to fill her empty life with love and warmth. They would have been a family together.

A hand squeezed her shoulder and she gasped, tearing herself away from her memories. Embarrassed to be caught in such an unguarded moment she wiped the tears from her grimy cheeks and looked warily up into the kind face of a police officer. "Do you have anywhere to go, kiddo?" he asked softly, again squeezing her shoulder, the motion almost comforting in her emotional state.

"No, just the state orphanage where I came from. I am Rayven Smith. The people who lived here were my foster family. I have no relatives." Dashing away fresh tears, Rayven sighed with deep regret. How could she go back to the orphanage now, after having known the comfort and welcome of a good home? She hated the orphanage. That cold stone building where sorrow breathed from the walls and hopes were frozen and shattered upon the floor.

The policeman looked into her tearstained face with deep regret. He felt her sorrow and tried to comfort her as best he could. "You'll have to come to the station where your social worker will meet you and take you someplace safe. You can ride with me, in my squad car. Would you like that, Rayven? When your foster parents get through this they'll come and get you." He smiled awkwardly.

She was such a small thing for her age, the kind policeman thought. How could he tell her that her foster parents were dead? He knew they must be dead by now. No one could have survived this long in that blaze. He'd been apprised of the situation upon entering the violent scene and knew Rayven was indeed alone now that her foster parents were dead. His heart constricted with pity for her plight.

Rayven sighed wearily. "There's no reason to patronize me, sir. I realize that my foster parents are dead." Her throat closed over more tears. "Thank you for being so kind to me, but if we could just go now I would be grateful."

The policeman looked into her beautiful golden eyes. He'd never seen any like hers before. He fancied that if he looked into them long enough he would never be able to close his own without seeing them looking back at him. There was such raging sorrow in the depths of her golden orbs, as if she bore the world's worries on her small shoulders alone. As she looked back at him with her eyes limpid pools of golden starlight, he knew he would never be the same. He would never escape the tortured longing of this child's steady gaze.

Rayven saw the bewildered confusion in the man's eyes. She knew she had stared into his eyes for too long. She knew how it affected people when she did that and she should have been more careful. Quickly she jerked her eyes away from his and reached instead for his hand in an effort to soothe him as well as her. He clasped her small fingers tightly. She felt him shiver.

"I'm sorry. So sorry," he whispered. The tremor in his voice was obvious to them both. The fact that his words had sounded like a plea did not escape the notice of either of them.

"You mustn't be, sir. We each meet our end in our own time. At least they were together." Rayven's heart stuttered as she remembered how alone she was now that they were gone. "At least they had each other at the end."

Together they walked hand in hand to his waiting vehicle. The glowing fire billowed its warmth at their backs. Leaving behind Rayven's hopes and dreams, burning on into the night.

Chapter One

Thirteen years later

Rayven glanced up from her clenched hands. Taking a deep breath she forcibly relaxed them, and tried to look like all the other tourists in the busy airport. An airline security guard smiled politely at her as she stepped forward to retrieve her luggage from the conveyor belt. She tried to look inconspicuous as she smiled back at him from behind her dark sunglasses. She knew that the security personnel would be on the alert for her presence. She knew they'd have sketches to identify her by, as well as detailed descriptions of her many aliases.

They would not, however, have descriptions of her present alias. She'd never used one quite like it. Normally she went for the understated—a prosthetic nose, the guise of a man, or the clever use of a wig and cosmetics. Not this time. This time she'd really outdone herself.

She'd changed her body shape with prosthetics, padding and fancy footwear, transforming her petite five-foot-three-inch frame into that of an overweight five-foot-seven woman. Her long black hair was concealed beneath a spiky blonde wig, and her molten gold eyes were hidden behind nondescript brown contacts and dark shades. Her normally sculpted lips pouted now, thanks to hasty collagen injections. A fake butterfly tattoo graced her left cheek and a well-placed swatch of flesh-like liquid latex concealed the scars at her wrists.

Hers was the misleading disguise of casual anonymity.

As she strode past the security guard she saw his eyes sweep the surrounding passengers and knew that her charade was successful, at least with this particular individual. Now if only she could meet with as much good fortune while she navigated her exit. As she neared the taxi area she carefully surveyed the area for more security and law enforcement officials. This would be their last shot at apprehending her, and she knew they would have their best people on the assignment.

Assessing the uniformed threats hovering about the exit she strode on as casually as possible. After walking through sliding glass doors and out into the warm air, she raised her hand to hail a passing taxi. Suddenly a hand clamped onto her arm.

Turning slowly, Rayven faced the security officer who had detained her. "Miss, you dropped this," he said in a heavily accented Cajun drawl. He handed her the tourist map that had fallen out of her coat pocket as she'd raised her arm for the cab.

Smiling, inwardly relieved, Rayven took the map from him.

"Thank you, sir. Wouldn't want to get lost in a great big city like this now, would I?" Her feigned New England accent was harsh enough to make the officer cringe slightly.

She peeked into his mind and heard his thoughts as if they were her own. She smiled impishly at him when she had assured herself that he posed her no threat. Her disguise had worked perfectly. She knew he was in a hurry to see her on her way. That was fine by her.

*****

Officer LeBlanc smiled benignly at the plump woman before scanning the area behind her alertly. All tourists seemed brash and ill-bred to him, and this plump Yankee was no exception in his opinion. But, he told himself, she was a visitor to his fair city, and New Orleans was a warm and welcoming place to all visitors. No matter how rude or ill-mannered they may be. After assessing their surroundings and assuring himself that his quarry wasn't in the vicinity, he generously hailed a cab for the woman and helped her load a bag into the trunk of the car.

"Enjoy your stay in New Orleans, Madam," he said as he held open the door for her. As he watched the cab drive away, he gladly turned his thoughts to his work.

He had been assigned to a very important international operation. He was searching for a notorious international thief, Lynx. Certainly an alias, but it was the only name they had to put to the fugitive who had thus far evaded the international authorities for the past ten years. Even with all the composite sketches of the many aliases Lynx assumed, the authorities knew it would be nearly impossible to apprehend the master criminal.

Earlier in the day however, an anonymous call had come through to police that Lynx would make an appearance in this airport. It was the first break in a long and grueling chase. Everyone's hopes stayed high and their eyes stayed alert to any suspicious character that passed.

LeBlanc grinned to himself. If he were the one to apprehend this notorious fugitive, he would certainly receive the promotion he longed for in his department. He'd have his fifteen minutes of fame in the international news. He would be a hero among men. Of course he knew it was an impossible dream. They didn't know if Lynx was male or female. From their sketches Lynx could be either, and they had no clue as to what guise the thief would take today. Lynx could be anyone in the airport. Lynx could be among them all now, and none of them would even know it.

He laughed to himself, pushing away his doubts. They had their best people on the job, no way was Lynx going to get by them today. No way.

* * * * *

Rayven Smith stepped into the room she had obtained at the Lafayette Hotel. She always enjoyed her visits here in New Orleans. Here was a place where magic and secrets ran deep, just as they did in her. Among these passionate people who still believed as much in their ancestral Voodoo as in modern secular religions, she felt safe enough to let down the guard she'd long ago erected to hide her strange abilities. She felt almost free. Almost.

Walking gracefully now without her prosthetic suit, which she had discarded at the cheap motel to which her airport taxi had transported her, she opened the doors to her terrace. She had taken two different taxis after tossing her disguise in a dumpster, each taking her on a zigzag route through the city before finally taking a third cab to her final destination. She took every precaution, no matter how much time was wasted, to prevent any interested parties from finding her hiding place.

She breathed in the warm sultry breeze. Though the air was hot and thick outside, she left the French doors open. She loved the sound of the city below, its busy noise helped her to feel less alone. A family strolling along the sidewalk below caught her eye. A mother and father smiled down into their child's eyes as they all held hands. They each laughed and talked together, sharing the sunny afternoon. Rayven smiled as the father lifted the child into his arms and bounced him up and down. She knew that if she concentrated enough she could hear their thoughts—full of love for each other—and feel their happiness as if it were her own.

Rayven sighed and turned back into her room. Such flights of fancy were not for her. She could never know the love of a family, could never stroll in the sun with such abandoned, comfortable ease. She was a wanted fugitive and a freak of nature besides, and nothing could change that. She needed to remember always that she could have no part of the happiness afforded to those who were pure of spirit. Her every chance at true happiness had been snatched away from her by a cruel and devious hand.

She hadn't wanted to return to the orphanage after the fire that killed her foster family at the age of fifteen. She hadn't understood when the police had turned their suspicions on her only a few short days later while her grief was still raw. She had believed that justice would prevail and that any attempt to frame her by persons unknown would be ferreted out by the police. It hadn't been. She'd been arrested and charged with arson and the murder of her foster parents.

She'd escaped the jail where she'd been held while awaiting trial. She'd simply looked at her guard and told him to unlock her cell and he'd obeyed. She had walked calmly through the building stared deeply into the eyes of any who noticed her and commanded them to ignore her. She'd chosen a car from the parking lot at random, hotwired it and driven away. After she'd gained some distance between herself and her prison she'd been confused as to how she'd actually done it. Why had the guards followed her command? Why had they let her escape? Her memory of the events had already begun to fade. She had escaped and that was all she cared to know.

At first she had wanted to prove her innocence and claim what remnants of her life remained back for her own. But her enemies had laid their evidence well. Her fingerprints were all over the gas cans littered around the house. Witnesses had attested to seeing her that night spreading the fuel that had made the fire spread so quickly, and Rayven could only assume that they had been paid quite a lot to lie so convincingly…or somehow been brainwashed into believing their own lies.

Worst of all was the motive that had been given for the crime. Her foster parents' bank account had been hacked into and thousands of dollars had been stolen. It had made perfect sense to the authorities. Rayven was a certified genius. It would have been child's play for her to tamper with her foster parents' bank records and steal from them.

What had not occurred to the police was that if she had wanted to commit so terrible a crime as killing her foster family, she would have been smart enough not to get caught. There would have been no evidence of arson, no fingerprint-laden gas cans, and no witnesses. Even more realistically, if she had wanted to steal money, she would have hacked into the accounts of another bank's customers simply to draw suspicion away from her, and stayed within the loving arms of her foster family.

Alas, it seemed that the police and FBI had not wanted to consider the possibility that she had been framed. It had seemed a clear-cut case to them, and she had been left to deal with the law enforcement officials like the threat they had turned out to be.

Her life had taken a drastic turn, forever changed that fire-lit night, which had ended her foster parents' lives. As a means to survive Rayven had been forced to turn to a life of crime in truth. She'd hacked her way into banking institutions, transferring funds into her own private, offshore accounts, using remote computers wherever she could have access to them. She'd stolen only from faceless wealthy entrepreneurs and businesses, trying to salve her guilt at the crime. Taking money only from those who would hardly miss the funds, she had used the ill-gotten money to leave the country.

It had been difficult being a young girl on the run. People took notice of one so young traveling alone, and she'd always looked young for her age, which didn't help matters much. She'd invented fictitious parents so that she could buy a place to live until she could figure out what she was going to do now that she was a fugitive. She'd bought the latest computer technology and once again used her technological skills to hack into the FBI's mainframe computers in Quantico. She'd at first only wanted to clear her name of the crimes she'd been charged with. She'd hoped that by gaining access to law enforcement computers she could search for clues should there be any to find.

Disbelievingly, she'd discovered that the American government as a whole now wanted her found. They'd feared that the most intelligent mind known since Einstein would be unstoppable as a murderous criminal. They'd put her face on the FBI's most wanted list and offered a hefty reward for information on her whereabouts.

Panicked, Rayven realized then that countless people who could identify her to the authorities had seen her during her flight from home and country. Not knowing what else to do, Rayven had learned all she could about the art of disguise. She'd learned the use of prosthetics, and implemented this knowledge to aid her in her flight from Mexico and subsequent flight to Europe incognito.

As the years had stretched on, her attempts at subterfuge had met with great success. There were only a few instances when the authorities had discovered her whereabouts. Rayven had barely escaped each time. But one thing had become clear to her during these brushes with discovery.

She had enemies.

Enemies who knew her habits, knew her aliases and knew almost her every move. They were the same faceless, nameless foes that had taken away her one chance at happiness with her foster family. They were surely the same enemies her dream companion, the black hawk, had warned her about.

Aware of the very real threat posed to her safety, Rayven had learned the art of self-defense. She was an excellent markswoman and could use any projectile weapon should the need arise. She was a virtuoso swordswoman and knife thrower, as well as a master of the kung fu and jujitsu styles of hand-to-hand combat. She was ever ready and willing to learn from an experienced instructor. Criminal or professional it hadn't mattered to her, so long as they had kept her instruction a secret.

At the age of nineteen, in a fit of desperation and loneliness, after her latest brush with law enforcement officials, Rayven had attempted the unthinkable. Knowing that her future stretched before her in an endless lonely struggle against discovery, Rayven had tried to take her own life. Her anguish and suffering had become more than she felt she could bear, and she had grown so tired of running from her faceless pursuers. And so, in a seedy motel room on the outskirts of Paris, she'd slit her wrists and waited for the cold oblivion of death to embrace her.

As her vision had faded and the last droplets of blood had pooled on the floor around her like a crimson flower, her friend the black hawk, absent since the night of the fire, had once again flown to her side.

"*A grifa*, what have you done to yourself?"

Rayven had felt his dark wings flutter about her face. Suddenly before her darkening vision her hawk had appeared to transform into a man who then kneeled down by her prone body. Oblivious to the blood staining his clothes he'd gathered her close in his arms. He tenderly brushed away a lock of blood-soaked hair from her face.

"Ahh my darling little one, is the pain so great that you would seek to forsake your very life? I promise you that one day, the time will come when you embrace your existence with a glad heart, and all this suffering you bear will be but a faded memory. You have a powerful destiny, my love, you have only to wait a bit longer." His silky hematite-colored hair swept down over the two of them as he pressed his warm lips to her now-cold brow.

"I will wait with you until you awaken, *a grifa*. You will not be alone in your dark sleep. Rest easy until your body heals, for heal it will. Though this cannot make much sense to you now, one day you will understand, I promise you. For now, though, you must rest and awaken renewed in spirit."

Rayven's heart had ceased to beat and her sight had dimmed to darkness. The vision of molten silver eyes burning into her mind was the last thing she could remember.

The next day Rayven had awakened alone to find the horrible wounds at her wrists completely healed but for thin silvery scars. There was no sign of the hawk, if indeed he had even existed outside of her imagination. If not for the dried blood on the floor she would have thought she'd dreamed the whole thing.

As she'd stumbled and crawled away from the proof of her extraordinary escape from death, a lock of blood-red hair had fallen over her eye. Crying out, she'd clawed and tugged at the alien-looking hair, as if trying to pull it from her scalp by its roots. Whimpering like a wounded animal, she had rushed to the bathroom vanity to look at her reflection. What she had seen there had scared her senseless. Where once her hair had been pure black, her long tresses were now streaked with deep red color wherever her lifeblood had soaked into it. No amount of soap or water would remove the stains.

As if her blood-branded hair were not enough proof of her mystical swim through death's dark waters, she then noticed another startling physical change. Her eyes had taken on an almost supernatural luster, a metallic shine much more pronounced than before. Where before her eyes had been merely startling or unsettling, they now branded her as something other than human. Without the use of colored contacts her eyes would now surely attract undue interest.

Other changes within her had become more apparent in the following days. Where before she could vaguely sense the thoughts or feelings of others, she could now look into another's mind at will and know exactly what they were thinking. If she concentrated hard enough she could easily control the minds of others. She could move objects at will without touching them, and she could make strange, inexplicable things happen all around her if she wasn't careful with where she let her thoughts stray.

Rayven forcibly pulled her mind from her memories and grounded herself once more in the present. For the past nine years she had kept a low profile. Never again had she attempted suicide, as she feared it was a hopeless endeavor for one such as her.

Her preternatural strength prevented her from perishing somehow, and she cared not to dwell overlong on the phenomenon. It was far too frightening. She didn't know how she'd become what she was now, or even what she was—for she knew she was definitely not a normal human, but she had learned to cope with her strangeness as time wore on.

Her life was what she'd made of it. Thankfully she'd had her hobbies to keep her amused, if not happy. Smiling to herself she went to her computer to do what she did best. Steal.

Chapter Two

Ysault Dimensional Plane
Ampilon Star System
Planet Varood

General Karis stood gazing out of his window. The dramatic beauty of the sunset beyond the glass went unnoticed as the man behind him continued to speak in a fearful tone.

"We failed to capture her, General. Intelligence suspects that she slipped by our agents using a new alias, one we were unaware of. I can assure you that next time—"

"Next time!" General Karis roared, turning to look at his second-in-command with a sneer. "There should never have been a mistake the *first time* you and your men were sent for her. How could you let a fledgling girl slip through your fingers? She was practically still an infant at fifteen! Now she's a woman grown, and smart enough to know when to run and when to hide." He sneered disdainfully. "Why is it so hard for your people to capture this woman? You've had several opportunities—multiple skirmishes with her, and yet still she eludes you! Perhaps you feel I expect too much of you?"

Lieutenant Devon lowered his eyes in shame as his General reprimanded him. "No, sir. However, you must understand, sir, that this woman is already using her *Awareness*. Were it not for this we certainly would have found her by now."

General Karis moved closer to the Lieutenant, using his legendary skills of intimidation on the cringing man, his pale green eyes cold and hard. "Her race has long since been destroyed, stamped out of existence. There is no one to guide her. She should not be able to use her accursed powers at all!" The General's eyes flashed. "She hasn't been properly trained. She is a fledgling, alone on an alien world. She is among mere mortals, a warring race, who would turn on her in fear and rage at the first sign of her strange abilities. You are mistaken in your assumptions, Lieutenant."

"What shall I do, General Karis? I have my best-trained men scouring the tiny planet in search of her. We have used all of our technological superiority to aid the lawmen on Earth to find her but to no avail." He swallowed nervously before continuing, "I can think of nothing else we can do. Perhaps we should just let her go and simply ensure that she doesn't leave the planet's boundaries."

"Do not presume to point out the futility of our operation to me! We must find her and discover how she escaped the slaughter of her people. How did an infant get sent across space and time without our invading agents' knowledge? How has she eluded us for so long?" The General snorted. "Once we have these answers we can rest easier in knowing that it has all been some fluke, some twist of fate, and we can execute her as we executed the rest of her accursed race so many years ago."

Lieutenant Devon waited in silence for his General's next command. He did not have to wait long.

"As to your question about what you should do next..." The General clapped his hands loudly and a secret panel in his study wall opened.

From the darkness behind the hidden door stepped a tall man wearing the blue uniform of the Galactic Communal Military. His four-foot frame, purple skin and snow-white hair and eyes revealed him to be a member of the race of Monabi. The Monabi were psychic bounty hunters who swore allegiance to none but the highest bidder. Reviled throughout the Galactic Commune, the Monabi were labeled untrustworthy liars and thieves. Their greed and duplicity were legendary.

"Sir, with all due respect, I hardly think we need fraternize with a Monabi *sludgeworm* to find the renegade," Lieutenant Devon sneered disdainfully down at the purple man, who hissed back at him to reveal shining black teeth.

"Well, Lieutenant, you have left me no choice in the matter. You say you have used all the technological means within your disposal. Perhaps technology will not help you with this mission."

Motioning towards the small purple man the General continued, "My new friend Dit here has promised his psychic tracking skills in service to the Galactic Commune. We shall see if he can help you expedite this matter posthaste."

Dit chuckled grittily. "I've never failed to locate my assigned prey. I'll bring this little woman to you, and you will pay me the credits you promised." Dit's green, leathery forked tongue licked rapidly at his lips. "We'll all be happy with this little business venture, I assure you."

General Karis nodded with a slight, derisive twist of his lips, "Dit's powers can help you to pinpoint the girl's life force and lead you to her. You will work closely with him, Lieutenant—" General Karis turned his burning stare to the Monabi before clipping out, "—to ensure his success in this mission."

General Karis again looked out his window to the sky beyond. "Do not disappoint me again, Lieutenant. I do not want to think of the harsh nature of the punishment I will have to devise to fit your failure, should you return from this new mission empty-handed. Now go."

Lieutenant Devon saluted smartly before he turned and left the General's office with Dit following behind him.

General Karis remained standing before the window as the two men left. As the door swung shut behind their retreating forms he turned to pace angrily before his desk. If only the Lieutenant and his men had succeeded in capturing the girl thirteen years ago, his worries would be over.

His teeth clenched at the thought of finally capturing the daughter of Empress Delphi and Emperor Thibetanus, the powerful rulers of the Aware. He could remember a time, before his obsession with stamping out the once great race of psychic beings, when the Aware had roamed their giant homeworld of Nye. Though they had seemed a peace-loving race, everyone knew that their powers were too great a risk to let them hold a threat over the Galactic Commune.

At a young age he had ascended to his rule over the Galactic Commune and its vast armies. Greedy for power and wealth, he had begun his campaigns against the many worlds of the Ysault Plane. He'd let his armies run unchecked through hundreds of worlds, subjugating them to the rule of the growing boundaries of the Galactic Commune. When it had come time to conquer the world of Nye he had faltered in his quest for glory.

For reasons he could not bear to even now contemplate.

For many years he had let the peaceful people of the Aware exist unharmed, until circumstances that even now brought a murderous rage to his eyes had forced his hand. His rage had demanded no less than the total annihilation of the people of Nye.

He had brutally and mercilessly gathered every man and woman in his huge army and unleashed them upon the unsuspecting Aware. Though possessed of great and unimaginable power, the Aware had been unable to withstand the onslaught of such massive force. Instead of merely engaging the fighting forces of the Aware, the Galactic Communal Army had ravaged the population down to the last man, woman and child. No one had escaped the General's wrath—none had survived his genocidal rage.

None but one, that is. Somehow, unbeknownst to General Karis, Empress Delphi and Emperor Thibetanus had secreted their infant daughter away from the slaughter and into another dimension. They'd sent her beyond his far reach to another planet many suns away. Spies from within the Aware's own ranks had later informed the General of the girl's existence and survival, before they too had been executed for being members of the accursed Aware race.

General Karis' obsession with stamping out all Awares had not permitted him to leave the girl to live out her life peacefully on the planet known as Earth. He knew how long the lifespan of the Aware could last, and though his own race's life expectancy was three to four hundred years, he feared that the girl could live well beyond even his grandchildren, should he have any. With such a long lifespan the possibility existed that one day she could learn of her origins, and perhaps come back, should her powers be strong enough to permit such a feat. He could not chance the risk that the girl posed to his future offspring's rule should she seek revenge against them.

Soon the young woman would at last stand before him, and if she were half the woman her mother had been, he would give her a choice; a choice that could mean life or death for her. Until then he would continue to hunt for her. With his attention focused on her discovery there was no way she could elude him for much longer. Until then he was prepared to wait, no matter how long it took.

She would be found and brought before him. It was her destiny.

Chapter Three

Rayven sipped at her coffee, hiding surreptitiously behind the morning's newspaper, outside under the bright New Orleans sunshine. Ever conscious of her surroundings, she scanned the small outdoor café for any signs of threat before turning back to her paper.

Breathing in the sultry morning air she smiled to herself. Despite her necessarily reclusive lifestyle, she reveled in the feel of the outdoors. Nature in all its abounding glory was often her bastion of strength when her spirit was low. She often took long treks into the forests of whatever hiding places she found herself in, and stayed there, basking in nature's beauty for several days and nights at a stretch. Closing her paper she rose from her seat, tossing her glossy, red-streaked onyx hair over her shoulder. Still alert for any hint of danger she turned and slowly strolled down the crowded pavement.

Living her life on the run as she did, she had learned to appreciate the little things in life. All around her, people went about their daily routines, tourists worried over what souvenir to buy or what attraction to attend next, businessmen and women rushed frantically about to this job or that. Rayven was just happy to feel anonymous and free among them. Separate and strange though she was, these people treated her like any other person passing on the street.

Her mind filled with the music of the innocent people surrounding her. She heard their thoughts like a million tiny whisperings layered over her consciousness. She smelled their sun-warmed skin and hair—the perfume of hopes and dreams. She felt their warm tufts of breath flutter over her skin like the delicate caress of a butterfly's wing. She heard their hearts pumping in a rising crescendo all around her, and her own heart struggled to find a similar rhythm.

A child with riotous golden curls passed her by, close enough for Rayven to lightly brush her hand near her corona of hair. The silken feel of it flooded Rayven's senses and filled her hungry soul with warmth and light. The child glanced back and smiled, as if she too had enjoyed the secret caress. Rayven's steps became lighter and more carefree as she slipped deeper into the heart of the swelling crowd.

* * * * *

"Are you sure this is the place, Dit? We've been searching this area for a fortnight and so far there's been no sign of her." Lieutenant Devon craned his neck above the swarming crowd, looking for any sign of their quarry.

Dit grinned, revealing his gleaming ebony teeth. "I'm sure. I can smell her psychic emanations on the wind." His nostrils twitched as if to attest to the truth of his words.

For the past several days and nights, ever since Dit had first led them to this sweltering city, Lieutenant Devon and five of his most highly trained men had searched for their prey. Hoping and praying that their mission would at last be met with success, they'd worked almost nonstop at their task.

Donning the costumes of the native people of the primitive planet, and hiding the Monabi's garishly purple skin under a dark cloak, the Lieutenant and his men had wandered through the city, seeking the renegade Aware. Though they had tried to disguise their appearances, going so far as to hide the silver bands with their tiny blue *Chama* stones at their brows under strange long-billed hats, the people of this world remained wary of the menacing-looking group. They had been given a wide berth in which to hunt their prey.

By the thirteenth night, though Dit had sensed several psychic emanations, their team had only encountered weak mortals of mediocre psychic talents. At first Dit and the

Lieutenant had feared that if their quarry was indeed a powerful psychic, she was somehow shielding herself from their detection. They had almost given up hope of ever discovering her whereabouts when, suddenly, the Monabi had at last sensed her.

In a violent paroxysm of convulsions, Dit had honed in on her presence within the heart of the city. Gasping and thrashing wildly in his effort to latch on to her psychic signature, he had been unable to pinpoint the Aware woman's exact location, but had led the men to within a five-mile radius of their target.

After his first painful attempt at direct contact, Dit had refused to do more than track her by her psychic scent. Lieutenant Devon had angrily tried to force the Monabi to connect with her again, but he had refused. Her mental signature was too powerful for Dit to attempt contact without a great risk to his life. However, Dit's methods at hunting out his prey through scent were still quite useful, and the Lieutenant had let his anger with the Monabi cool.

The Lieutenant cared not how they found the elusive Aware, so long as they did find her. At last, after many years of searching, the Lieutenant felt their mission would soon be over, their renegade Aware safely in their custody.

Lieutenant Devon looked behind him to the five men who waited there. "All right men, this is it. Look lively now, and remember that the General wants her taken alive. Only hurt her as much as you have to."

Spreading out, trying to blend in with the local crowd, the Lieutenant and his comrades awaited Dit's next directions. Dit's purple head peeked out from his cloak's concealing cowl, and lifted into the wind like a hound on the hunt. He inhaled deeply of the air, his milky white eyes seeming to dim. Walking forward he led the group of men purposefully through the milling crowd.

Halting suddenly Dit hissed to the Lieutenant, "She approaches!"

Not sure what to expect, the Lieutenant and his men tensed and readied themselves for their first confrontation with their quarry. They did not have long to wait.

"There she isssss," hissed Dit, pointing unsteadily to a figure emerging from the crowd.

Lieutenant Devon gasped as a beautiful, dark-haired angel strode into the morning sunlight. She was nothing like the monster he had been expecting to see. Though his parents had been in the Great Aware Massacre, he'd never heard much about the Aware. He'd known of their immense and potentially destructive psychic abilities, but he'd never known what they looked like. He had expected a vile and corrupt-looking woman, perhaps not unlike the vicious little Monabi beside him. Certainly he had not anticipated the vision of purity now before him.

As if sensing his intense regard, the woman looked up directly into his eyes. Her steps faltered and time seemed to slow between the two of them for what seemed like a small eternity. A flash of comprehension lit her eyes.

All hell broke loose.

* * * * *

Rayven's heart was still full of the warmth of the child's smile as she continued walking through the crowd. One day, she promised herself, she would be free just as those who surrounded her now were free. Able to come and go as she pleased, freed from the constant fear of discovery and capture. She just had to find the right haven, far from the reach of law enforcement officials. She would be free. She vowed it.

Suddenly a prickling sense of nearby danger raised the hairs on the nape of her neck. Raising her eyes to look ahead she locked gazes with a young man wearing a ball cap pulled low over his brow, a few paces yet from her. Instinctively she scanned his mind for any hidden threat.

Not understanding at first, the strange images downloading rapidly into her brain from his, she didn't react as quickly as she should have. From deep within his thoughts she discerned images of strange planets, frightening alien creatures, and schematics from the most unusual weaponry she'd ever before seen. For a moment she mistakenly assumed that she was glimpsing images from the last movie the man had seen, or perhaps from the last book he had read.

Then, however, she noticed the men tensed closely behind him. They, too, wore the exact same type of ball cap as their leader, and their eyes darted fearfully around them. She noticed a very short figure wearing a dark cloak that was far too heavy for the sweltering New Orleans morning.

Searching the little man's mind she saw his fear and awe of her, and his desire for the reward her capture would bring to him. However jumbled and foreign the images she read in his mind or in the taller man's before him, she knew then that they had come for her.

Suddenly one of the more nervous-looking men in the group pulled his ball cap from his head to reveal a high forehead banded behind a platinum circlet with a tiny dark blue jewel resting along the center of his brow. For a moment Rayven felt drawn to the strange jewel, as if it called to her on some primal level. Not certain how she knew, Rayven realized that his concealed circlet was some sort of powerful weapon that would be used against her.

As if in response to her realization of the threat before her, a violent flash of bright blue light pulsed and shattered the sidewalk mere inches in front of her feet. All around Rayven, people began to shriek and run, panicking at the explosion of light and sound.

Rayven's mind seemed to calm and slow the scene before her. As always was the case for her in a dangerous situation such as this, she distanced her thoughts from her jumbled emotions to better concentrate on the best course of action. Calmly turning to the small man in the group, Rayven instinctually aimed her thoughts and compelled him to do her bidding.

Without hesitation the little man turned, his purple face emerging from its shadowy hiding place, and launched an attack of flailing fists and biting teeth upon Rayven's attacker. Growling like a wild beast, the purple man latched violently onto the larger man's vulnerable throat with his gleaming black fangs and ripped the tender flesh in a torrent of blood and sinew. Her attacker fell under the brutal onslaught, drowning in a flood of gore.

Rayven turned, her actions almost too quick for human eyes to discern, and ran through the frightened mob of people. Behind her the purple man screamed as another of the men tried to disengage him from his victim. Unable to separate the small man's jaws from the throat of the now-dying assailant, the taller man snapped the purple man's neck and tossed his limp body aside before sinking to his fallen comrade's side in a futile attempt to save him.

Three of the men gave Rayven chase, shoving aside any who stumbled into their path. Rayven darted blindly down crowded side streets. She led her pursuers on a twisted path through the shrieking crowd.

She came upon a dead end and, in an amazing feat of inhuman agility, she jumped several feet straight into the air to grasp at an overhead ladder. Swiftly she scaled the fire escape and jumped onto the roof of the building. Focused and confident, she ran the length of the roof and, without pause, jumped to another. Using her phenomenal preternatural speed and strength, she soon outdistanced her still-grounded pursuers, jumping fluidly from rooftop to rooftop as she ran.

Jumping to yet another building Rayven headed directly for the fire escape ladder on the farthest side. Not even pausing to climb down its rungs, she lightly grasped the poles to either side of her with her hands, braced the soles of her shoes against them and slid rapidly down. Landing lightly on the balls of her feet, she continued her rapid flight through the bowels of the city.

Ducking through a littered alley and out onto the street beyond, she quickly searched the area for any evidence of her pursuers. There was no sign here of the violent struggle that had taken place several blocks behind her. There was no sign of her would-be captors.

Walking once again among the throng of New Orleans' population, Rayven tried to look casual and relaxed as she sent her mind seeking outward, searching for some sign as to the whereabouts of her hunters. Sensing their agitated presence a few short blocks behind, she quickly darted to the nearest parked car. Focusing her awesome telekinetic power she unlocked the secured car and brought the engine to roaring life. Appearing serene, for all the world like any other common motorist, she drove down the street and away from her pursuers.

*****

Lieutenant Devon and his remaining men halted breathlessly. Searching the surrounding area frantically, he could find no trace of the Aware woman's whereabouts. Angrily he turned to his comrades, his eyes blazing.

"How could you have let this happen? Why did you let Kimo attack so haphazardly? Weren't one of you close enough to stop him?" he shouted.

None of the men answered, fearful to say the wrong thing and enrage their leader more.

"Ensign Tybb, you were supposed to use your *Chama* stone and release a brain trace on her. Did we accomplish *that much* from this fiasco?"

The young man who the Lieutenant had addressed thrust his shoulders back, standing at attention. "Yes, sir. I was able to put the trace on her while her mind was preoccupied with the Monabi's. We should be able to track her without difficulties now."

Lieutenant Devon sighed in relief. He was grateful that all hope was not lost. With their psychic implant deeply embedded into the woman's brain, they should be able to track her easily to within a thousand spans. He would not return to Varood and the General empty-handed. He would not fail in this important mission. Success would soon be at hand, he vowed. It must—his very life might depend upon it.

Chapter Four

Ysault Dimensional Plane
Sord Star System
Planet Hostis

Setiger raised his bronze head from betwixt the woman's spread thighs, his sensuous coral lips glistening with the evidence of her fragrant arousal. He smiled slowly as her dilated onyx eyes dazedly met his. Licking his lips, savoring her sweet flavor, he crawled slowly up her quivering body to settle his rock-hard cock into her wetly dripping pussy. As he entered her body on a savage thrust she mewled and clawed his back in a paroxysm of ecstatic pleasure.

Despite the fact they were not true mates, and therefore most unlikely to produce offspring together, the two lovers met here each night in the warmth of her bed feathers to try to trick nature into gifting the woman with a child. Their goal was not unlike that of the other couples nestling in the feathery boughs of the purple *Neffan* trees nearby. They sought to repopulate their dwindling race by copulating as often and with as many partners as was possible.

Thankful that his noble task had added benefits, Setiger reached for the woman's plump nipple and tugged teasingly. His hips began a circular grinding motion in and out of her drenched pussy, sending waves of ecstasy through both of their writhing bodies. Growling harshly in his throat he threw his long hair over his shoulder, embedding his shaft more deeply into her now-audibly slurping channel.

While one thumb and forefinger pulled and squeezed her nipple, Setiger let his other hand pull his partner's legs firmly around his thrusting middle before reaching between their bodies to stroke the swollen berry of her clit, nestled in her moist curls. Soon his hand was drenched in her flooding juices and he felt the walls of her pussy begin to quiver more strongly about his massive cock.

Keening into the night, the woman beneath him quivered in the throes of her orgasm. Secure in the heady knowledge that he had helped her to find her woman's joy, despite the fact that they were not true mates and therefore a feat near to impossible for most, Setiger let loose his passion. Pounding furiously into her silken heat, his skin slapping loudly against hers, he released a violent flood of glistening cum deep into the tunnel of her cunt.

Careful, lest his muscular body crush her own, Setiger collapsed to lie at her side. He grunted in satisfaction. Turning to face each other they smiled and softly laughed together, while their pounding hearts slowed their frantic rhythm.

"Indeed, Ursus, yours is the sweetest pussy I've ever fucked. I vow if we did not impregnate you this night, it is a certainty you will never accept my seed," he said quietly to her.

"Setiger, we have been copulating for near to five years now. Even regularly accepting two more lovers besides you into my womb, I have yet to conceive."

Her voice trembled before she continued, "There have only been two women out of our numbers who have managed to produce a child from an unmated womb. I do not think we are going to succeed in this endeavor…no matter how pleasurable the trying may be." The last was said with a faint smile and no small amount of heat in her dark eyes.

Setiger frowned at her words. Though he'd never spoken of it aloud, with Ursus or with any of his many other partners, he feared her words to be true. Their numbers were drastically small, and only a few children had been born into their population in the past twenty-eight years. During the Great Aware Massacre, only a hundred Aware had managed to escape the slaughter of their people by secreting away to the farthest reaches of the dimension to a tiny, uninhabited planet they called Hostis.

It was rumored among their numbers that the Emperor of their people had received word of impending invasion by the Galactic Commune just before the Great Massacre occurred. It was also rumored that the Emperor and his Council had managed to warn many off-world Aware of the danger and sent them into hiding among the various planets of the galaxy. The suspicion that there were others of their kind scattered among the stars kept their hope alive. If they could one day venture off their new world without fear of destruction by the Galactic forces, they might be able to reunite with their misplaced brethren.

After the great Galactic Communal Army had struck, the Emperor's Chief Counselor, Draco, had opened a tunnel through space as the battle had escalated. He had saved as many Aware as he could manage, sending them hurtling through the portal, before it had suddenly closed, sucking him through to the other side as well.

Though many of their people were able to transport themselves through space, Draco had likely been the only one powerful enough to hold open the portal, undetected, during the brutal invasion of the Galactic Communal Army. Draco still mourned the fact that he had been unable to save more of his slaughtered race.

Though their newly adoptive planet was named in the ancient tongue, a word meaning *seed of hope*, as the years went by the survivors had found little in the way of hope. Soon after their escape, after they had counted their great losses, the survivors had realized the greatest problem ahead of them would be that of repopulating their species.

The race of the Aware was an ancient and powerful one, possessed of mystical and magical powers, revered and feared by all other races. Their great powers were of no help however, were in fact more of a hindrance to the population problems they now faced. Throughout evolution their kind had developed certain genetic propensities, which would only enable them to produce offspring when two people were psychically compatible, and only with a member of their own race. Only by a proper mate's seed could a woman hope to conceive offspring. Very rarely had there been exceptions to this rule, which was the reason why the surviving Aware now copulated freely and frequently amongst themselves.

They hoped against hope that somehow their genetic makeup could be fooled, allowing them to repopulate their dwindled race. However, as Ursus had pointed out, only two unmated women out of thirty had conceived in the last twenty-eight years. If their people had been able to gestate a fetus more quickly, the six properly mated couples in their numbers would willingly have attempted to produce more children than their normal thirteen-month long confinements would presently allow.

Since their wild flight from certain destruction twenty-eight years before, a total of only seventy-eight children had been born, bringing their total number to one hundred seventy-eight Aware. Despite their intentions, the mated couples within their population had been unable to produce as quickly or as successfully as they had hoped to. It seemed that no matter how often a mated pair rutted between the bed feathers, a female Aware could only conceive offspring at certain times of the moon's phasing.

With none but twelve of their population safely mated, and the rest of their numbers unable to produce offspring amongst themselves, the Aware's desperate hopes of repopulating their species seemed next to impossible.

Setiger shook his brooding thoughts forcibly from his mind. Knowing his lover needed reassurance he gently reached out for her soft breast to cradle it within his palm. "Ursus, don't despair. Soon will come a day when our Empress will return to us, to lead us once again into freedom." He let his mind caress hers soothingly. Sharing with her his glowing memories of better days.

"Setiger, what if it's true what some say, that she is a myth? A fable told to us by our leader Draco, to keep us in high spirits."

"Ursus, do you not trust our chosen leader? Know you not that he would never lead us astray with such a vile lie?"

"It has been twenty-eight years and still he does not go to claim our lost Empress. How could he not have restored her to us by now if she were really out there among the stars in exile from us?"

Setiger lightly squeezed her breast, feeling her nipple stab demandingly into his palm. He thought of their sweet, plump taste and his mouth watered. His cock lengthened and hardened as a wave of lust shook him, but he forced himself to concentrate on their conversation.

"I promise you that our leader would not lie so cruelly to us. He has his reasons for waiting to claim our ruler. I know that he, too, anticipates her safe return to us. He is merely waiting for the right time to retrieve her from her exile."

"I believe what you say, Setiger, yet still do I fear for the future of our people. I only wish Draco would let us venture off-planet, that we may try to search for more of our own kind among other worlds. Perhaps other Aware escaped the Great Massacre as we did, secreting away to planets far beyond the reach of the Galactic Commune." Ursus' breath shuddered on a sigh. "We have been in exile for far too long, unable to search for more survivors of our race."

"Try to have faith, Ursus. Our time will soon come. We will not always remain in hiding." Setiger bent his sleek head and licked at her nipple and let his hands stray over her lush body.

His roaming hands became more demandingly provocative as Ursus' eyes clouded with desire. "Now let us speak no more of such dark matters," he whispered huskily, "I have much more pleasurable issues to discuss with you."

With a feral grin he flipped her much smaller body over, landing her on her stomach. Raising her hips high he spread her labia wide with his fingers and thrust his turgid erection into her already dripping channel.

"Aaah, Fates, but I love how your cunt drips for me, Ursus," he growled into her ear.

Ursus gasped as all thoughts fled from her mind. Her lover's thick cock pounded ferociously into her, and she moaned deep in the back of her throat. Hitching her hips up higher to accept him more deeply, she desperately clutched her bed feathers in her grasping hands.

It was a long and pleasure-filled night for the both of them.

Chapter Five

Rayven drove the rest of the day, her only objective to get as far away from the threat in New Orleans as possible. She stopped only once to dispose of her stolen vehicle and purchase a new one, in an effort to reduce the threat of local law enforcement getting involved in the chase, should her stolen car attract notice.

In the back of her mind she feared that no matter how far she ran, her pursuers were now easily tracking her over the distance she placed between them. She could still sense their dogged pursuit of her. Like a buzzing fly on the outskirts of her consciousness, she was ever distracted and irritated by it.

She knew she wasn't up against any common government threat anymore. She was certain that her pursuers, whoever they were, had not been human. Somehow, for whatever reason, it seemed she had attracted the unwanted attentions of beings far unlike any she'd ever faced. As strange and impossible as that may seem, she reminded herself that she, too, was more than a mere human. As evidenced by her own preternatural powers, there were forces unimagined at work everyday.

"'There are more things in heaven and earth, Horatio, than are dreamt of in your philosophy'," she said under her breath with an ironic little smile.

She had long ago suspended her disbeliefs about what was possible in the world. Though she didn't yet understand this new threat she faced, she would do whatever it took to evade capture. She could do no other than try her best to remain one step ahead of her hunters.

As the day turned into night, Rayven's mind began to cloud. She felt exhausted to the point of collapse. Knowing that to stop now could mean allowing her pursuers the opportunity to catch up to her, she forced her eyes to remain open. She had no time for rest.

Her body, however, had other plans. After dozing behind the wheel for what seemed like the hundredth time, Rayven drove her car into the nearest rest area off the highway. Defeat a bitter taste on her tongue, Rayven leaned back in her seat to catch some much-needed sleep.

Unbeknownst to her, deep in slumber as she was, her weariness had not been a natural one. For not far behind her, traveling faster than any radar could detect, came her hunters. The five men rode strange-looking motorcycles, or *dronerunners* as they called them, which hovered a few inches off the ground and traveled at high speed. A side effect of the deviously implanted psychic brand in her mind forced her to slow and sleep, as her hunters tracked her with dark purpose.

"She sleeps now, sir. She's not far ahead of us," Ensign Tybb told the Lieutenant through the microphone in his *runner* helmet.

"Excellent, Ensign. What's our ETA?" Lieutenant Devon asked.

"Approximately seven minutes, sir."

"Remember to use a deep stun on her, we don't want her waking up during a crucial moment. We have to quickly subdue her and use our *Chama* stones to open a portal to home," he said referring to the blue stones in the circlets upon their heads.

The five men raced onward to secure their prey.

*****

Groggily, Rayven's eyelids fluttered at a sound just beyond her car door. Her usually alert brain struggled against an almost overpowering compulsion to stay asleep. Without understanding how, she knew that her would-be captors had found her. She sensed them stealthily approaching her car, and struggled mightily to awaken.

As the driver's side door opened, Rayven spilled inelegantly out onto the pavement. The man stooped down, clasped the front of her linen shirt in a hard grip, and hauled her up roughly against him. Rayven's bleary vision took in the scene of the man before her and the four militant men behind him. For a certainty it was the men who had accosted her this morning. What was left of them anyhow, she thought with no small amount of satisfaction, still trying to pull free of the sleepy haze clouding her mind.

"Ensign Tybb, Officer Myer, open the portal now," the gruff voice above her head commanded two of the men beyond them.

As a brilliant blue wave of light projected forth from the two men's silver-encircled brows, a gaping maw opened in a dark vortex before them. All about them the wind whipped into a frenzied howl. An unimaginably powerful force began to pull at them, making everyone stumble awkwardly forward.

Abruptly, Rayven's clouded mind came to into focus once more. Raising her eyes defiantly to those of her captor, she hesitated a mere microsecond before she shoved her fist viciously into his nose, snapping cartilage and bone. He cried out and released her, clutching his face as blood spewed forth in an arc of gleaming crimson.

Whirling in a fury of movement, fighting against the sucking force of the vortex still held open by the two men furthest from her, Rayven launched an attack against the man closest to her. He moved to meet her halfway. Rayven ducked his widely swinging fist, and threw her hands out in front of her.

Rayven had intended to pummel the man's vulnerable middle with her fists. Unexpectedly, as she swung her hands out in front of her, her hands did not form into fists at all—nor did they make contact with her attacker's stomach. Instead, a blaze of electric white light flew forth from her now-upraised palms. The blindingly bright display pulsed outward so strongly that it propelled Rayven back several inches. However, it did much more to her attacker than push him back as it did her.

Screaming now, the man flew several feet into the air. Encased in pulsating, white-hot light, his body began to convulse. His screams ended in a frothing gurgle as his skull audibly cracked, and blood erupted from his mouth. The bright light dimmed and receded to nothing, leaving the man to hover in the air one second longer before falling to the pavement below with a meaty splat.

Rayven watched the whole scene with horrified disbelief. She'd never suspected herself capable of such a deadly feat. She suspected that the whole event had probably been instinctual and that she would be unable to perform such magic at will. She had never directly killed anyone with her power before. She had never imagined her power could be used in so destructive a manner.

All around her was chaos. The two men behind her determinedly struggling to hold open the raging vortex with their *Chama* stones, their leader who was still groaning and staggering, clutching his broken nose. Rayven was oblivious to these things. She had eyes only for the blood-soaked heap on the ground before her. With her attention fixated upon her fallen victim, Rayven did not see the fifth man approach her from behind. In a blaze of light projected from the circlet upon the man's head, Rayven fell stunned to the ground.

The last thought Rayven had before succumbing to the dark oblivion that beckoned her was that should she ever learn to control her newfound destructive power, she would be strong enough to rule the nation should she choose to. Perhaps even the world…

Recoiling from the horrifying thought, Rayven embraced unconsciousness.

Chapter Six

Ysault Dimensional Plane
Ampilon Star System
Planet Varood

Rayven awoke to find herself flat on her back in a small room. She made to rise before she realized that she hadn't been on the floor, as she'd first surmised after all. She was laying spread-eagle on a warm slab of reddish translucent plastic, which she could see through clearly to the floor if she turned her head. The dais she rested upon was raised a few feet from the floor by what appeared to be a pulsing flow of air. A similar, though more flexible, material to that of the slab beneath her had been used to tie her wrists and ankles.

Gasping, Rayven realized that she was completely nude. Who had taken her clothes and why? If her captors thought that removing her clothing would discourage her from escaping they were sorely mistaken.

Struggling against her bonds, Rayven's eyes raced about her to take in her strange surroundings. She was in a small closet of a room. The only objects in it were her and the strange plastic dais upon which she lay. There was a heavy wooden door beyond the floating slab, which she could see if she raised her head to look beyond her secured feet.

Unable to dislodge or loosen her unusual handcuffs, Rayven tried to focus her telekinetic powers and untie them. Confused when she failed to loosen her bonds in this fashion, she tried again. And again.

Nothing happened.

Nothing.

How could this be? She'd never failed to harness the use of her powers like this before. Her phenomenal abilities were always obedient to her command. They'd never completely deserted her before. What was going on?

Jerking wildly now at her restraints, Rayven tried to bring one of her wrists to her teeth in the hopes of biting through the strange material. Her wrist, raised high over her head, would only move a scant couple of inches before the plastic-like binding would tighten and prevent further movement. The same was true of her other wrist, and her widely spread ankles.

A feral growl escaped her clenched teeth. Not knowing what else to do, Rayven began to buck violently to and fro, as far as her bonds would allow. She hoped to dislodge the floating dais from its hovering position above the pulsating shaft of air, which flowed from the floor. She thought that perhaps if she caused the slab to fall to the ground it might shatter and free her.

Several moments later, Rayven was breathlessly forced to admit defeat. The floating slab refused to budge. Frantic now, Rayven tried to calm herself in order to better assess her situation. She had to escape, but *how*?

Jerking her head to look at the door, Rayven's nude body stilled as the door swung inward to admit two men.

Recognizing the younger of the two men as the leader of those who had captured her, Rayven flashed him a darkly feral smile. His eyes glared furiously back at her over his bandaged nose and cheek, and the blue stone in his headband glinted like blue fire. As Rayven stared back unwaveringly, his eyes shifted away. But not before they darted derisively over her exposed flesh.

Enraged by his audacity, Rayven again tried to use the power of her mind. She tried desperately to enslave the man to her will, but to no avail.

The second, older man walked closer now and spoke, "You can't use your *Awareness* while bound with *Kiel* ropes, you know. You'll only tire yourself if you try." A small smile played about his mouth.

Rayven felt her skin crawl as the man's eyes blatantly roved over her body. His physical form would have been most pleasant to look upon with its dark hair, sculpted face, and strong muscular physique. It would have indeed been quite handsome…except for his eyes. Deep within his jewel-green eyes lay a dark and vile sickness, which Rayven could easily sense, even without her extrasensory power as she was.

Not deigning to speak to her captors, Rayven met his disturbing stare, her gaze fierce and defiant. Though she could understand his language well enough despite his strange accent, she didn't understand his meaning. His words made no sense, and she was sure if she bothered to ask he wouldn't explain. She simply looked at him, maintaining her silence.

"What is your name?" he asked gruffly.

Rayven refused to answer. She broke her gaze from his and turned her face away.

The man reached out to roughly grasp her jaw and force her to look back at him. "You will answer me or you will suffer. I leave the choice to you. I don't have time to play games with you," he said firmly.

Rayven gathered a pool of moisture in her mouth and spit it squarely into his face. Seeing him recoil, she smiled craftily at him, eyes blazing her satisfaction.

The younger man with the broken nose gasped and made a move towards them.

"Don't," roared the older man, wiping spittle from his face.

"Leave us, Lieutenant," he gritted out. "I would have this time alone with our captive before her execution." The last was said with a relishing smile aimed at Rayven. When she showed no outward reaction he sneered.

"But General Karis, sir—" the Lieutenant protested before he was cut off.

"I said leave us, Lieutenant!" the enraged, red-faced General roared loudly.

The Lieutenant left without another word, firmly closing the door to the small room.

Alone now with a man she strongly suspected might be mentally unstable, Rayven shifted uneasily on the slab. The General struggled noticeably for control of his anger. Bringing his features to a semblance of calm assurance, he again approached her.

"I realize, now, that you know not what a dangerous position you are in. You have lived on a primitive planet your whole life, unaware of the circumstances behind this event." He leaned conspiratorially closer to her.

"You've been running your whole life, my dear. Running blindly from enemies you do not know. Have you never wondered why? Why you were singled out from so many other people to live the life you led? Have you never wished for the answers that elude you as to why your life has been naught but one long struggle against capture? I can well imagine that you have dwelled on these issues every day of your life. Let me give you the answers you seek, my little renegade. Let me reveal to you your darkest secrets—let me help you to discover the monster you are deep down in your soul.

"You are not a native of Earth, my dear woman. You are, in fact, not a member of the human race at all. You are what is known as an Aware, an accursed breed of beings from a planet called Nye, found here in the Ampilon Star System. You are a powerful psychic, with amazing talents even I do not know the extent of." He paused, his eyes sweeping over her rhythmically rising and falling breasts.

Rayven tried to remain outwardly calm as her mind reeled under the effect his words had on her. She was from another planet? Such a thing was not possible. What type of mind game was the General trying to play with her? Perhaps he really *was* mad and believed his insane tale. His eyes were cold and hard, and seemed empty of all human feeling. She would not be surprised if he killed her now, without a hint of any emotion or remorse.

"Your awesome psychic abilities are known as *Awareness*, and they are the most powerful abilities of any race in the Galactic Commune. Sadly, my dear, you are the last of your great race. They were all killed during a great war, instigated by the Emperor of your people." The General's eyes greedily searched her face for some trace of emotion, his eager countenance belying his professed sorrow over the extinction of her people. He reminded her of some evil bird of prey, searching for tears on which to feed his dark appetites.

"You have been hunted since your birth, my dear, because of who and what you are. Your kind are so devious and hardhearted that you cannot be trusted among normal humans, you cannot be trusted not to cause death and destruction wherever you go. And so we've sought you out, to protect our fellow humans from your dark powers, and to bring you to justice for the misdeeds of your brethren."

Rayven's muscles hardened at his cruelly spoken words, and she tested her bonds once more with her mind, hoping for some chance at escape. The General noticed her concentration on the bonds at her wrists and smirked, his gaze full of arrogant condescension.

"You might wonder at the oddity of being unable to use your *Awareness* to escape. Let me assure you that you haven't permanently lost control of your powers, it's merely the *Kiel* bonds working against you."

Rayven glared at the offending *Kiel* bonds securing her wrists. She assumed that not only were her bonds made of this strange material, but also the slab upon which she lay as well. She didn't know why he was so amicably telling her these things, but she suspected his reasons were anything but altruistic. Her suspicions were confirmed as he continued.

"You might also be wondering what it is about the *Kiel* that makes it so effective in preventing you from using your *Awareness*. It's really quite simple." He grinned leeringly at her.

"As you probably don't know, members of your race were unable to use their psychic powers against each other while in human form. No one is quite sure why, it's just one of those strange evolutionary puzzles. However, we do know that the seat of this survival trait was found within an Aware's blood and skin," he paused and let his words sink into Rayven's mind before continuing.

"So, in an effort to protect ourselves from your kind, humans have developed *Kiel* armor and restraints using this knowledge." He smiled bitingly. He placed his hand tauntingly on her throat before moving his hand slowly down to squeeze her breast. His breathing hitched and his eyes glazed.

Rayven thrashed under his vile touch, her effort to remain unresponsive forgotten. He cruelly pinched her plump nipple, laughing softly at her struggles.

"You see, my succulent pupil," he continued. "Before an Aware's body has a chance to deteriorate and turn to dust, we harvest their corpses of skin and blood. *Kiel* is a material fashioned from the flesh and blood of an Aware. Unable, as you are, to fight against one of your own flesh and blood using your *Awareness*, the composition of the *Kiel* is what makes it so effective a defense against your psychic gifts."

Rayven gasped, sickened, as the General continued almost gleefully.

"We take the skin and blood from your people, and boil it with a mixture of quartz sand at high temperatures until it forms a viscous liquid. This liquid is then molded into many different items which we like to use when confronted with your kind, such as armor, weaponry, and of course restraints such as the ones which now hold you."

Rayven's shock forced her to speech at last. "But I thought you said I was the last of my kind. Why would you need such devices at hand if that were true?"

The General's eyes closed, seeming to savor hearing the melodious sound of her voice. "Well, we haven't had to use such devices for the past twenty-eight years, of course."

"What do you plan to do with me?" Rayven asked. Shamelessly, she now used her voice as a weapon, seeing how it affected him. She hoped that if she appeared compliant she could use her voice to seduce him into letting her loose. She let her body relax under his groping hand, allowing her breast to soften under his touch. She struggled to conceal her distaste.

The General's breath hitched and he moved closer to her. She could tell by the dark look on his face that her acquiescence had aroused him further. As much as the idea repulsed her, she tried to appear as if she were not adverse to the idea of trading her body for his leniency.

"Well, it's complicated," he rasped out in answer to her question before moving his dark head to her breast.

Rayven's mind reeled as the General's hot mouth scorched her erect nipple. An impulse to launch some sort of attack against him warred with her usual iron control over her emotions. Rayven concentrated with all of her might on maintaining her façade of submission. It was one of the most difficult things she'd ever had to do.

Moaning softly and arching her breast into his mouth, Rayven tried to appear submissive to her baser sexual response to him. All the while she carefully planned her escape, should the chance arise.

General Karis slurped at the coral berry crowning her breast. He let his hand wander slowly down her midriff, savoring the feel of her silky soft skin. He released her nipple with a wet, popping sound and surveyed what his ministrations had wrought on her body.

Her nipple glistened wetly, engorged with blood and trembling with her every breath. Her face was lightly flushed and her eyes appeared hooded with arousal. She appeared to be enjoying his attentions, a thought which more than pleased him.

Perhaps she will be more amenable to my proposition than I had hoped, he thought smugly to himself.

Rayven waited for the General to remember their conversation, while she tried to appear in thrall to her desire of him. She didn't have to wait for long.

"Tell me your name," he commanded.

She demurely lowered her lashes, thinking the whole time about how much she wanted to rip his condescending tongue from his mouth.

"Rayven," she quietly answered him, knowing he would try to verify the truth of her words with the Lieutenant when he later left her. She did not want to get caught in a lie and shatter the appearance of her submission to him, should he question the validity of her responses to him.

She didn't know if she believed all that the General was now telling her, but she sensed that *he* believed in the truthfulness of all that he had said. Admitting to herself that his explanation of her origin explained a lot of unanswered questions, she pushed aside her doubts for later contemplation.

"Rayven," he breathed her name throatily on a sigh.

She detested the sound of her name on his lips.

"What if I told you there was a way for you to avoid execution at our hands? Your kind is guilty of countless misdeeds against the Galactic Commune, but your only crimes have been against the people of Earth, thief that you are. You were just an infant when your people launched an attack against our armies." His roving hand lightly traced patterns over the soft swell of her belly as he spoke.

"If you were willing to cooperate with me just a little, I could see to it that the charges of treason against you were dropped. After all, it would hardly be fair to condemn you for the misdeeds of your whole race, now would it?"

Rayven said nothing, waiting to hear what he had to say. She had a sinking feeling that it would not be pleasant, this alternative he dangled before her. Even if the alternative meant surviving her intended execution.

At least, she consoled herself silently, she could go along with what he wanted until she found a way to escape. Within reason, of course.

"I am a very powerful man, Rayven. I lead the great Galactic Commune and its vast armies. I can see to it that you are long-lived and wealthy beyond your wildest dreams. Or I can have you killed for a traitor, in shame and pain, if you choose not to fall in with my plans for you."

"What would you have me do?"

"Oh, it's no great sacrifice, I assure you. In fact it will be more of an advantage for you than myself, I would wager."

Rayven steeled herself for what was to come next.

"All you have to do, my beautiful little *Aware,* is swear allegiance to the Galactic Commune and to me...by joining me in the bonds of marriage."

Chapter Seven

Ysault Dimensional Plane
Sord Star System
Planet Hostis

Draco shook his sleek dark head. His hematite-colored hair shimmered in a glinting waterfall down his back. He looked out over the small crowd before him. They were likely the last of their kind, these few Aware gathered before him. And if things did not soon improve, if they failed to find their missing members and prospective mates with which to reproduce, they would remain the last. Slowly dying out, fading from existence.

He allowed his molten silver eyes to rove over the people waiting patiently for him to speak. With hair and eyes like precious stones and metals, his people had always stood out vibrantly among the other members of the Galactic Commune. Which was why they dare not venture off-planet now, for their race was readily recognizable.

Their legendary beauty and power had made them much sought-after lovers before the Great Massacre. Their incredibly sensual natures, in and out of the bedroom, had compelled many to seek out their favors. By using these traits, as well as their advanced intellect and mental prowess, hopefully those Aware that had been off-world at the time of the Great Massacre had found a way to ingratiate themselves with the peoples of other worlds. Or perhaps they had fled to the outer reaches of the galaxy, far beyond the boundaries of the Galactic Commune, and found safe harbor among the planets nestled there. Alas, he did not know the fate of his lost brethren.

Draco worried that his people's last hope for repopulation was in vain. He feared that, even with the warning given to those who had escaped the Great Massacre, they likely had been found and executed by their enemies. He wished only that he could have learned something of those survivors during the past twenty-eight years. Sadly, he was not powerful enough to find them.

Draco pushed his worries aside. He had other, more pressing, duties to attend before he and his people could search for the other survivors of their once great race. He reminded himself of his duty to his people to restore their lost Empress to the throne.

Only the Empress could reunite them with their lost brethren. Only she had the strength and power to sense their presence over time and space. Only she had the power to defeat their enemies and restore freedom to her people. Even were the whole of the surviving Aware race to combine its powers, theirs would but be a shadow under the awesome force of her fully developed *Awareness*.

Draco must go to claim her from her exile on Earth. He must help her to at last delve into the full potential of her power, to harness her great strength, which could at last crush the Galactic Commune.

He rose to his towering seven and a half foot height. Even among his people, who were taller than many other races, he was considerably larger than most. He sighed to himself before beginning. "Thank you for coming before me this rising," he said.

"I know you have all been anxious these past twenty-eight years during our exile. I thank you for being patient with me. I am your chosen leader, meant to rule in our Lady's stead while she is away from us. I have done the best that I can to help see us through such a difficult time."

Draco's closest friend spoke out. "You have done a fine job leading us, Draco. Were it not for you we would not be here now."

"I thank you for that, Setiger." Draco bowed slightly to him in acknowledgment.

"I agree with Setiger, Draco. Though we have all suffered, you have suffered the most, carrying the weight of our worries upon your shoulders without so much as a word of complaint," added Draco's brother, Avator.

Draco turned to his brother, his silver eyes roving over Avator's seven-foot-three-inch frame, bloodstone hair, and lapis eyes. He nodded arrogantly to his sibling, the only sibling out of seven others to survive the Massacre. They had both lost much during their trying ordeal, though they had been luckier than most to have a family member survive. The two brothers had remained strong and focused upon their goals, refusing to let their grief overwhelm them while their people needed them.

"We have all suffered, 'tis true, brother. Soon, however, I hope to see an end to these dreadful times."

Turning back to the crowd Draco continued, "I have spent the last moon rising in the company of my Chief Counselor, Onca." Draco motioned to a muscular, dark-haired man on the outskirts of the crowd.

"After much contemplation, we have decided it is at last time for me to go forth and claim our Empress from her hiding place." He waited patiently for the deafening roar, which spewed forth from the crowd, to die down before he continued.

"I know many of you have doubted the truth of my story, that I secreted the Empress away following her birth. I assure you that I have not misled you with this tale. Not all of you know the circumstances surrounding our Empress' exile, so please allow me to tell you what I may.

"It is true that thirty years ago I was a member of the Emperor's closest council. It is also true that shortly after the birth of his daughter, we received word that the Galactic Communal Army planned to launch an attack on our people." Draco paused to survey the effect his words had upon his people.

Seeing that he had his people's undivided attention he went on with his story.

"While we had the chance, we cautioned away as many off-world Aware as we could, warning them of the impending danger. We told them they would need to flee from any backwash of violence from the Galactic Commune, and lie in wait for word from us before returning to our homeworld of Nye. I do not know what has become of these missing members of our race. I only hope that they are hiding still, safe from the danger our enemies seek to visit upon them.

"Knowing of the mate-bond between his daughter and me, Emperor Thibetanus also bade me ensure the safety and survival of our infant princess, Rayven, should it become necessary. Less than a day later, our enemies attacked en masse, slaughtering our people with their *Kiel*-armored soldiers and weapons."

Draco closed his eyes on the wave of rage and pain at the memory of his people's decimation at the hands of the ruthless army.

"As it became apparent to our ruler and his mate that our people would fall under the crushing onslaught of our invaders, Emperor Thibetanus and Empress Delphi commanded me to remove their daughter from danger. I opened a silent gateway in time and space, seeking out a proper hiding place for our precious infant princess. Finding a tiny green planet far beyond the boundaries of our galaxy and dimension, I sent her through the gateway to safety."

A young woman named Manna moved forward in the crowd to speak. "Why did we not follow her when we left? Or why did you not retrieve our lost ruler after we arrived here?"

"At first it was because I feared our discovery and subsequent destruction at the hands of the Galactic Army. Later, when it seemed we were safe, I sought out the Empress to claim her. She had reached fifteen years of age, and already she stood out among the people of her adoptive planet, with her unusually vibrant eyes and hair and her advanced intelligence—"

Yet another member of the crowd before him interrupted Draco. "How has she survived this long, anonymously, among the people of this planet?"

"Please have patience, Jagur, and I will explain all the soonest."

Draco reprimanded the man with a hard stare from his silver eyes. He had learned much in his many years as ruler, and the cardinal rule was to never allow those subjects that he ruled to be impertinent. It undermined his power and weakened his necessary iron hold upon control. Jagur bowed his head respectfully, and subsided into the crowd once more.

"Our Empress is even more powerful than her parents and our seer, Onca, prophesized. She has been without proper training these past years, but already she has learned much on her own.

"She has become quite adept at controlling her great *Awareness*. She disguises her appearance with the use of colored lenses over her eyes and fake hair over her own. She has not attained the great height that is common in our race, and though I fear that this is because of her foreign diet and climate, this deficit in height has greatly helped to mask her among the people of her adopted planet. She has adapted very well to her surroundings, given the circumstances.

"As I was saying, thirteen years ago I went to claim our Empress, only to discover that our plans at subterfuge had failed. Somehow, spies from within our own ranks had discovered our plans to hide the heir to our throne and revealed them to the Galactic Army, just after the Massacre. Our enemies had been given thirteen years of opportunities in which to hunt her down. But they had not yet succeeded when I arrived.

"At first, only mediocre agents were sent to destroy Rayven. I suspect it was because the Galactic Army had not yet mastered the art of inter-dimensional travel, though how they even developed such a skill in the first place is beyond my knowledge, and they did not want to sacrifice more skilled Galactic agents should their travels end in mishap.

"I revealed myself in totem form to Rayven and warned her of the threat to her safety. I decided not to remove her from her adoptive planet, knowing that any attempt to do so would alert the Galactic Army to my presence. Instead I helped her to escape the immediate threat and encouraged her to be mindful of future attacks."

Draco paused to reflect upon what he had just said. How he wished he could have done more to help his mate than he had. He blamed himself for her loneliness and heartache. If he hadn't directly made contact with her, using his mind, strengthening the mate-bond between them, she wouldn't have felt so adrift when deprived of his presence.

Though she probably didn't know it, his distance from her had caused much of the unhappiness in her young life. Among their kind, once mates connected with each other's minds, they longed strongly thereafter for more contact. It was almost agony to be apart from one's mate, once bonded.

However, he knew he'd had no choice but to appear to her in the way that he had. She would never have heeded his orders to flee if he hadn't appeared in such a way that she mistook him for a psychic vision from her own mind. He knew she didn't believe him to be real, instead believed him to be her "spirit guide", a projection of her subconscious imagination. He would have spared her the unnecessary anguish of a separated mate, but it was the only way to ensure her continued survival.

Shaking himself forcibly from his brooding thoughts, Draco again addressed his people.

"She has remained safe from her hunters these past two decades. Now that we know we cannot successfully repopulate our race without seeking our off-world members, we must come out of hiding at last or we shall fade into extinction. We must claim our Empress so that she can lead us to our lost brethren, as only she has the power to sense our missing members across time and space. She will lead us out of hiding at last." The people gathered before Draco cheered upon hearing such news.

Draco's Chief Counselor, Onca, stepped forward now to address the crowd. His onyx-rimmed ruby eyes roved the crowd before speaking. "As many of you know I am a *Seer*. I possess the gift of the 'far-seeing eye', and I can oftentimes see what the future may bring. Though the road of the future is not paved in stone, and though I do not always receive a precognition when it seems we would need it most, I have never beheld a vision that did not later come true.

"Many years ago, when our late Emperor and Empress first mated, I beheld a vision of the future. I saw an image of the Empress Rayven, heir to the throne of *Aware*, standing before the massive Galactic Army. She held death in one hand and rebirth in another. There was an aura of unimagined power surrounding her, bathing her in a white-hot light, shaking the very foundations of the planet upon which she stood. At each shoulder stood the spirits of her parents, and their power ran through her like a raging river, wild and untamed.

"I knew then that she would be one of the most powerful rulers we had ever known. I knew that our people would face great evil at the hands of the Galactic Commune, and that our great Empress and Emperor would not live to see us through it. I knew our triumph over this evil lay in the hands of their child as our future ruler."

Onca waited patiently as the crowd murmured wonderingly over this new information. When the disquiet subsided he continued.

"These next few months after the return of our exiled Empress will be difficult for us all. We must each of us help to prepare Rayven for her destiny. She needs patience and training, to learn to harness the great *Awareness* within her. We must set aside our worries and sorrow and look now to the future."

Draco clasped Onca's shoulder in a strong grip. He nodded respectfully to his trusted friend and advisor before again addressing the crowd.

"I will go now to claim Empress Rayven from her exile. The Fates willing, she will lead us into the light," Draco's voice became as hard and unyielding as steel, "to Freedom."

Chapter Eight

Ysault Dimensional Plane
Ampilon Star System
Planet Varood

Rayven looked at the General in astonishment. Her mind racing over the words he had just spoken to her, with such a self-satisfied expression on his face. Surely he had to be joking!

He wanted her to *marry* him?

General Karis chuckled at her stunned expression. "I know it's a bit sudden, my dear, but let me assure you that I do not offer you such an honor lightly. I realize that we do not know each other, yet, but that will soon change. I have every confidence that you will make me an excellent wife."

Rayven felt her stomach plummet at the thought.

"I knew your mother, you see, and I am certain that after extensive training, you will be every bit as beautiful and refined as she. You already have the look of her, so all that remains are your poor manners which we can train out of you with relative ease." He trailed his hand across her velvety midriff, petting her as if she were some kind of docile animal.

"You knew my mother," Rayven breathed, looking deeply into the General's eyes for any sign of truth to his words, ignoring the flood of hope that welled within her. She didn't dream for one moment that she could believe anything the General told her, but she couldn't deny the flare of gullibility she felt when he mentioned her mother.

The General's eyes glowed as he saw Rayven's eager response to his words. "Yes, my little renegade, I knew your mother," he verified. His hands stroked absently along her exposed body. "Long ago…ages ago, it seems." His voice ended in a whisper.

Rayven struggled to concentrate on his words and not his disgusting touch. The General's eyes seemed to look off into the distant past, seeming to forget her presence as he continued.

"She was the most beautiful woman in the known galaxies. Rare and radiant, her smile could send a man to his knees. I knew the moment I saw her, while visiting on her planet of Nye, that I had to have her.

"Alas, it was not to be. Though she could have grown to love me given the chance, she was stolen from me by *Him*. Seeing my desire for her hand, Emperor Thibetanus forced my sweet Delphi into a marriage with him…" His voice faded away, and his eyes glazed blearily.

Rayven felt a prick of *Awareness* in her mind. She sensed that there was some truth to the General's tale, but there was a trickle of doubt in her brain as to his complete honesty. Perhaps he *had* known her mother, but had events surrounding her parents' marriage been as the General had said? Rayven wagered that all was not as he told her.

Rayven sensed that his perception of the truth was largely affected by his unstable mind. Her powers may be useless to aid her in her escape but they were still with her, and they bade her to take the General's words with a large grain of salt.

She wanted desperately to ask specific questions about her parents, but she realized that whatever answers he may offer her would be only half-truths at best. At least she had a name for her mother and father now. *Delphi* and *Thibetanus*. Rayven clutched the knowledge to her heart, letting its warmth spread through her and imbue her with strength.

"Shortly thereafter, you were born. I knew then that she had been unfaithful to me from the first. You were born a mere three months after the royal wedding. Then came the Great Massacre, and your mother and father were killed along with all the other Aware."

Rayven, alert to every nuance on the General's face, asked him, "Why would the Emperor launch an attack against an army that could decimate their entire population? You said he launched an attack. Against whom?"

The General seemed to come back from his recollections to regard her steadily. His cold green eyes hardened before he spoke, and he clenched his fists tightly at his sides.

"Against the Galactic Commune, of course. He knew how I coveted his wife, and to ensure that she didn't leave him to be with me, he attacked us. I fear his jealousy over his wife's affections blinded him to the danger he placed his people in."

Rayven saw a sudden and startling vision in her mind of the General waging war on her people. She could sense that it had not, in truth, been her father who had instigated the attack. The slaughter of her people had been the General's goal from the first. Upon hearing of the early birth of Rayven, the General had realized at last that the Empress had not reciprocated his obsessive passion for her.

General Karis had felt Delphi had betrayed him by mating with Thibetanus during his dogged pursuit for her hand. He had not cared that Delphi did not wish to marry him, that she had in fact deeply loved Emperor Thibetanus. He had felt slighted and allowed his jealous rage to decimate an entire race.

Rayven also perceived an image of her mother and father standing before the triumphant General on a vast battlefield littered with the dead and dying bodies of their people. They regally faced down their enemy, tall and straight, enfolded protectively in each other's arms. Her father's onyx hair flew wildly in the wind and his amethyst eyes flashed defiantly.

With a flash of pain deep in her heart, Rayven witnessed a scene from the General's own memories…

"So, Thibetanus, was it worth all this slaughter, your marrying my chosen bride?" The General swept his hand over the bloody

battlefield around them, his other hand clutching a glowing white sword.

The Emperor straightened his impossibly broad shoulders. "She was not a prize to be won by you. Your obsession has made you blind to the horror you have caused." His glowing amethyst eyes hardened menacingly.

"You will come to regret the deeds of this day," vowed the defiant Emperor, "I promise you this, General Karis. You, yourself, will know the needless suffering that my people have endured. It will be visited upon you a thousandfold before this is done."

General Karis roared his rage at Thibetanus' words before he viciously beheaded the great Emperor of the Aware.

As her husband's body had teetered and crumpled, Empress Delphi had screamed in pain and rage. Turning to the General, she hissed out a curse that chilled the blood in his veins.

"I condemn you to endless suffering, Karis. You will forever pine for me, for the love that I would never give to you. You will wake at night calling my name, knowing that you can never have me. You will never be able to mate with another woman without imagining me in her place. Every moment of every day you will think of me and wish for things that could never be."

Upon uttering her last words, the Empress threw herself upon the General's Blazesword, beheading herself upon its razor-sharp edge…

Pulling herself from the horrific scenes unfolding in the General's memories, Rayven experienced a rage unlike any she'd ever known before.

"You killed them," she said, her voice flat and lifeless.

"I had no choice. It was war. I wish I could have spared your people but they fought like beasts to the death. Such a tragedy." The General shook his head as if in regret over the waste of so many lost lives.

Rayven felt a flood of heat engulf her body. She felt her rage pour through her veins like liquid fire, feeding off itself, and growing in its intensity. The burning rush of pure adrenaline and psychic power brought pain flooding through her body—as if her skin were too tight to contain the sheer volume of it. Rayven welcomed the pain—fed off it even as she welcomed the return of her powers. Feeling a surge of this hate-spawned power raging unchecked through her body, Rayven "pushed" at the General with the power of her mind.

In a violent, sudden fury of movement, the General flew backwards to impact roughly against the wall—his head connecting against the stone with a resounding smack. Rayven's power had been reawakened despite the *Kiel* bonds, and its sheer intensity was unlike any she'd ever known before. The astonished look on the General's face contorted into a mask of rage and fear as he struggled against the crushing unseen force that prevented him from moving or calling out for help.

"You killed my parents, you fucking asshole!" Rayven's usually well-modulated voice ended on a choking scream.

She used her reawakened power to open the bonds securing her wrists and ankles. Jumping lithely down from the dais, she rushed at the General. Taking his throat in her hands, uncaring that she'd lost control over herself, she ruthlessly began to squeeze the life out of him. In her mind she built the image of the General's lungs shrinking and rotting, and her enemy started to convulse as he gasped for the air to fill his dying lungs.

"Did you *really* think I would just blindly believe that load of shit you just tried to feed me? Fuck that and fuck you! I'm going to kill you for what you've done, and I'm going to enjoy every sweet minute of it. Do you hear me? I'm going to *kill* you!"

Her fingers viciously squeezed his bulging neck, the awesome power of her *Awareness* keeping him firmly held against the wall. The General's face turned red, purple, blue—all the colors of the rainbow, before he started to pale, and his life force began to wane. Rayven felt a surge of dark satisfaction, and tightened her already superhuman hold upon his swollen neck, digging into the muscle and cartilage beneath his flesh.

The door of the room swung suddenly inward, shuddering on its hinges as a swarm of uniformed soldiers, alarmed by the sounds of struggle, filed into the room weapons at the ready. Releasing her death grip on the General's neck Rayven turned and flew at the soldiers. As she ran, she simultaneously and instinctively used her mind to compel the men with guns to turn and fire at one another. Two unarmed men made as if to physically attack her, only to be thrown heedlessly out of Rayven's way as she dashed from the room.

Rapidly assessing her surroundings, Rayven let her body flood with power. Using her preternatural skills to guide her through the bowels of her would-be prison, Rayven ran for her life. She darted down corridor after corridor, taking in the strange-looking gray stone of the walls around her and the odd light sources above her head. Instead of electrical lights, soft light emanated from flat disks floating just below the ceiling.

We're not in Kansas anymore, Toto, she thought to herself with an almost insane urge to giggle aloud.

Heedless of the stares of confused military personnel as she passed, she wasted no time dwelling on the fact of the nude spectacle she presented, her mind focused solely on the need to flee. She did, however, notice that many of the staring people were anything but normal-looking. She noticed green, orange and purple skins interspersed with the more familiar white, black and brown ones.

Using her powerful senses, she sought the outermost wall of the keep. Sensing it a few corridors ahead, she sprinted onward. Despite the fact that she now strongly suspected that she was indeed on a different planet, as the General had suggested, she sought a window from which to escape. She hoped that once she reached the outside world beyond, she could then reassess her situation and perhaps find a way home.

Home. What *was* home now? Was it the planet on which she'd lived her whole life, or that unknown place of her birth, Nye? Brushing these thoughts from her mind for further contemplation, Rayven raced on through the alien fortress.

As she rounded a corner, Rayven was suddenly compelled to stop her wild flight. Her feet slid and skidded upon the cold stone floor because of her abrupt cessation of movement. A strange compulsion—a feeling that took hold of her mind and will in a flood and left her numb, caused her body to turn as if it were pulled by invisible strings. She slowly approached a small dark door to her left, a feeling of intense dread filled her form and soul. She tried to resist the strange feeling within her, a feeling that beckoned her to look beyond the door to whatever lay inside—but to no avail. She wasn't strong enough to disobey the strange summons that had robbed her of her self-will. Hands shaking, still futilely struggling against the overwhelming urge to open the door, she reached for the cold iron handle and turned it. It was locked.

Not understanding why she felt such a strong need to enter the room, and frightened because of it, Rayven used her already depleted reserves of power to trip the lock and opened the door.

At first she could see nothing, as the strange floating lights were dimmed within. She felt a strongly emanating warmth from within the room, beckoning her deeper within. Her heart stuttering in fear and trepidation, Rayven reached out her hand only to encounter a small velveteen bag, filled with what felt like thousands of tiny marbles or stones.

Wanting only to flee this strangely foreboding chamber and whatever lay inside it, Rayven heeded the compulsion that drove her. She stole one small stone from the bag, her fingers clutching desperately at the strangely red-hot pebble, before she turned and fled in horror from the darkened room.

Once she reached the hallway, she breathed a sigh of relief and let her heart resume its normal rhythm before resuming her run to freedom. Her strange feelings in connection with the room faded from her mind—as if it were naught but a remembered dream or nightmare, but she continued to clutch the stone firmly in her tight fist, knowing it must somehow be important for her to keep it safe. For whatever reasons, she could not say, her powers had commanded her to take the stone for her own. Later she would study it and try to understand what its significance was.

Rayven ran swift and sure down the winding tunnels. Sudden weariness beat at her like a thousand hammers. Her mind was dulled—her great surges of power against the General and his men had taken a mighty toll on her usually vast reserves of strength. She was emotionally and physically drained. She didn't know how much longer she could run, but she knew she had to try and reach some sort of safety before she could rest.

So much had changed in the past few hours, that she could hardly sort it all out in her mind. Had it only been a few hours since her capture? How long *had* it been since the General's men had taken her from her car? She had no idea.

"Halt!" A voice behind Rayven shouted, numerous footfalls steadily approaching.

Darting around a corner Rayven spotted a twisting stone staircase. Hesitating only long enough for her *Awareness* to assure her that beyond this staircase lay freedom, she quickly raced up the stairs. Glancing down the expansively winding staircase, Rayven spotted half a dozen uniformed men hot on her trail. They were led by the Lieutenant whose nose she had broken earlier.

"Halt or we will be forced to fire!"

Not pausing in her flight, Rayven ducked as stone splintered from a laser blast over her shoulder mere seconds later.

Glimpsing the door just ahead of her, Rayven put on an extra burst of speed, ignoring the now-numerous laser blasts flashing around her. Reaching the door she burst through it, dislodging its heavy wooden bulk from its hinges with her unchecked strength. She looked around and gasped at the scene that unfolded before her dazed eyes, stumbling to a clumsy halt.

She was on the roof of a great stone castle, not dissimilar in style to those castles found on Earth. Its biggest difference was that it rose thousands of feet up into the air. Rayven ran to the parapet and looked out over the castle's vast height. The low stone balustrade afforded her a dizzying view overlooking wispy clouds at a height that would put a small mountain to shame.

From what she could see from the surrounding countryside below the thin cloud cover, the physical characteristics of the land below differed little from those of Earth. There was a vast expanse of rolling green hills dotted by tall green trees. Blue water sparkled cheerily in the sunlight from small bodies of water in the distance.

Rayven could have almost believed she was simply in another country were it not for one very noticeably alien characteristic. Far off over the horizon hung two suns low in the sky. One was a huge ball of yellow light, not unlike the Sun of Earth. The other was a smaller, pale blue ball that glowed like some kind of strange jewel resting low in its blanket of clouds. The strange suns, coupled with the glimpses she'd had earlier of strangely colored humanoids, and the immense height and size of the castle in which she found herself, confirmed her suspicions.

She sank down to lean heavily back against a stone slab. She was on another planet. Another *world*. Her mind reeled with the realization.

How was she ever going to get back to Earth? What was to become of her? She felt lost and alone, certain that she would never feel safe again. One thing was for certain, she thought when she caught sight of her pursuers as they crashed through the door. She wasn't going to stay here and be executed by some madman and his fanatic henchmen.

Jumping up from her crouch, Rayven climbed to the top of the parapet. She dizzyingly braced herself as she once again surveyed the scene below, the heels of her feet teetering out over the edge of the stone wall beneath them. How in the world could she hope to safely escape? She was too weak to use her powers against them right now—just the thought of calling upon them made her weary with the effort. She had no idea where to run from here. She couldn't see any other avenue of escape besides the door behind her pursuers.

"Halt and we will spare your life," Lieutenant Devon commanded.

Rayven snorted defiantly and tossed back her head proudly. "Why bother? You're only going to execute me as soon as you have me in custody once more."

"We will let General Karis decide your fate, as soon as he is able. You crushed his windpipe, you know. We had to summon a doctor to revive him."

"Do you think I care at all? I only wish you'd waited a few seconds more before interrupting your General's murder. Then your damn doctors would have been unable to revive him at all!"

"Do not dare to be impertinent with me! You have no way to escape us. Your choice is to die now by *las-shot* or to come with us and pray for the General's leniency." Lieutenant Devon moved forward in an effort to grasp Rayven's wrist, a translucent *Kiel* bond dangling from his hand.

Rayven frantically swept her eyes about, hoping in vain that there was another door nearby that would afford her a chance at escape. When she saw none, her heart sank within her breast. She sent her mind seeking outwards, hoping for some miracle that would aid her.

If only my dream hawk were here to guide me now, she thought sadly to herself.

But he wasn't there with her, and he couldn't be, not really. Oh yes, she knew that he had never been real to begin with. He'd merely been a physical manifestation of her subconscious yearning for a friend in her youth. No matter how real he had seemed, she knew that he'd been a figment of her imagination.

As much as they managed to comfort her, Rayven pushed aside her thoughts of the black hawk to concentrate on the dilemma before her. Seeing no other alternative as the

Lieutenant approached her with his dratted *Kiel* handcuffs, Rayven did the only thing she could do to avoid capture.

She jumped.

Chapter Nine

Ysault Dimensional Plane
Sord Star System
Planet Hostis

Draco rose as his people cheered around him. He would make haste in his preparations for claiming the Empress. He had a strong feeling of urgency, a sense that all might not be as it should with his mate. He felt that the sooner he retrieved her from her place of exile and began her training for the throne of her people, the sooner he could claim her for his own and shelter her from those who wished her harm.

Who am I deceiving? he thought to himself. *The sooner I claim her, the sooner I can rut with her until she cannot walk straight*.

Of a certain, his libido had been raging at him almost nonstop. His species was a highly sensual one, and having found his mate he was more than ready to consummate their physical union. He had been aware of his mate's existence for almost three decades now, and his sexual urges were becoming exponentially more powerful as each year passed. His frustrations grew daily, and no mere wench could cool the fire in his veins—no matter how accommodating her cunt or mouth might be. Only his mate could satiate his sexual hunger. Only Rayven.

It was past time he claimed Rayven, brought her to his bed feathers, and eased the fearsome ache in his loins.

Suddenly Draco's body stilled, and he sensed a sudden, wrenching disturbance within his mind. A sudden shrieking wail sounded long and loud within his brain. His teeth clenched at the roaring sound. He darted his eyes over the crowd and saw that they, too, were hearing the awful psychic transmission. Each face in the crowd winced and contorted as the sound rose impossibly louder in volume before abruptly stopping, leaving a black wall of silence in its wake.

As Draco stood gasping he heard a whisper brush along his mind in a mournful tone that sent a chill of foreboding down his spine.

If only my dream hawk were here to guide me now…

Rayven! He would recognize her psychic voice anywhere. His mate was in dire trouble, and she desperately sought his aid.

Draco turned and met the stunned eyes of Onca. Knowing that as Rayven's mate, he had been the only one to hear her last whispered words after her untrained mind-seek, he sent a private thought to the mind of his friend.

"'Tis Rayven, she seeks my help. I must go to her anon. You and my brother must watch over our people. If anything should happen to us…"

Onca nodded, knowing that should Rayven and Draco not return he must assume the role of leader of their people. He was the most powerful of their people after Draco, and it would be his duty to find a way to free their people if they should lose their Empress and her consort.

"It will be as you wish, my friend. May the wind be at your back, and good luck by your side."

Upon hearing those words from his second, Draco transformed himself into the form of a giant black hawk and transported himself immediately to his mate's side, leaving Onca to explain the powerful mind-seek and its origin to their stunned people.

* * * * *

Rayven fell, arms outstretched as though in flight. Her mind reeled as she saw herself plummeting towards the low cloud cover at a speed that brought stinging tears to her wide eyes. The wind lashed her cheeks, her hair flew around in disarray, and she fought the wild urge to scream out her fear.

She tried desperately to slow her fall using her *Awareness,* but to no avail. She had exhausted herself in her earlier struggles with the General. Knowing she faced her impending death splattered on the ground below, she went limp and let the wind take her where it willed. She was too weary to fight the inevitable.

As she passed through the first layer of clouds a faint motion caught at the corner of her vision. Surrealistically she caught sight of the form of a giant black raptor racing towards her on the dizzying wind. As the bird of prey rapidly approached her she felt her heart jump within her breast.

The black hawk! He had come for her, as he always had when she needed him most. Hearing his wild call on the wind, she almost laughed aloud in her relief. She had never been so happy to see anything in her life. Even if he was a hallucination, she somehow felt that he could keep her from harm.

As she sped onward in her dizzying plunge, the black hawk finally reached her and circled comfortingly around her, brushing her naked skin with his soft feathers.

"You came," she sent the words with her weary mind.

"Did you think I would not, having heard your call to me? I could never let harm befall you, a grifa. *Come, Rayven, do not fight my will that I might lead you to safety."*

The black hawk dived before her and Rayven saw a vast vortex open below, directly in their path of flight. It roared and wailed, and pulled at her even more strongly than the force of the planet's gravity, speeding her flight and pulling her within its boundaries. Sensing that through the gateway lay salvation and safety, she closed her eyes and let the suctioning darkness envelop her.

Cold…it's so cold, she thought.

She opened her eyes and saw racing flashes of light interspersed in the raging darkness. She caught an image of the black hawk riding the raging wind with her. A thousand points of freezing light pricked at her skin, flashing wildly all around her. Her eyes watered from the cold and from the bright illuminations.

Needles of bitter cold stabbed at her eyes, face, and body. Her flesh felt hard and frozen, like a deadweight slab of ice. Blackness began to swim before her eyes, and she feared that she would lose consciousness in the deep void. She tried and failed to slow her spiraling velocity, but the effort only pained her more. She fell and fell, forever into frigid emptiness. Her thoughts broke on a scream.

"Do not fight it, Rayven, it's better if you don't fight." The black hawk's words did little to soothe her fractured mind.

Rayven's breath was sucked forcibly from her lungs and her heart shuddered under an onslaught of fear. She sensed that she was traveling at speeds heretofore unimagined by the scientists of Earth. What lay in wait for her at the end of her terrifying journey? How would she stop her dizzying plunge through this strange doorway?

Abruptly her headlong flight seemed to slow and Rayven had the strange vision of an approaching heavenly body. A planet appeared before her, so much larger than her familiar planet of Earth, that it would have dwarfed it into a miniscule size. It was awash in hues that she had never seen or imagined before, interspersed with impossible shades of blue and lavender and green.

Her eyes closed involuntarily as the huge planet loomed ever closer. She experienced a few more moments of the freezing cold vortex violently shuddering around them before feeling a slight popping sensation—almost as if she were breaking bodily through a fleshy membrane. Suddenly she was through the wormhole and plunging feet first into impossibly blue water.

The water felt warm after her plunge through the freezing gateway, and it closed over her head on a welcoming swallow into its depths. Rayven plunged downward, the force of her fall taking her deep into the heart of the water. After her ordeal within the dark tunnel, she felt the foolish urge to stay beneath the warm waves forever, safe in a cocoon of thick blue warmth, before jerking mentally away from the thought. Rayven hesitated only a moment more as the last of her shock wore off before she kicked her feet and made for the surface.

Flinging her hair back from her face as she broke on a wave, she looked around for any sign of the black hawk. It was nowhere to be found. After searching to make sure the bird had not also plummeted into the water and perhaps been trapped there, Rayven decided that perhaps the bird had not been with her at all. She must have somehow found the power within herself to open the gateway to another world.

And what a world it was!

The water beaded off her skin in bright azure droplets. It seemed to be thicker than the water she was accustomed to on Earth. It smelled of crisp ozone and virgin snow. Risking a taste, Rayven felt it wash over her tongue in delight. It tasted divine. It was so sweet and clean that Rayven, suddenly thirsty, gulped down more. She had no idea when she'd last sated her thirst, and now she made up for lost time, gluttonously drinking her fill. Sighing with bliss she floated for a few moments, resting in the tranquil waves.

She felt a burning in her palm and realized that she still grasped the tiny pebble from the forbidden room in her palm. She looked at it, careful not to drop it into the water. It looked like one of those strange blue stones her captors sported in their silver headbands. It was dark blue, with hidden starlit facets. It was no larger than an apple seed, and was almost hot to the touch. Just looking at it made her feel strong, safe, and secure—though why this was so she could not have said.

She clutched it once again in her palm, careful now, for the stone seemed to want to burrow sharply into her skin as she grasped it. She was uncertain why she felt so protective of it, but was determined not to lose it in the deep blue waters.

Catching a glimpse out of the corner of her eye of a shoreline a surprisingly short distance away, she swam towards it gratefully. Safe at last! Though she didn't know where she was, she was sure that none of her hunters would find her here.

She wasn't sure how she sensed this, but as with most things she just accepted it and moved on, knowing that questions would get her nowhere.

Reaching the soft white sands of the beach, Rayven lay in the lapping waves at the shoreline. She rolled onto her back laughing gleefully—madly, and clutching at the sun-warmed sand with her empty hand. Looking up at the warm orange sun above her, she sighed happily. Wherever she was, it was beautiful.

She sat up and looked out at the vast ocean before her. It was so blue that it hurt her eyes to look at it too long. Looking up in the sky Rayven could see softly calling water birds flying out overhead, hunting the waters for prey. A sultry warm breeze tickled her hair and kissed her sun-drying skin.

A shadow loomed over her, startling her, and bringing goose bumps to her skin in its cooling shade. A soft cloth of flowing white material was draped loosely over her shoulder, shielding her nakedness. She gasped and flew to her feet, whirling to face the person who loomed behind her.

Her mind fell blessedly blank. She knew her jaw hung slack as she took in the sight of the overwhelmingly large man before her. He was so gorgeous that she actually felt her mouth water. She'd never seen such beauty on a man before.

He was at least seven and a half feet tall, with broad, strong shoulders and long silvery-black hair. Hematite was the closest color she could think of to describe its preternatural beauty, remembering the silver-sheened black stone from Earth.

He was possessed of an impossibly muscular chest, which was clothed in a loose black shirt laced casually down the middle, leaving a large expanse of flesh bare to her gaze. Hairless bronzed skin peeked temptingly out at her from the gaping laces of his shirt. His waist tapered gracefully into his tight black pants, which appeared to be made of some sort of buffed animal hide not unlike leather. His legs were long and strong, and their muscles rippled powerfully under her hungry gaze.

Catching sight of the growing bulge at the front of his skintight pants, Rayven's wide golden eyes flew up to meet his glowing silver ones. Remembering her nudity, she hastily gathered the ends of the white robe he'd given her tightly around her tingling body. Unable to tear her gaze away from his mesmerizing one, she stood there for what seemed like an eternity before he spoke.

"Do you like what you see, beauty?"

His voice brushed over her like warm black velvet. Its compelling melody tingled along her skin, bringing her nipples to erect and tingling points. She imagined giddily that he had somehow invaded her body with his voice, touching secret places that had never even seen the light of day, and awakening within her desires she'd never felt before, enslaving her to him with its tempting promise of forbidden pleasures.

He approached her slowly, dwarfing her in his shadow and reaching out a beautifully long-fingered hand to her face. His hand softly caressed her jaw, and her eyes closed at the exquisite feel of its warmth. He gently but firmly tilted her head back, her damp hair fluttering out over her back in the wind. A small, soft moan escaped her throat as he dipped his sculpted lips down to taste of her.

His lips were firm and smooth as silk. They burned against her own, moving like a whisper against her mouth. His tongue slipped past to tease and stroke. His wild untamed flavor washed over her in a dizzying wave. She imagined she could stay that way forever, with his hand cradling her jaw and his lips plundering hers.

"You're ripe for fucking aren't you, little one?" he whispered against her lips, teasingly flicking his tongue over them in a small taste. "You seem as eager for your claiming as I."

As if to prove the truth of his darkly muttered words, his hand began to move over her body, teasingly pushing aside the folds of her concealing robe. His fingertips traced circles on her delicate collarbone before traveling lower, pausing to lightly run the pads of his fingers across the throbbing peak of her full breast. He moved his hand lower still, his lips never ceasing to move seductively, and his knowing fingers moved towards the burning, melting ache between her quivering legs.

As he reached his destination and dipped his fingers temptingly into her wetly dripping heat, Rayven suddenly came back to herself with a jolt. Thrusting away from him with trembling fingers that until that point had clutched at him desperately, she stumbled and fell.

What the hell had she been thinking? What was happening to her? It felt as if she had no will of her own. She'd just wilted into his embrace like some hothouse flower, more than ready to spread her legs and have sex with him. With a complete stranger!

An unbelievably sexy and gorgeous stranger, her traitorous libido pointed out giddily.

The gorgeous man smiled, his eyes twinkling knowingly, as if he knew her every thought. He reached out his hand and, ignoring her struggles, brought her to her feet with an almost practiced ease.

Rayven felt the wind kiss her exposed breasts and belly and gasped as his gaze scorched a blazing path down her sensitized skin. With clumsy movements she grasped the ends of the strangely fashioned robe and, trying not to lose the small blue stone still held firmly in her hand, she struggled to hide her nudity from his hungry gaze. He moved closer to help her, as her fumbling hands made a tangle of the strange ties on the seams of the loose garment.

"*Oompf*! Quit it," she bit out as she struggled to bat his hands and hide herself at the same time.

He merely chuckled at her efforts, the dark, masculine sound washing over her like a splash of liquid sunlight. He brushed her hands aside and rapidly laced up the ties to her garment. When he was finished, he stepped back and she stood enfolded in a flowing white shirt, with straight laces up the middle. It was not dissimilar in fashion to the shirt he wore, though it reached to the tops of her knees and therefore looked more like a short gown on her.

"Thank you," she said, trying to gain some dignity, in spite of her earlier lapse of good sense.

"You're welcome," he said with a small twitch at his mouth.

Not knowing what else to say, Rayven simply stood where she was, looking everywhere but at him. She put the stone she was clutching with white-knuckled intensity into a small pocket in her strange garment, freeing her trembling hands. Her lips burned and her lower belly ached with unfulfilled desire. She'd never felt so embarrassed, or awkward…or aroused. Her brain was like a puddle of insensate goo in her head. For the first time in her life, her intelligence deserted her.

"So, um, where am I?" she asked.

"Hostis." He appeared to enjoy her discomfort. His eyes twinkled and a corner of his mouth twitched as if he were fighting the urge to grin at her dishabille.

"Where is—oh never mind! Who are you?" Rayven gritted her teeth at her ineloquent words. For the first time in her life she felt like a dense fool.

"I am Draco," he said to her in his sexy midnight voice, bowing slightly to her from his towering height.

"I am Rayven," she said raising her chin regally, her tone suggesting it was a great boon for her to offer him her name.

"Yes, I know—" he smiled openly now, revealing straight white teeth, "—I have been awaiting you for some time now."

"What do you mean?"

He shrugged his broad shoulders, leaving her question unanswered. Rayven gritted her teeth as he chuckled softly. She wanted to walk right up to him and smack him squarely in his beautiful face. How *dare* he laugh at her? He had no idea who he was messing with, and as soon as she was well rested and back at her full strength, she'd take great pleasure in showing him.

Suddenly he leaned in closer to her and grasped her shoulders before she could make an effort to step away from him.

"Oh, I know exactly with whom I am dealing, tiny one. It is you who are unaware of just whom you are dealing with." So saying, he swooped down to kiss her roughly and quickly on the lips.

Gasping, Rayven again tried to pull away. This time he released her shoulders, allowing her to put some space between them.

"You read my mind, y-you big sneak! How dare you—you've no right." Her usual eloquent vocabulary deserted her once again as she stuttered up at him. Her hands fisted at her side and she stomped her foot in agitation.

"Temper, temper, tiny one. You must learn some control or you'll never be taken seriously," he laughed in her face as she sputtered.

Pushed beyond the limits of her already strained temper, she rushed at him in a fury. So far today she'd been manhandled by a lunatic General, been told she was an alien, been informed of the slaughter of her parents and of the extinction of her entire race. She'd been shot at by bizarre weapons, she'd jumped from a building the size of a small mountain, fallen through a wormhole, crash-landed on an alien world and had nearly been ravished by the most gorgeous hunk of male she'd ever laid eyes on—who could also read her mind! Enough was enough, already.

She attacked him out of sheer frustration, fists flying. Before she could pummel his sexy chest with her fists, however, he grabbed her hands and anchored them at her sides with seemingly no effort. Trying to squirm out of his hold, she lashed out at him with her bare feet. He merely laughed and lifted her by her arms, several inches off the ground, to bring her to eye level with him.

"I'm bigger, stronger and faster than you, *a grifa*. You cannot hope to bring me low with brute force. You are tired and need rest. We will continue this confrontation when you are more yourself."

"You asshole, don't you *dare* talk to me that way," she cried, struggling against his gentle but immovable hold.

"Sleep, Rayven. Sleep and dream sweet restful dreams…" His heated silver eyes bored into hers.

Suddenly a wave of dizziness washed through her, one she couldn't fight against, nor did she wish to. His eyes were so mesmerizing, his voice dark and textured. She forgot why she was angry, forgot what she'd been saying. She was lost to all but the heady compulsion in his eyes.

Sleep…sleep…sleep.

She gave in to the weariness that pulled at her. Closing her eyes she went limp in his arms. She slept.

She dreamed of him.

Chapter Ten

Ysault Dimensional Plane
Ampilon Star System
Planet Varood

"What do you mean she disappeared? She can't have just disappeared. She should be splattered on the rocks at the foot of this castle! Look again, Lieutenant. Use the brain trace you placed upon her to track her, anything, just find her!" General Karis roared in a gravelly voice from his sick bed.

"Sir, we removed the trace, so that she would think more clearly during your interview with her. Everyone knows that implanted traces cause fatigue and disorientation. It was for your benefit that we did this."

"Well, find her. I don't care how!"

Lieutenant Devon looked at the General's still swollen and purple neck as the palace doctors attended him. General Karis had received a concussion, a crushed windpipe and two slipped discs in his spine from his altercation with the renegade Aware woman. The injuries seemed minor, considering how quickly the Aware probably could have dispatched his life should she have so chosen. What had held her back? Was she truly a novice, or was she playing some game? The Lieutenant did not know.

"Sir, my men have searched the grounds twice. There is no sign of her body, and she could not have escaped on foot. There is no ground cover for miles and our lookouts would have seen her. She has disappeared."

The General's face turned an ugly shade of red as he gritted out, "Look again, Lieutenant. She can't have vanished into thin air, and our scans detected no interstellar gateway opening, so she didn't escape that way either. Now find her, and if your incompetent men cannot find her torn and bloodied body on the ground, have them span out and search the surrounding area."

Lieutenant Devon saluted smartly and rushed to do his leader's bidding.

"She can't have just disappeared," the General whispered angrily to himself. "It's impossible."

"General Karis, you must calm yourself." The doctor by his bedside checked his pulse and shook his head. "Your men will find her, never fear. Now just lie back and relax. Let your body heal and rest, so that you may return to full health."

The bruised General subsided from his all-consuming rage as his doctor pumped painkillers into his system. As he drifted off into a drugged sleep his doctors left him to his rest. As his head surgeon closed the door behind him the doctor thought he heard the General breathe a word softly in his sleep, though he had no idea what it meant.

"Delphi..."

Chapter Eleven

Ysault Dimensional Plane
Sord Star System
Planet Hostis

Rayven slowly awakened from her deep sleep. She was lying in a scrumptiously soft bed of fragrant purple feathers. Overhead, ebony-colored branches heavily laden with the same strange feathers swayed gently in the warm morning breeze. She looked around at the opulent tent surrounding her and rose from her comfortable bed.

She was still wearing the strange white shirt Draco had given her. Draco, of the delicious velvet voice and sexy body. Draco, the seducer and mind reader.

"Bah," she grouched aloud as memories of her embarrassing encounter with the gorgeous giant washed over her, staining her cheeks with a hot blush.

A slight movement at the opening of her unusual shelter caught her eye and dragged her from her musings. A head with brown- and blonde-streaked hair the color of tiger's-eye poked through the tent opening followed by an exquisitely beautiful pair of onyx eyes and elfin features.

"I heard you stir, Highness. If you are well rested, I have brought you proper clothing to don. When you are dressed I will take you to break your fast."

Rayven ignored the woman's strange greeting. "Who are you?"

The woman smiled shyly. "I am Ursus, Highness, and I am at your service. Shall I help you to dress?"

"Why are you calling me Highness? My name is Rayven—just plain Rayven."

The lady's gaze suddenly shifted away. "All of your questions will be answered the soonest, do you dress now and join us in the Gathering Tree."

Rayven frowned. Highness? Gathering tree? This woman wasn't making much sense to her, but hey, *When in Rome...*

Reaching out for the black and red gauze the woman held out for her, Rayven studied the woman. She was one of the most beautiful people she'd ever seen. Her hair was an impossible mixture of shades and shone like a mirror, her skin was a flawless gold tone, and her eyes were dark as onyx stones and heavily lashed. Though she was bent down through the small opening to the feathered tent, Rayven could tell that she was very tall and willowy.

Breaking her gaze away from the vision before her, she looked at the strange garments she held. From what she could tell, it might be some sort of skirt and shirt, thought she wasn't certain. It consisted of several diaphanous ties and long swatches of cloth.

"How do I put this on?"

The beautiful woman grinned at her perplexed question. "I will show you, Highness."

Short moments later Rayven glanced down at her new clothing. It looked like a belly dancer's outfit, complete with sexy, revealing harem pants and a backless bustier. Rayven felt naked and exposed, and though the material was opaque, it left little to the imagination.

The leggings were slinky and fluid, black against her thighs, with slits from just above the ruby-red ankle cuffs all the way to her hips, revealing her long and toned calves, thighs and hips. They rode low on her waist, the wide ruby-colored waistband coming to just below her silver navel ring. Her top was tied at the nape of her neck and middle of her back, the front was black with splashes of ruby color with tiny black beaded fringe framing the vee of its hem over her midriff. Otherwise, her whole back, shoulders and arms were left bare.

"I look like a harem girl," she moaned aloud, wishing she had a mirror to assess the damage done to her modesty.

Ursus laughed softly. Though she wasn't sure what Rayven was talking about, she suspected she had a good idea. The Empress was very alluring in her new clothing. Ursus knew that when Draco first glimpsed his mate, he would be hard-pressed not to claim her before the whole assembly this morning.

"You will be glad of it when the sun is at its peak. It gets very hot here, and you will stay cool despite the heat of the day in this ensemble. All of our women dress this way—though some wear even less, and the color brings out the highlights of your hair, Highness."

"What's it made out of? It's like silk but not so fragile," Rayven asked, ever curious about new and unknown things.

"I know not of this silk, Highness, but 'tis true the material is quite durable. It is spun from harvested *syabean* hulls." At Rayven's questioning look she explained, "*Syabean* is a type of fruit, which grows on a vine along the ground. The sweet fruit is housed in a stringy outer shell, which is broken open and shucked of its strands. The strands are spun into threads, which are then woven to make cloth. We call the cloth *evansai*, which means breath of steel, as it is light as air and yet most difficult to tear."

"Will you show me the *syabean* fruit? I'm eager to learn all I can about this new world."

"That is good to hear, Highness. You will learn much, for we are also eager to teach you what we may. Come, break your fast and meet your people. We have been anxious for your return."

"My people? What do you mean you've been waiting for me? That guy Draco said the same—" Rayven faltered as Ursus slowly shook her head.

"All questions will be answered at the Gathering Tree, Highness. I have already said too much and have only succeeded in confusing you more. Come, follow me."

So saying, she scooted backwards out of the tent and waited for Rayven to follow her. Not knowing what else to do, Rayven crawled out of the opening in the feathered tent and stood up with Ursus. Stepping back, Rayven realized she had to look up at least a foot to meet Ursus' twinkling eyes.

"You are a tiny thing, Highness. Indeed, I feel like a giant next to you and I am one of the smallest of our numbers." She smiled to show she meant no insult.

Rayven searched for a fitting reply before her breath caught at her first glimpse of her surroundings. All thoughts fled her mind as if blown away on a wind.

She was standing on a black wooden walkway that grew out from one massive ebony tree trunk and connected to another one. On and on, the path stretched between hundreds of similar trees, all of which were laden with purple feathers instead of leaves. Round tents, like the one in which she'd awakened, were perched here and there between the tree's mighty branches. A warm light emanated comfortingly all around them, casting flickering shadows over the richly colored surroundings. Tiny golden and silver lights floated on strange appendages that hung down from vines intertwined around the trees and walkway, like millions of twinkling Christmas lights.

It looked like a vast city enfolded in purple feathers and warm starlight. Rayven walked to the edge of the walkway and gazed down into a soft black void of space. It seemed as though the trees were so high up she couldn't see the ground below. The trees were exponentially larger than the largest redwoods on Earth, so Rayven assumed it was possible that they were indeed high enough that the forest floor was out of sight below.

"Go on, Highness. Reach out and feel it—you won't fall," encouraged Ursus.

Rayven reached out a hand, expecting to feel only empty space. A ripple broke out upon the strange surface that met her hand, like small waves in an otherwise still pond. It was unlike anything she'd ever felt before, and she had no words to describe it.

"What is it?" she breathed.

"These *Neffan* trees are sentient beings. They will not let us fall from their great height and be harmed, so to protect us should we stray from the paths provided, they have erected a shield to prevent us from plummeting off the edge. They are very nurturing, something for which we have often been grateful. They provide shelter for us from the elements—in the hot season it is quite cool beneath the feathers, and in the cold season it is warm and comforting."

"What do they get in return?"

"They do not need anything in return, Highness. For some beings, selfless giving and the goodwill it evokes is reward enough. These *Neffan* trees have no predators or enemies, they merely *are*. It is enough for them that they can provide for our comfort and safety."

"How romantic." Rayven gazed about her with a sense of awe and reverence.

Ursus laughed softly, a tinkling sound in the tranquil quiet. Motioning for Rayven to follow her along the ethereal pathway, she led them deeper into the maze of feathers and lights. They walked for what seemed to Rayven like miles, Ursus' impossibly long legs eating up the distance while she hurried to keep up. Though they continued to travel deeper and deeper into the treetop city, Rayven still could not see to the end of it. It seemed to stretch on into forever.

At last they came upon a tree even larger than those surrounding it. Several pathways led into it from all different directions, and strange light-encrusted vines covered every possible inch of the great tree's ebony trunk. It was like a bright beacon shining happily and reassuringly to all who could see.

Before Rayven and Ursus passed through an archway that went into the heart of the tree trunk, Rayven couldn't resist running her hand over a nearby low-hanging vine of twinkling light. It was cool to the touch, though it glowed with an unmistakable warmth. As Rayven studied the vine before her, several other vines moved closer to her, causing her to gasp. Seemingly thousands of tiny lights moved to her hands and hair, bathing her in warm starlight. Rayven grinned in delight.

Ursus smiled and shooed away the vines from Rayven's hair. "Do not tease them so, Highness. These *emalaya* vines love to show off their beauty to newcomers. Verily, 'tis a fact that when we first arrived here I would sit for hours playing with them, myself. They were quite the little flirts and loved the attention."

"They are very beautiful. Like tiny captured stars."

"Indeed they are, Highness. Now come, we are already late."

Rayven followed Ursus into the heart of the tree, her heart feeling lighter than it ever had in her waking memory.

The feeling wouldn't last for long.

* * * * *

Rayven gasped at the sight that met her dazed eyes. Stretched out before her lay a great feasting table that seemed to have been fashioned out of stone. How such a monstrosity had been carted up here to reside in the treetops, Rayven could not guess. Great high-backed chairs made of the same stone rested at the table's sides.

Behind the chairs stood many men and women of towering height. As Rayven took in their expectant faces they each bowed or curtsied to her in turn. Rayven had never seen so many beautiful people before. Their hair and eyes were vibrantly colored, like many different jewels, stones and metals. They all stood tall and straight, their bearing proud and regal.

Not knowing what else to do, Rayven nodded slightly to the gathering before her, as Ursus led her to the far end of the table. Rayven could feel their eyes watch her every movement, and struggled to remain calm under their intense regard. She noticed that the women present were wearing outfits similar to the one she wore, though some were much more risqué. Some women merely wore small swatches of gauze at their breasts and mons, which revealed considerably more than they concealed.

The men wore varying degrees of clothing, some wearing clothing similar to what Draco had worn on the beach. Other men wore loose-fitting genie-style pants and loose shirts that looked like pirate or poet shirts, with gathered wrists and elaborate collars. Still others wore no shirts at all, boldly displaying their gorgeously muscled chests and bronzed skin.

Rayven's cheeks flushed with heat as she took in the sight of so much displayed skin. *They sure know how to make a man here,* she thought to herself, picturing Draco's rugged beauty vividly in her mind. As if in response to her musings, at the far end of the table stood Draco in the flesh.

At least he's not flashing his chest everywhere, or I'd probably faint, she thought to herself. As his silver eyes twinkled and a grin tugged at the corners of his exquisite mouth, she realized he'd probably read her mind again. Rayven cringed at the mortifying thought.

As Ursus reached Draco's side, she suddenly took Rayven's hand in hers. She placed Rayven's hand lightly into Draco's with a great show of ceremony, and he enveloped it into his much larger one. Ursus moved back to an empty seat a little farther down the table, and Draco raised Rayven's hand high in his own.

"Our Rayven has at last returned to us!" his voice decreed in a booming melody over the assembled people, inciting them to cheer in a deafening roar.

Rayven tried to tug her hand from Draco's, but he held her firm. Not understanding what was going on, Rayven decided to wait for her answers as patiently as she could. She was at the mercy of these strange and beautiful people, and could not afford to offend them.

When the cheering died down, Draco turned to her with a gleam in his eyes that looked very much like pride. Perhaps he was merely grateful that she chose to wait for his explanations. Or perhaps it was something more?

Draco's booming voice sounded through the great hall once more, "Come and let us break our fast, that we may get to know our Empress the soonest."

Empress! So that was why Ursus had called her Highness this morning. These people must know of her heritage. Perhaps they would have answers to the many questions she had about her past.

As the people sat in their stone chairs, food appeared on the table before them as if by magic. Dishes of strangely colored and textured foods were passed around from person to person, and the delicious aromas of many exotic flavors assailed her nostrils and made her mouth water. Draco tugged at her hand, which he had yet to release, and led her to sit beside him at the head of the great table.

Once Rayven was seated, she was afforded a better view of the people around her. It seemed that men greatly outnumbered the women here, and though the women were much taller in height than she, they still seemed small next to the towering, muscular males.

Rayven's cheeks blushed as her gaze swept over several couples who were sharing the same chairs. The women sat upon the males, legs spread on either side of muscular, masculine thighs, and the males proceeded to feed the females succulent fruits and berries. The display was too personal for her to glance overlong, but before she looked away she noticed with shock that more than one couple seated thusly were engaged in a sexual act.

With shocked fascination Rayven saw one particular couple passionately mating as thought their exhibitionism were the most natural thing in the world—clearly uncaring that all could see their love-play. The man bounced and rocked the woman slightly on his lap as he reached around the woman to knead and cup her breast.

He bared the plump globe, pulling it from beneath its scanty covering, while he fed her ripe purple berries with his free hand. The juice dripped in a dark violet streak down the woman's chin as she gasped and moaned. The juice trickled onto her chest and drew Rayven's eyes lower to her stomach and spread legs. The woman's loincloth had been nudged aside and Rayven could clearly see the man's exceptionally huge cock as it lay half buried in the woman's glistening pussy. The woman had grown so aroused that her juices flowed freely down over the man's massive cock and balls. Rayven had never seen such a shameless display, but nevertheless she still felt a pool of moisture between her own legs as she continued to stare at them in fascination.

She felt a hand brush her thigh and jerked back to look at Draco. She realized that his hand had been there for several moments, and that she'd been too enraptured watching the couple as they mated to notice it. Draco had managed to knead her thigh just enough that her legs had instinctively opened slightly, and he now preceded to insinuate his hand between the apex of her thighs.

"What are you doing? Stop that right now," she hissed, and tried ineffectually to nudge his hand away from its seat against her mons.

He bent closer to her. "Do you like to watch them, *a grifa*?" he whispered into her ear.

"N-no. I'm just shocked, that's all. It's like staring at a car wreck—you don't want to but you can't help it. Now keep your hands to yourself!"

"I think you are lying." He ignored her command and her struggles. "I can feel the wet heat here beneath my hand. Your *evansai* is thin and you're drenching me through your clothes."

"Draco," Rayven brokenly whispered, anger, embarrassment and all-consuming desire warring within her, "please let me go. Don't embarrass me in front of these strangers."

Draco hesitated but a moment, as Rayven's gold eyes refused to meet his, and her cheeks flushed with her tangled emotions. Then, with one meaningful press of his fingers against her tingling, swollen clit, he pulled away. His hand felt moist with her obvious arousal. Rayven looked at him with relief, and he felt a primal urge to shock her once more before he could let the moment pass.

Rayven tried not to look as Draco brought his hand to his face and breathed deeply of her scent, but her eyes were caught and held captive by his. With a savoring look in his burning eyes, his tongue darted out and licked the traces of her fluids from his hand and fingers. Rayven felt a clenching in the center of her body, and with it came a new gush of fluid between her labia. With a shaking breath, she broke free of his gaze and hastily looked away. She struggled for calm, but her heart raced, and her mind reeled with desire and uncertainty.

As if the planet hadn't just tilted on its axis beneath them, Draco calmly and nonchalantly turned back to the meal set out before them. "What fares shall you sample, *a grifa*? I would see to it that you remember your first meal among us with great delight. We have many dishes for you to choose from." He swept his hand outward to encompass the entire feast of foods before them.

Rayven swallowed harshly, but she was more than determined to let the strangely—dangerously—arousing incident slip from her mind, just as it had apparently gone from his. She struggled to speak in a tone as unaffected as his, but knew that she failed. "I don't know. I don't recognize any of the food here. Do you perhaps have any *syabean* fruit? Ursus told me about those and they sounded interesting."

Draco motioned with his hand and a platter of bright green fruit appeared before her.

"You will take a liking to the *syabean* fruit, as it is sweet and succulent." Draco leaned closer to her to whisper his next words in her ear, causing a delicate shiver to race up her spine and her heart to race anew. "Though it is not so sweet or succulent as your tender lips, beauty…or your honeyed juices."

Aloud he continued, "Is there naught else you desire, Highness? Nothing else you wish to sample?" His eyes burned a molten path from her eyes to her lips and then downward to her breasts.

"Your tongue on a plate perhaps," she said with deceptive sweetness, reaching with unsteady hands for her *syabean* fruit.

"I am sorry to disappoint you, Highness, but we do not partake of meats. Only fruits, grains, nuts and roots." His eyes twinkled with humor.

Rayven gritted her teeth before she bit down on her fruit. It tasted like a combination of oranges and blueberries and was quite delicious. Closing her eyes in pleasure, she sighed appreciatively and reached for more.

"I see you like the *syabean*, perhaps you should also try these other fruits as they are quite palatable as well," he suggested, before handing her a large assortment of oddly shaped and colored fruits. Suddenly his eyes became thoughtful, and he said, "We will try to start you off slowly, so your digestive system does not suffer over these strange foods. I know not what foods you are accustomed to, but I wager they are not so exotic as these. Would you care for some *tearwine*?"

"What's *tearwine*?"

"It is water from the lake into which you fell yesterday, mixed with herbs and berries. It is quite refreshing, I assure you."

Remembering her great liking for the water she had drunk yesterday, she nodded and accepted a stone goblet full to its brim. She drank half of the chilled liquid in one greedy draught. Draco obligingly waved his hand over her goblet and it was again filled to the brim.

"How do you do that? You just wave your hand around and things appear out of thin air."

"Can you not also do these things?" he asked her, looking deeply into her eyes. Their earlier play seemed forgotten, and he appeared quite seriously interested in her answer.

"I can make things move without touching them through telekinesis, but I can't just create something from nothing," she said, realizing she'd never discussed her strange abilities aloud before. She was surprised she sounded—and felt—so comfortable while doing so.

"Perhaps you have never properly tried, *a grifa*."

Rayven thought on his words a bit. She realized that indeed she had never attempted to test her powers this way, and she suddenly couldn't wait to try. She saw that Draco's goblet was drained of his *tearwine* and she waved her hand over it as he had done to hers. She "pushed" with her mind, willing more liquid to appear in the empty goblet. Nothing happened for a long moment.

Suddenly, all around the room drink goblets started to overflow with *tearwine*, the liquid bubbling and spilling out over the table and onto the floor. Rayven jerked her hand back in mortification and made to rise from her seat. All around her lay puddles of *tearwine*. Her eyes scanned the shocked visages of the people about the table. All around her was silence. Even the couples locked in a fornicating embrace had ceased their motions and passionate cries.

Then, startlingly, a great cheer rose up among the diners, and Draco smiled down at her, openly pleased. He reached for her elbow to guide her back into her seat beside him.

"I am so sorry. I didn't know that would happen," she said in a shaky voice, mortified beyond belief.

"Rayven, do not apologize. You have just displayed the greatness of your untapped power to all that are present," Draco's voice rose so as to be heard above the roar of the crowd, his tone full of patience and good humor.

"It takes great control to 'create something from nothing' as you so charmingly put it. We call it *blaithen*, which strictly means 'create'. You not only *blaithened tearwine* in my goblet, you did it to all those around you. This is difficult enough to do on a small scale, and yet you have so grandly exhibited your power that you have put even our strongest members to shame. You have great *Awareness,* and you need only learn to control it. Once you learn control you will become a great ruler over us all."

Draco was speaking to her like she was in on some great secret—as if she were supposed to know all that he was talking about. All of her good intentions to wait for his explanations for the bizarre events unfolding around her fled as if on a puff of wind. Rayven could stand the wait no longer. She had to have answers to the endless questions storming in her mind, and she had to have them *now*.

As if he sensed her frustration and determination to demand answers, Draco waved his hand and demanded silence in the hall. Immediately all the cheering stopped, as if a switch had been turned off. Rayven noticed that those couples that were still glued together at the genitals disengaged from one another and took to their own seats. If nothing else, Rayven admitted to herself, these people greatly respected the man next to her. She could almost see his air of command, as if he were born to lead many. He wore his responsibilities like a mantle of honor, and his subjects were clearly loyal and devoted to him for it.

In the still silence that now reigned over the gathering, Draco turned once again to her. He stared deeply into her eyes for a long moment, as if sizing up her strength of mind to handle what was next to come. Giving away nothing, and hiding all her emotions behind a neutral mask, Rayven boldly met his steady gaze. Finally he spoke, without taking his eyes away from hers.

"You were taken from Earth by General Karis," he began, while at the mention of the General's name several members of the assembly gasped. "Did you meet him? Did you speak to him?"

"Yes, to both questions," she answered, impatience lacing her tone.

"What did you think of him? What did you talk about?"

"Why are you asking me this? Don't I have a right to ask my questions first?"

Draco's silver eyes burned deeply into hers. "I promise that all will be revealed to you shortly. I could take the information I seek from your mind, but I can see you would prefer that I do not. Our people have a need to know the details of your capture, so please share the tale with us."

Rayven thought for a moment. She didn't know these people, or their motives for seeking information of any sort from her. What she did know, however, was that they had treated her well thus far. Though Draco's overwhelming kisses and caresses yesterday and then again today had unnerved her, he had treated her with honor by taking her to his people's home without causing her any harm. He could read her mind with apparent ease, if she wasn't careful to shield around him, yet he didn't out of regard to her wishes in this instance.

Ursus, the only other person here with whom she'd had opportunity to speak, had been courteous and attentive to her needs. She'd seemed nice, and non-threatening.

The General and his men, conversely, had been openly hostile and desirous of her immediate execution. No matter what the General had told her during her short stay in his fortress, it could not hurt to share it with Draco and his people. Despite her ignorance of the bizarre situations in which she'd recently found herself, she knew who her enemies were and they were not the people here with her now.

"You ask me what I thought of him? Honestly, I believe he is an unstable and evil man. He is the kind of person who would only be happy in life if he were surrounded by the weak and easily subjugated. He cannot stand to be thwarted in any way, no matter how trivial the matter at hand. He feels that ruling power is his due, and he will not tolerate it being proven otherwise."

Draco smiled suddenly. He put his hand softly over hers and looked up at his people.

"Our Empress is indeed a wise judge of character," he said proudly.

Rayven tried in vain to tug her hand away from his, his warm touch and words of praise setting loose a flutter in her belly.

Draco curled his fingers around her smaller ones more firmly, stopping just short of crushing her fingers with his strength. "What did you discuss? Did he harm you in any way?" At his last words, his teeth clenched and a dangerous light shone in his eyes, causing Rayven's heart to stutter in trepidation.

A murmur rippled along the assembly at the mention of her possible injury at the General's hands. Rayven could plainly see that they were outraged on her behalf, and she hurried to reassure them.

"No, he didn't hurt me." She refused to divulge the details of his roaming hands and mouth, and otherwise he hadn't even been given a chance to hurt her in any way.

"He just spoke to me about where I came from. He didn't make much sense at all, and though I admit I didn't believe much of what he said, there appeared to be some truth to the things he told me. What those truths were I am not sure. He was completely off his gourd. Crazy, you know?"

Draco nodded his head slightly in agreement.

Rayven took a steadying breath before she continued. "I saw images from his memories… I saw him kill my mother and father."

Draco's impossibly long black lashes closed over his bright eyes like a small dark cloud. He looked as though he were truly sorry for her having witnessed such a thing, though why he should care so much Rayven could not guess. Suddenly his eyes flashed open again, a hardness within them that Rayven had never seen in any person's eyes before. It seemed as though he could easily kill with such a gaze from his molten silver eyes, were he to will it so.

"I am sorry you were cursed with such a terrible vision, *a grifa,*" he whispered for her hearing only. "I would that I could have spared you from such a thing."

Rayven's eyes softened as they looked into his. No one had ever offered such caring words to her before. The strange emotions his softly spoken words evinced in her heart confused and frightened her. She cautioned herself against reading too much into his offer of comfort. She was unaccustomed to interacting with other people, and mustn't be too naïve when offered kindness from strangers.

It would not do well to become vulnerable to such a man. He would easily dominate her heart if she let him, and she refused to allow him such power over her. He was not the type of man who would allow her much freedom, this she could easily sense. He would instead try to bend her to his will and force her submission. She had not lived a life imprisoned by forces beyond her control, just to hand her first chance at freedom over to a man as dominating as he.

Rayven pushed her musings aside. With Draco's penchant for reading her thoughts she could not afford to ponder such dangerous things.

"Do not be sad," she said in a steady voice, "I have long since come to terms with the violence of life…*and* death. My parents died together, and if the General's memories can be believed, they died bravely as well."

Draco pursed his sensual lips. He nodded before he addressed the assembly as a whole, though he never took his eyes from hers.

"Let us do our duty to our lost Emperor and Empress, and share the memories we have of them with their daughter. We are the last survivors of our race and can do no other than honor them as is their due."

Rayven's eyes widened as she looked into Draco's.

"I thought I was the last…"

"So far as the General of the Galactic Commune knows, you are the last, Rayven. That, at least, we have to our advantage. We have been in hiding for twenty-eight years now, waiting for your return to us before we could at last make our way out of exile.

"There are other Aware besides we few, who have hopefully gone into hiding on other planets in safety. You, Empress Rayven, were born to lead us out of our enforced retreat from the Galactic Commune. Only you are powerful enough to help us defeat the armies that will seek our destruction once they learn of our survival. Only you can help us to find our other lost brethren, and reunite us all once more. The destiny of your people rests within your hands."

Chapter Twelve

Rayven let the shock of Draco's words wash over and through her. Here she sat, at last among kindred spirits, people who had the same strange powers as she, and they expected her to *lead* them?

"I'm not powerful enough to lead you, and I wouldn't know how to go about it even if I were," she said, ignoring the startled gasps of the people around her. "I can't explain to you what sort of extrasensory powers I have. I can barely even control them at will. You must be mistaken, Draco, I cannot possibly help you wage war on an army..." Rayven stumbled into silence, her heart racing in fear over the mere thought of being responsible for the lives of these people.

A muscular man with blue-black, waist-length hair leaned closer at her side. "Highness, you are untrained it is true, but we can all sense your great strength. We will help you to tap into your slumbering gifts, we will teach you to control them. Let go of your fears, and trust us to guide you. You will mature into a great leader. This I have foreseen."

Rayven stared into his hypnotic eyes. His irises were the color of blood-red rubies, rimmed in the blackest obsidian. His eyes should have made him look like a monster from a fairy tale, but instead they made him appear exotic, otherworldly and beautiful. He was meeting her stare levelly, something she was very unaccustomed to from someone other than Draco, having lived her life among normal humans who were generally, instinctively afraid to meet her gaze.

Without knowing why, Rayven felt compelled to delve more deeply into his jeweled gaze. She felt as if she were drowning in the ruby depths of his eyes, could not pull herself away from the urge to lose herself within them. Everyone around her faded into the background, and her surroundings were cloaked in a ruby haze. Images began to assault her mind with unrelenting force. The scenes were memories from deep within his mind that she, in some magical way, was now witnessing.

She saw images of the people in his past, of happier times before the Great Massacre of their people. She saw images of the women he'd loved, of the friends he'd lost, of his large family—all of whom were now dead. She saw the burden he bore with his great precognitive gift, and how he had blamed himself for not foreseeing the destruction of his people in time to save them.

She then saw an image of him standing on a great precipice overlooking a barren wasteland of ash and smoke, his hair a flapping curtain of darkness in the whistling wind. It was a glimpse of their homeworld of Nye many years after the war that had decimated it. It was a dead planet now, where the psychic scars left in the wake of an unimagined wave of destruction ran deep and ugly, never to heal.

She saw him raise the blazing metal of a blade up before his eyes, his fingers running reverently over five gaping holes in its hilt. It looked as though tiny gems had been pried from their resting place with clumsy disrespect. She could tell from the anguished look on his face and the negative emotions she sensed washing through him, that the missing gems had been removed against his will, and that they had meant a great deal to him. She was angry on his behalf that anyone would dare to steal treasured heirlooms from his weapon without regard to his wishes.

He had secreted away from Hostis, without the permission of his leader, to find this family sword. This information made itself known to her on a whisper from deep within his mind. He had risked much to go back and retrieve the sword, a great heirloom with mystical powers and much sentimental value to him. He had found it after endless days of searching amongst the rubble of his once great home, but the sacred stones that had rested for generations upon its hilt were gone. The marauding members of the Galactic Communal Army had taken them for some nefarious and dark purpose.

As if sensing her presence within his memories, the man with the ruby eyes forcibly pushed her from his mind, sending her back into her own body with a near-painful jolt. Blinking at him dazedly, Rayven helplessly reached out a hand to him. Her anguished empathy was etched clearly upon her countenance as she sought to comfort him, only to have him draw roughly away. His rejection of her touch squeezed a fist around her heart, and she pulled her hand back with a lump in her throat.

"I didn't mean to..." she started, wanting to apologize for invading his private thoughts, but he cut her off with a brisk nod of his head.

"It is all right, Highness, I can see you did not know what you were doing." Rayven's eyes widened as she heard his voice clearly in her mind. Looking around her, she could tell that no one else heard his words and that he had intended it that way. *"Please do not reveal my secret. I know I should not have ventured to Nye without permission, but I wanted to retrieve the* Blazesword *of my ancestors. It was wrong of me to do this, I know, but I was weak and gave in to my selfish desires."*

Rayven nodded slightly to let him know she understood, her eyes forgiving him his earlier rejection. She could understand his need for some remnant of his family and his past. She had been there to see his reaction to the raping of his ancestral sword, and she knew he had paid for his lapse in good judgment upon leaving Hostis without permission. He had suffered much.

Rayven jerked as Draco placed his hand upon her shoulder comfortingly. Had he read her thoughts while she'd been in the other man's mind? Had he seen what she had seen? She hoped not, for she knew that Draco would have been most displeased with the man for disobeying the obvious rule that no one leave their new planet. She had a feeling that his displeasure was something to be avoided at all costs. He seemed too dangerous a foe to wish on anyone, no matter their sins.

"Do not let Onca frighten you with his words, little one," Draco said. "We will all help to guide you on the road to discovering your hidden *Awareness*, and though the journey will be long and difficult I have every faith that you will far exceed our expectations of you."

Rayven looked at Onca, and then at all of the other expectant faces surrounding the great stone table. She had a sinking feeling that each person here had suffered just as much as she had in the last three decades, if not more so. They had all lost family, friends and loved ones. They had seen the destruction of their entire planet, and been forced to flee in secrecy to an alien world in order to survive the vicious slaughter of their race. How could she deny them their last hope for freedom and survival? How could she in good conscience deliver such a cruel blow to so proud and noble a group of people?

"Tell me everything," she said, and felt the arms of fate enclose her in their unrelenting embrace.

Chapter Thirteen

Rayven paced back and forth along the walk way outside of her room. Ursus had led her back here to await Draco and his promised tour of the treetop city. The past few hours she'd spent listening to Draco's story of her birth and subsequent separation from her people had flown by rapidly. All the strange and wondrous things that had been revealed to her were replaying themselves over and over in her mind.

She was no longer alone!

She had a family now, an amazing and magical family that had suffered from her absence just as deeply as had she. These people did not find her strange or alarming, far from it. They respected her for her intelligence, and revered her for the strange gifts she possessed. These were people who understood and shared her many unusual traits. Though she could hardly believe it, she had at last been accepted into the welcoming arms of others who were not entirely unlike her.

However, not all thoughts were as sunshine and rainbows within her mind. Though she had been given the great gift of acceptance and understanding—things she had been yearning for all of her life—she had also been given a terrible burden to bear along with it. If all of Draco's words were to be believed, these people needed her desperately to lead them on a campaign to take back their lost freedoms and avenge their slaughtered people.

Rayven had never been responsible for anything other than her own safety before now. She had always been a loner and a wanderer. She'd never even owned a pet or held a steady job. Now, suddenly, these people—*her people*—expected her to be their Empress and leader. How in the world was she going to find the strength to do that?

All of Draco's talk about her unimaginable power and hidden strength frightened the life out of her. How could she possibly control the same immense power as Draco? Rayven shuddered with an innate fear of the magic supposedly hidden deep inside her. He must be mistaken. There could be no mystical training powerful enough to dredge up those unplumbed depths she was supposed to possess. If only he would listen! She'd struggled to make him see reason, but he'd have none of it.

Draco's reply had been seared into her brain for all time. "You are a novice Aware, untrained and untested. I have sensed a core of steel within you like none I have ever known. Onca, my Chief Counselor, has foreseen your destiny as one of the greatest rulers we have ever encountered. Trust in me, and I promise you, you *will* triumph!"

Rayven quailed at the thought. She didn't know what frightened her more. That she wasn't this great, destined ruler her people had hoped for her to be, or that she did indeed have some deeply buried power that had lain dormant her whole life just waiting to be brought forth and unleashed in some deadly hailstorm upon her people's enemies. Was she a pitiful failure, destined to help bring about the deaths of the last remaining members of her race? Or was she a warrior queen destined to bring death and despair to those who had dared visit such destruction upon her people?

She had no answers to these questions. She wasn't sure she wanted to know the answers. Of one thing, however, she was certain. She would try to help her people find the peace and ease of suffering that they sought. Somehow.

* * * * *

"Why did you not reveal your true relationship to her?"

"I did not feel it was the right time, Setiger. Let us leave it at that."

"Draco, she must be told. Surely she will hear it from someone else sooner or later, and then she is likely to resent you for not telling her you are her mate."

"Setiger is right, Draco, she must be told."

Draco, Onca, Setiger and Avator sat together in the now-empty Gathering Tree. The four looked like warriors of old with their battle-weary eyes and darkly serious faces. Huddled close together as they were, their vibrant coloring and large, muscular bodies were almost too beautiful to gaze upon. No one could have mistaken them for other than what they were. They were men who knew duty and wore its weight well upon their broad shoulders, they were fiercely loyal and protective to those in their care…and they would make dangerous and formidable foes to any who dared cross them.

Draco sighed wearily. "I know that she must be told, and she will be soon enough. However, I did not want to add more weight to the burdens I had to place on her shoulders this morning. She has enough to worry her as it is, without being told she is expected to bond for life with a man she does not properly know."

Onca pounded his fist upon the table in frustration. "What of the others? Someone is going to mention it to her and then what will you do? I do not know the minds of women well, but I do know enough to wager that she will believe you are trying to trick her into an illicit relationship by not telling her firsthand. She'll think you had no intention of giving her a choice in the matter."

Avator snorted. "As if she really had a choice. Her soul is linked to Draco's. She cannot help but to mate herself to him. You saw how she responded to his attentions at the feast—though she was angry with him, she was beyond aroused. We could smell her lust like heady perfume. She will come around to the idea."

"But she does not understand our ways, Avator. She has not been raised among us. She will fight this tie to him if we press her too hard, seeing it as a challenge to her independence," said Setiger.

"Quiet, the lot of you," growled Draco. "I will see to it that our people do not tell her just yet of her tie to me. I will do so now, if you will but give me peace."

Draco closed his eyes and opened a mental pathway on which he could silently communicate with his people en masse, though he was careful not to include Rayven in the mental conversation. He commanded his people's silence on the subject of his relationship with Empress Rayven, offering no explanations why and expecting their complete obedience to his wishes.

"You are far too comfortable in your role as leader, my friend. You grow more arrogant as the days pass. I cannot wait to see the struggle you will have with our Empress when you at last try to bring her to your side as mate," Setiger chuckled.

Avator thumped him roughly on his back, sending him teetering from his chair. Setiger took the abuse with his usual good humor, and laughingly launched a mock attack, catching Avator under the jaw with his fist and felling him to the floor.

"Cease your play at once! What if our Empress were to see you behaving thus?" Onca, ever the levelheaded member of the group, admonished the wrestling men.

Properly chastised, though still grinning widely, the two men returned to their seats, none the worse for wear.

Draco rolled his eyes to the ceiling searching for patience. "Today I will begin Rayven's training. I will take her on a tour of the city and introduce her to everyone, and then I will lead her outside and begin to teach her the use of her powers. When I am certain she can handle the pressures of being our Empress, then and only then, will I inform her of her role as my mate."

"Be sure that you do, Draco. We cannot afford to have even one mated couple deny the urge to procreate. Do not wait too long before you claim her and get her with child."

Draco leveled a hard stare at his Chief Counselor. "I will not endanger her life or the life of my child by impregnating Rayven before our troubles with the Galactic Commune are over. I do not want to put her at risk if I can avoid it. Our women are fragile during their pregnancies—their powers at their weakest. I could never forgive myself if she or our child were brought to harm because of my actions. I will not risk it."

"We would not suggest that you do so, Draco. However, we do not know if we will survive this new war with the Galactic armies. Why not grasp what happiness you may find now, while you have the chance? Claim her as your own, merge your souls as one, and share with her your love. You may not get another chance to do so." Avator's eyes were haunted and full of sorrow.

Avator's mate, Lamiya, had been killed during the Massacre, and though he was glad that his brother had a chance at happiness, he could not help feeling the bitter sting of all the lost years since his own mate had died. There were so many things that had been left unsaid between them, and he felt the hollow ache in his heart over her memory. He had loved her, but had waited to claim her until he was ready, wanting instead to travel to the far corners of Nye, seeing all the sights of his homeworld before settling down to raise a family. He had taken it for granted that she would always be waiting for his return, never expecting to lose her to death in a war. Now his chance at happiness was over, and his beautiful Lamiya was gone forever.

Draco saw the haunted look in his brother's eyes, and knew its cause. Perhaps Avator was right. If nothing else worthwhile had come from the slaughter of their people, it had at least taught the survivors that life was a precious commodity. Their natural lifespan was so long that they had often taken time for granted before the Massacre, but now they understood how fragile and inconstant life was, and how every moment should be treasured. Every day was a precious gift and should be treated as such.

"I will think on all that you have said, my friends. Trust me when I say I will not be rash in any decisions I make. I will do what is right for our Empress and our people, doubt it not."

So saying, Draco transported himself to his mate's side, ready to begin her training. He found himself eager to help her assume control of the throne. Once she was comfortable in her role as ruler he would then claim her for his mate. He would lay siege to her body—to her heart and soul, and together they would grasp at whatever happiness they may…before it was too late.

Chapter Fourteen

Rayven turned another circle in her agitated pacing and was almost knocked over as she stumbled squarely into a large masculine rib cage. She gasped and teetered backwards hastily. Looking up…and up farther still she looked into the mercurial eyes of Draco.

"Don't do that! You nearly gave me a heart attack," she griped in a shaky voice. No one had ever made her feel as uncomfortable or clumsy as Draco seemed able to. Perhaps it was simply because she was unused to being among other people, and it made her jumpy. Perhaps it was because he touched her so freely—as if he owned her and had the right to do so. Perhaps it was more.

Draco bowed slightly, a small twist at his mouth. "Do not be alarmed, Highness, I will be more careful of startling you in the future."

Rayven gritted her teeth. He made her sound like some fragile bird that was frightened of its own shadow. She hated the strange flustered feelings he always evoked in her with his presence.

"Just don't sneak up on me, okay? I'm not used to being around people, and I don't want to accidentally hurt you." There! Maybe tough talk like that would warn him off a little…she hoped.

"But how else will you accustom yourself to the presence of others if we must tiptoe around you?"

Oh well, so much for putting some distance between them. He'd paid her threat as little heed as a fly buzzing around his head. Rayven raised her chin a notch and stared regally at him, unknowingly mirroring the stubborn stance her mother had been famous for amongst her people.

"Just forget it. Now—I am to understand that you wish to give me a tour? Will I get to see the grounds beyond these trees, or do you not often venture from the grove?"

Draco's eyes flashed dangerously as he drank in the sight of her. She was so beautiful that she took his breath away. The temptation she presented was a sore test to his self-control. Her golden eyes flashed, her chin set stubbornly, and her cheeks flushed with emotion.

He'd never been so stricken by lust as he was then, when he scented her floral spice on a small breeze. It was difficult for him to think of anything beyond bending her back over his arm and laying his burning lips to the pulse in her throat. He had to forcibly shake his thoughts away from the temptation of claiming her right then and there.

Bringing himself back from the precipice of desire with no small effort, he answered. "We are not confined to the shelter of the trees, if that is what you are asking. Our kind often communes with nature, and we enjoy roaming about the countryside, admiring the flora and fauna. Even on Nye we were not confined to stone or wooden homes as so many other humanoids seem to be. We often slept out among the stars, enjoying the natural beauty of the earth and sky, basking in the peace and serenity of nature."

Rayven thought back to all the times in her life in which she'd much preferred the welcoming outdoors to the plush comforts of an impersonal hotel suite. What he said made sense to her on a primal level, and struck a chord of kinship within her for these people who shared so many traits with her. Some of the feelings of loneliness that had haunted her all her life faded from within her heart.

"Let us proceed then. I find I am eager to learn as much from you as I can."

Draco's cock lengthened and hardened in a rush of warmth at the double entendre in Rayven's innocently spoken words. He tightened the reins on his normally iron control. He would not cloud the situation by giving in to his baser needs. No matter how strong they may be.

Draco reached to take Rayven's hand into his much larger one. Her bones felt as fragile as a flower's petals, but he knew that was as far from reality as it was possible to get. He had looked into her memories while she lay sleeping in his arms through the past night, and he had seen the many physical trials she'd had forced upon her body.

She was a skilled warrior, even without the use of her *Awareness*. Though Draco had been anguished at her desperate need for such knowledge to protect herself, he had also been beyond pleased at her perseverance and success in the deadly arts. His heart had swelled in pride over her accomplishments.

Rayven tried to pull her hand from his. She could feel strong emotions emanating from him through his touch, and the intensity of their nature confused her. It made her uncomfortable, and strangely aware of her own body. She'd never felt so exposed around anyone before, and she didn't understand the strange fluttery sensations she felt whenever he came too close to her. She knew about desire, she was not totally naïve, but it seemed to her that these feelings were too strong and out of control for it to be mere desire she was experiencing.

Her breath caught in her throat as Draco tightened his hand around hers. He didn't hurt her, but neither would he let her go. He flashed her a look from his molten silver eyes, the expression in their glittering depths inscrutable to her. She swallowed and tried to calm the jolt of her heart at his close regard. He reminded her of a panther, graceful and ever ready to pounce. She stared levelly back at him, before he fluidly turned away and led them down the winding pathway between the many *Neffan* trees. His every graceful motion reminded her of a dangerous predator whose instincts were barely held in check, and sent her pulse racing.

Looking closely from underneath the black fringe of her lashes at Draco's profile, she was struck by how timeless he looked. She had noticed throughout the feast that morning that now and again his eyes would look like ancient bottomless pools of starlight, and at other times he would look young and almost free of worry.

"How old are you?" Had she meant to blurt it out like that? Of course not, but he needn't know that. Rayven strived to meet his mildly surprised glance with a look of nonchalance.

"I am almost nine hundred years old," he said neutrally, as if they were discussing the weather.

Rayven's eyes flared and her mouth parted on a startled sigh.

"How can that be? You don't look over thirty! Do you reckon the passage of years the same as I?"

"Yes. Our years are equal in passage of time to what you are accustomed to on Earth." He smiled over her incredulous expression. "Our kind can live for many thousands of years in a natural lifespan. We do not age much past our thirtieth year, usually, which is why you have seen no ancient-looking people among our numbers. The oldest among us is a man named Stoar, who is close to five thousand years old now, though he looks no older than I. We had many elders before the Great Massacre whose lifespan would have doubled that, but alas they are no more."

Despite the shock he'd just delivered her, Rayven's heart constricted over the sorrow she heard in his voice. She was struck again by how much her people had suffered and lost because of the General's lust and jealousy.

"You must think I'm a child," she said. Suddenly she understood why he seemed inclined to treat her as if she were much younger than he.

"You are considered to be a youngling among us, it is true. But you are strong for your age, and you are our ruler, and because of this we expect more from you than we would someone of a like age."

"How do you die if you do not grow old? Do your biological functions merely fail or do you contract disease and die?"

"We do *not* contract disease, Rayven—" his lip curled in disgust over the thought, "—nor do our bodies fail us. There just comes a time in our lives when we simply feel the need to travel to the other side of existence, to the land beyond the living. We take the time to gather our family around us and we have a great fare-thee-well celebration. When we die, our souls travel to the hereafter, but we try to leave behind pieces of our spirit to guide our descendants in their times of need."

"Wait a minute...you're saying you can choose when you die? Why give up life when you can hold onto it forever?"

Draco paused and stood before her, gathering both of her hands in his.

"How can you ask this when you yourself were willing to give up the gift of life not so very long ago?" His fingers caressed the silvery scars at her wrists, his touch as light as the brush of a butterfly's wings.

Rayven looked away from his compassionate gaze. She didn't know how he knew of her attempted suicide, but that he did shook her to her soul.

"That was different," she said in a shaky voice.

"How was it different, *a grifa*? You were weary of your mortal coil, and sought to leave the pain of your life behind you. There comes a time to all when the mantle of life grows heavy and tiresome to don. It is the way of all things."

"Why didn't I die then, if I chose to?"

Draco deliberated on his answer. He did not wish to lie to her, and yet he could not tell her that by her being mated to him he had the power to keep her from dying by her own choice. He was certain that she had no clear memory of him at her side in his human form the night of her attempted suicide. She did not remember his holding her throughout her twilight sleep, as he had commanded the lacerations at her wrists to heal and her heart to pump more blood to sustain her.

He had felt such fear that night. As he had lain sleeping in his feathers on Hostis he had received a vision of Rayven lying in a pool of blood, dying alone and in sorrow. He had raced to her side, across time and space, and barely arrived in time to prevent death from claiming her. His heart had nearly stopped with fright and shock. The knowledge that she had been so tormented that she'd chosen death over life had torn a gaping hole in his soul.

He had planted a compulsion deep in her mind to keep her from attempting such a thing again. He'd known then that he would not be able to live without her. He would have followed her into the afterlife willingly if he had failed to save her in time. Thankfully such a sacrifice had not been necessary, and she had recovered rapidly from her brush with death.

"Perhaps you were not ready for the eternity of death, Rayven. Perhaps you chose the familiar trials of life over the unknown. The reasons behind your survival do not matter. What matters is that you are here now, among us where you belong. The past horrors of your life are over now, and we must face the future together."

"The future may hold even worse horrors than my past ever could. That's what I'm most afraid of."

Draco brought her hands to his heart and looked fervently into her glittering gold eyes. "At least we'll all be together. Together, we at least have a chance."

Rayven's heart faltered under his impassioned stare, but she found to her surprise that she agreed with him. If she died in the coming war she had that one consolation to hold close. It was better to die among friends and family than to die alone in a dirty hotel room, as had almost been the case for her nine years ago. No matter what the future may bring, she was where she belonged at last. She and her people would face the hardships to come together, as any family should.

Draco's eye softened at her look of acceptance. He sighed in relief and continued down the pathway, her hand warmly grasped in his.

Chapter Fifteen

Draco led Rayven down the many twisting pathways in the city within the purple treetops. People came out from their feathery tents, which Draco called *Bitos*, to greet them. It was as if they had been waiting all morning in the hopes of meeting her, and each person greeted her with enthusiasm and great deference. In her life, Rayven had only met a handful of people whom she could recall by name, and this was a new experience for her, meeting so many in a few hours.

Despite the fear she felt over her people's expectations of her, she couldn't fight her natural inclination to help them from their enforced exile. Everywhere she turned someone had a wistful story of lost family and friends to share with her. A surprising number of people she met had memories to share with her of her royal parents, how regal and just their rule had been, how kind and unselfish they were to their subjects, and how joyously they had celebrated Rayven's birth. Each story touched a place within Rayven's hungry heart.

Though it seemed like there were many people to meet and greet, she was not oblivious to the obvious fact that there were so few of her kind left. There couldn't be more than two hundred to her way of thinking, and while the number might seem large in her mind, it was as nothing compared to what the population had been before the Great Massacre. This she knew.

As the day wore on she met some couples with toddlers and teenaged children. She couldn't remember seeing them at the feast, and assumed it was because of the open mating amongst their parents. The children were each beautiful and unique, with coloring as vibrant as that of their parents'. Rayven had always loved children, but had never had the opportunity to interact with them before. She hoped to get the chance to rectify that soon, with these children.

"Do we procreate like humans?" she couldn't resist asking.

"What do you mean? Do we copulate? Do we fuck?" He smiled, eyes twinkling as she blushed. "Yes, we fuck."

"That's not entirely what I meant. I mean how do we give birth, that type of thing?"

"We have children much like any other member of the mammalian species. You, as a female, have a womb in which the fetus gestates safely. Your confinement or pregnancy lasts about thirteen months, and you pass the child from your womb into the world when it is ready."

"Thirteen months! How can the women stand carrying around the excess weight for so long? It must be tiresome to say the least."

Draco looked perplexed for a moment, then Rayven felt a slight brush of movement in her mind, like a warm and fuzzy caress against her brain, and recognized instinctively that he was reading her thoughts. He was trying to understand what she meant by her comments. Suddenly he threw back his head and laughed, a melodious sound that caressed her skin like a plush drape of dark velvet. Her breath caught in her throat.

Draco wiped tears from his eyes as his laughter subsided into deep chuckles. "Our women do not grow large with their pregnancies. How absurd! When we are housed inside the womb of our mother, we are not yet physical beings, so we do not take up much space. We are more spiritual…like tiny balls of light. When we gestate, we use the time not to grow physically, but mentally and psychically. We take much power from our mother, which weakens her *Awareness*, and through this siphoned power we become strong enough for the rigors of birth."

Rayven ignored his amusement over her naiveté. "But if we're not physical beings, what do we look like when we are birthed?"

"Well, when our spirit comes forth from the womb we are nothing but bright spheres of golden light. We are accepted into our mother's and father's arms, and they use their *Awareness* to will us to assume a physical body. Thus we are gifted with our physical forms."

"How is the fetus or spirit or whatever, passed into the world from the womb? Is it through the birth canal and cervix?"

Draco paled at her words. "By the Fates, no! Who would want to pass anything like that through the cervix? And what of this birth canal?"

As Rayven opened her mouth to answer he threw up his hands to stop her. "Nay, do not say it, I can see in your mind to what you refer." He blinked in shock over the images he witnessed in her mind.

"We pass through the wall of the womb, which is below the beat of our Mother's heart, just above her stomach." It was Rayven's turn to gasp and look dismayed. "It is a painless experience I assure you, far from it. From what I have been told, it is almost like a sexual climax in its intensity. Both the mother and father share in the boundless joy of the birth."

Rayven grabbed at her chest, imagining the horrors of a strange light seeping forth from there and becoming a child. Would it be enjoyable as he said, or would she be so frightened by the whole alien aspect of it that she would suffer from it? She vowed never to find out. No matter how desperate her people were to increase their population, she would definitely not be giving birth in such a manner.

"How...how does the woman's egg get fertilized if it rests so far away from the...well from the sperm's point of entry?" Rayven hated that her words faltered and trembled. She would *not* be embarrassed for asking such a direct question of him. She refused to be.

"Your body absorbs the ejaculate of a mate, and transports it to your womb, where it is accepted or denied by the resting life-force of a potential child. This is how you conceive." Draco hated that the mere thought of her body accepting his semen sent the blood pounding from his heart to his loins. She had asked him a pertinent question and he would *not* get flustered over it. He refused to.

"So *that's* why I've never had a period," she said as if struck by some great revelation. "I thought there was something *very* physiologically wrong with me, but I didn't really care to find out what was wrong because I was afraid that a doctor would know I wasn't exactly…normal in other ways."

"What's a period?" Draco asked, clearly confused.

Rayven gave him a hard look and sent him a picture of what she was referring to with a slight "push" from her mind. Draco turned an odd shade of green under his golden skin, and she couldn't help laughing over his disgusted expression.

"Do all humans have such strange biological functions in their bodies?"

"I assume so. All mammals on Earth have similar cycles, and they give birth through their birth canals. It's just the way things are."

Draco looked skeptical but took her at her word. "I for one am glad that our women do not have to suffer such tortures. Why would any woman from Earth wish to go through such agony?"

"Well, I guess the urge to perpetuate the species is a strong one, and it overshadows the risk of pain involved." Rayven fell silent as she pondered her own words. Therein lay the motivations for all living beings. The need to reproduce was paramount to the evolution of a species. Though she was frightened by her newfound knowledge of her people's method for procreation, she knew that one day she too would long for a child. When that time came she would willingly suffer whatever hardships she had to in order to produce one.

Looking at Draco, Rayven was struck suddenly by the thought of how lovely his offspring would probably look. He was the strongest and most handsome male specimen she'd ever seen in her life, and she couldn't help wondering what he would be like as a lover and a father. Her heart turned over at the thought of passing their child into his arms one day.

She had to struggle to pull her mind away from such tempting thoughts. She reminded herself that there was too much for her to think about, aside from what this man would be like in her bed and heart. She didn't even know him, and such blatantly sexual thoughts were out of character for her. Or at least they had been before she'd met Draco on the beach the day before.

The time for pursuing a personal relationship would have to come after she settled the affairs of her people. She must learn to guide them as best she could, and help them to find their lost brethren. Then she could see to her own needs…if she could just figure out what those were.

Chapter Sixteen

"I have many questions to ask you, but there is one that has been weighing heavily on my mind since I spoke to the General," Rayven said later that day, after she had met every single one of her people.

"Ask all the questions you like. I will try to answer as truthfully as I may."

Rayven moved to sit on a small bench-like outcropping in the trunk of a large *Neffan* tree. Draco still would not release his hold on her hand, and he was forced to sit with her or pull her arm from its socket as he towered over her. Rayven smiled secretly to herself as he quickly perched next to her on the bench. It was obvious, though Draco was overbearing and stubborn, he did not wish to cause her any physical discomfort.

Rayven thought a moment on how to phrase her question. The General had said so many things to her, and she didn't know where to begin picking away at his half-truths. It almost seemed an effort in futility.

"General Karis mentioned that he and my mother were suitors, of a sort. The way he spoke it seemed as if the whole massacre of our people was a direct result of his jealousy over losing her to my father. He said I was born shortly after their marriage and that my mother had betrayed him. How much of this is true?"

Draco's sensuous lips thinned as he answered. "The General's perception is clouded by his own ego. Empress Delphi, your mother, never showed any interest in the General. It was he who pursued her, blinded by his lust for her beauty. He did not see that Empress Delphi and Emperor Thibetanus were mates, and therefore much in love.

"When your parents married, they had already been mated for years. When your parents discovered that they were expecting a birth they decided to marry within the laws of the Galactic Commune, so that their union would be legally recognized throughout the galaxy. So that your birth would be sanctioned by the government, making you the undisputable heir to our throne.

"When the General heard of Delphi's marriage and your subsequent birth, he lost control and launched an attack against us. His overpowering jealousy was the reason for the war—this is true. I'm not at all surprised that you could see this. I have often wondered how the General has been able to justify his zealous behavior to his subjects. It would make things so much easier for us, were he to be assassinated by a disgruntled citizen of the Galactic Commune, but alas we have had no such luck."

"On Earth there was once a leader not unlike the General. After his armies had subjugated several countries, he was at last defeated, and those in league with him were severely punished. Throughout his reign he had loyal armies at his command, but after the war it seems as if the entire world woke from a great sleep and at last saw him as the monster he was. It has ever been a mystery to historians—how he could inspire so many people to follow his lead, despite his cruel disregard for human life. He almost succeeded in wiping out an entire race of people, and yet there were many who still revered him and willingly fought in his armies. Perhaps humans, as a whole, are easily blinded by mass delusions of grandeur. We'll probably never know."

Draco agreed with her. Humans, he knew, were a strange lot—especially so when in large groups. Trying to understand how they thought or reasoned would have been a waste of time, and would have been to no great purpose. He just hoped that when the General fell, his subjects would come to their senses and help to restore some of the heritage they had lost through the many wars and world dominations under the General's rule. Only time would tell what fate had in store for all of them.

"You mentioned that my parents were mated. I noticed that there were a few mated couples among the people I met today. If we are so desperate to repopulate our species, why aren't there more paired couples?"

"We do not mate in the way you are thinking, Rayven. For our kind there is more than just love involved in choosing a mate. We are largely spiritual beings, and though we are quite sensual in nature, we cannot choose a proper mate on the basis of mere physical compatibility.

"With our kind, copulation without a mate-bond is often a shallow, unfulfilling experience. We can find sexual release, though it is often hard for us to find it—especially so amongst our own kind. Our biology has made it thus, so that we are even more inclined to search for our proper mates.

"Before the Massacre, our people were looked upon with awe, for we were known to be skillful lovers. We've had to be, to gain what satisfaction we can from an unmated coupling. It isn't always easy to find one's destined mate, and sexual release is essential to the health of all humanoid beings, a fact even our advanced race cannot escape.

"When we are born, we are incomplete—our souls are but half of one whole. We spend our lives searching for the other half to our souls, to at last feel completed. When we find our true mates, they are the perfect accoutrement to our incomplete souls. We know our mates, often on sight, though sometimes it takes longer to realize who they are. There is only one match for each soul, and until we find that perfect fit we cannot produce offspring and we cannot know love with another."

Rayven stared hard at Draco in amazement. She felt bombarded with all the new information she was learning. It seemed as if her life had been spent in darkness and she had at last been given a light to guide her way. She'd never given love and marriage much thought, she'd been too busy running for her life. She had, of course, yearned for the tender feelings that were denied to her by the strangeness of her lifestyle, but she'd never thought to expect anything beyond a brief sexual affair in her life. Now, here was a man telling her that somewhere out in the stars, she could find a soul mate?

"Is that the main reason why you want to be able to travel off-world? To search for a mate to have children with?" The very thought made Rayven see a red haze. The thought of Draco with another woman made her almost livid with rage, and Rayven refused to dwell on why this was.

"In part, yes." Draco heard Rayven gasp and wondered what she was thinking. He could not always see clearly into her thoughts, and would not be able to fully rest within her mind until they mated.

"We cannot produce offspring outside of our own species, our biology is not compatible with other humanoids. However, we do hope to find mates for our unmated members among the ranks of our missing brethren. We have no other choice if we wish to procreate."

"Do you think I might have a mate, out there?" Rayven couldn't help asking. The idea seemed both foreign and wonderful at the same time.

Draco stared deeply into her eyes. Molten silver met flaming gold and held for the space of a heartbeat.

"I am certain of it, Highness," he said, his thumb stroking the palm of her hand.

Rayven trembled and she dragged her gaze away from his, the effort leaving her breathless and dazed. She'd never felt so out of control with her emotions before, and struggled to calm the wild flutter of her heart. For a moment she'd felt a wild sexual pull when looking into his eyes. Her breasts had swelled and her mons had burned. Whether he'd meant to or not, Draco had been affecting her thusly since they'd met. Rayven thought back to their wild kiss on the beach and wondered wistfully if she'd ever get another taste of his exquisite lips.

"So how do we find these missing Aware? How do we know if they've survived over the years?"

"You will know where to find them and how, when the time comes. When your powers are fully awakened, you will be able to call over the distance that separates us from our lost people. No Aware that is alive could refuse to heed your call. They will come to us or, if that is beyond their power, you may send out scouts to retrieve them."

"Just like that? I can make a call and they'll come? Why don't we try to do that before the war, so that we are at our fullest potential when we face the General's army?"

"Because it would be better, do we perish under the onslaught of our enemy, that those few who may yet have survived the Great Massacre be allowed to continue on as they have been, away from the carnage and death we may face. Because our victory over the Galactic Commune will not be swayed either way by our numbers or show of force. Whether we win or lose will depend solely on you, and the strength of your slumbering *Awareness*."

"Gee, thanks so much for helping to lighten the burden for me, Draco," Rayven's voice was dripping with sarcasm.

Draco smiled, but his eyes shone with a sudden sternness. "It is better that you know what to expect. It will serve no purpose to have you ill-prepared for the battle to come. I will not lie to you, Empress, not about your duties to our people. There's no point in training you, if you are unaware of the importance of your lessons."

"How, exactly, do you expect to train me? Because I'm telling you, what you see is what you get. I don't have some great slumbering giant power within me."

All of a sudden Rayven was torn by the image of her destructive surge of power lifting and crushing one of the men who'd come for her on Earth. She'd definitely been surprised by that new and fearsome surge of *Awareness*, but that murderous display was in no way powerful enough to fell an army—of that she was certain. Draco and his people must be mistaken.

However, a tiny whisper in her mind warned her that if Draco was right, and she *did* have great power at her fingertips, then she would be forever changed when she learned to wield it. It frightened her to her soul that she might be some sort of killing machine and be unaware of it.

Draco saw the images running through her mind, and felt her overwhelming fear. He grasped both of her shoulders in a firm grip and lowered his head so that they were on eye level.

"All great power comes with a price, Highness, this is true and cannot be undone. When you learn to control your hidden powers, it *will* change you forever, but it will not make you a monster. You will merely have to learn discipline and assume the duties to which you were born."

"I didn't ask for this," she whispered, ashamed of her weakness before this great man.

"Those who are truly great and just, rarely wish for power. So long as you remember this, and do not lust for power like some addictive drug, you will make a great leader. The mantle of leadership is a heavy one, and no sane person should ever wish to don it. However, someone must lead so that others may follow, and if you are careful, *a grifa*, you will lead your people down the righteous path, and find a certain peace within yourself—despite the hardships you will face."

"Why can't you lead them? I've only known you a short while but I can already see that you're more powerful than I am, you could easily lead them to freedom."

Draco stroked a lock of hair tenderly from her face. Her eyes were haunted and glowing, the sight causing his heart to constrict within his chest.

"I would that I could take this burden from you, Rayven. I cannot. But this I promise you—I will never leave your side and I will always be here to guide you should you need council. All of us, all of your people, are ready to serve you in any way you may need. You will not be forced to face this peril alone, but it is true that the ultimate victory over our foes rests within your hands, and this cannot be otherwise. You were born for this purpose.

"I will teach you how to search within yourself for your powers. I will show you how to call forth upon the elements of nature—for they are our strongest allies. I will show you how to open gateways between worlds, and how to use your psychic mind to its fullest potential."

"I think I may have opened a tunnel yesterday, but I'm not sure how—it's what brought me here. However, I don't think I could do it at will without training." Rayven tried to push aside her doubts, vowing to prove herself worthy of her people's devotion.

Draco smiled secretly to himself. His mate had no suspicions that the great black hawk of her dreams was, in fact, himself. He liked having this small secret from her, though he knew she would not appreciate his deception were she to find out.

"We shall see, *a grifa*. For now, let us venture out under the open sky and begin your lessons. The rest will take care of itself."

Rayven blinked and suddenly found that she was standing in a barren field with Draco at her side.

"How did you do that?" she asked him, her eyes dazed.

"Lesson One—teleportation. This will be one of the easier and more useful skills I can teach you. From here we will progress to planetary teleportation and then intergalactic teleportation. When you're ready we'll move onto the more tedious lessons."

"Well, gosh, don't start out *too easy* on me, okay?"

Rayven's sarcasm fell on deaf ears. Thus her training was begun.

Chapter Seventeen

Sweat dripped freely into Rayven's eyes, as she tried to hold steady the levitating forms of Draco and Onca high in the air. For the past three weeks she had practiced such exercises of control from dawn to dusk, with only a break for meals in between the long hours of training.

Each night she collapsed with screaming muscles onto her pallet of feathers and slept like the dead.

Each morning as the sun rose, Rayven and many of the other women ventured to a nearby stream to bathe. Afterward Rayven always went off to her training field, a vast stretch of flat, almost desert-like barrenness contrasting vividly with the surrounding fields of healthy green grasses, for another long day of instruction with Draco.

As the days wore on, her solitude with Draco was broken by frequent visits from Onca. Rayven soon found herself taking instruction from Onca as well as Draco, and before long Setiger and Avator had joined them.

Before the second week came to a close, a sizable crowd had gathered around to witness the Empress' instruction. It was a little unnerving for Rayven, at first, having witnesses to her many failures. However, it greatly boosted her spirits to hear the roaring praise from her audience when she succeeded in mastering a new power, so when Draco asked if she wished for him to send her growing audience away, she bid that he let them stay. After all, she reasoned to herself, these people largely depended on her successes. And if she was a flat-out failure, she wanted them to have no illusions that she hadn't at least tried to live up to their expectations.

Though Rayven could hardly believe it, Draco and Onca had assured her that she'd been steadily improving as the lessons progressed. She couldn't help but feel that her progress was too slow, and thus a disappointment to those around her. No one had seemed openly disappointed with her performance so far, but she still felt her inadequacies weighing down on her self-confidence. Especially when she witnessed Draco performing the feats he wished to teach her with little to no effort. Such as today, when Draco had informed her that he and Onca would be instructing her on levitation.

He'd effortlessly levitated her high above his head and twirled her gently in the air before setting her back on her feet, leaving her shaken but thrilled. It had felt to her like an exciting rollercoaster ride, without the safety harness, and she'd been eager to learn the skill. However, when it came time for her to try, she'd dropped Draco time and time again after levitating him only a few inches off the ground. She'd found it difficult to keep her spirits up, but by the end of the day she'd shown some improvement.

Now, as the sun was setting in the sky, casting bright orange and scarlet hues over the countryside, Rayven found herself able to levitate Draco and Onca over her head for several seconds at a stretch. Unfortunately, she had been unable, thus far, to lower them gently to the ground as Draco had done with her, and she suspected their feet and rumps were bruised from their many harsh landings. No matter how hard she concentrated she couldn't aid them in a softer landing on the ground.

"Concentrate, Rayven!"

Draco and Onca had wavered precariously in the air, causing Draco to call out the harsh command. A week ago Rayven would have cringed over the sternness of Draco's deeply booming voice. Now, she simply straightened her shoulders and raised her hands instinctively, as if by doing this she could hold them up more firmly. It didn't work—half a second after the words were out of Draco's lips he and Onca came crashing roughly to the earth.

"By the Fates, woman, do you have any idea how much that hurts?" Draco growled as he rubbed his offended posterior and rose from the ground.

Rayven's muscles were trembling from her efforts, and her breath was a harsh wind in her lungs. Despite the fact that Draco had told her time and time again that her *Awareness* was dependent on her psychic faculties and not her muscles, she still couldn't keep herself from locking her body when she was using her power. She wiped the sweat from her brow with unsteady hands.

"Why don't *you* just cushion your fall then?" she said in an exasperated voice.

"Because, Highness, then you wouldn't feel the guilt of hurting us in your failure," Onca answered with a grimace as his knees popped when he stood.

"Then don't blame me for your bruises. It's not like I'm failing on purpose."

"Try again, Rayven, and this time concentrate more on our landing," Draco instructed her, arrogant authority dripping from his velvet voice.

Rayven gave a shuddering sigh and collapsed to the ground, putting her head in her hands wearily. Luckily her audience had left for the day, to prepare for the evening meal, and there was only Onca and Draco to witness her lack of grace. Unlike the first meal she'd shared with them, not all of the Aware's food was prepared by *blaithen*, and the Aware often set out to gather native fruits and grains for the evening's repast, which were made into succulent and exotic dishes that Rayven greatly enjoyed. Now she was glad of the absence of her people, so she could lower her guard and let her weariness and frustrations show.

"I can't do it anymore! I'm tired and I'm achy and I want a bath. I'm so sweaty my clothes are sticking to me like glue and I hate it!"

Draco snorted. He knew she was close to the breaking point of her control, and he sensed that this might be a new key in teaching her the depths of her power. He was growing tired of hearing her deny the strength of the *Awareness* hidden within her, and had been searching for a way to prove her denials unfounded. Willing to test his theory, if not especially eager as his posterior still throbbed from the bludgeoning it had taken throughout the day, he pushed her further.

"Quit your whining. You'll rest when I say you may. Now try again."

Rayven's eyes flashed brightly in the deepening twilight. "I will not! I need a break now, before I pass out from exhaustion."

"Are you truly this weak, or is it merely being among humans that has softened your will?"

"How *dare* you," Rayven hissed, rising angrily to her feet. "I didn't ask for this damned training of yours. You forced it on me, and now all I want is some time to rest. That doesn't make me weak! We've been going at it for three solid weeks without a break—anyone would be tired by now."

"I am not tired," Draco taunted, his eyes hard and derisive. He turned to Onca who was slowly backing out of the line of fire and asked, "Are you tired, Onca?"

Onca rolled his eyes skyward, seeking patience. He didn't particularly want to be included in this test of wills, but if Draco willed it then so be it. "No, Draco," he said. His voice was the personification of innocence. "I'm not tired at all."

Draco turned back to Rayven and sent her a cold glare. "Perhaps you should quit wallowing in lazy self-indulgence and focus on the tasks at hand. Then you will not tire so easily."

Rayven's mouth gaped, her eyes going wide with incredulity. Draco sounded like some kind of impatient parent or schoolteacher. Her body was weak and sore, and her fatigue was growing more and more heavy as the days wore on, and she couldn't understand his attitude towards her in the least. She had worked tirelessly and given her all each day without complaint until now…and he dared to call her lazy?

"That's it! I've had it with all your supercilious commands. I refuse to sit back and let you mock me. If I'm your ruler then I command you to back off and let me rest this instant!"

"You have not yet earned the right to rule me, Empress. I have my doubts that you ever shall. How can you hope to rule an entire race of people when you cannot even learn the basic skills necessary to survive on your own?"

"I don't believe this! One minute you say I'm destined to be the greatest ruler you've ever known and then you tell me I'm a weakling who hasn't even earned your respect. What is your damn problem? All I wanted was a break from all this endless training. Just one evening where I'll have some time to myself before I collapse from exhaustion like I do every other night."

"When you are ready to assume the throne you will hardly ever have a moment to yourself. You must accustom yourself to hard work, or you will never be fit to rule. Now try it again, and this time do not drop us or I will have to bend you over my knee and give you the spanking you so richly deserve for you childish attitude," Draco gritted out his last words, hoping the threat would at last push her over the edge of her usual iron-control. He didn't know exactly what he expected from her…but he was certainly unprepared for what he got.

Rayven saw a red haze before her, and her jaw clenched at the humiliating thought of his threat of a spanking. She couldn't believe his audacity in threatening such a childish punishment. Her temper got the better of her and her self-control slipped a notch. She forgot how tired she was, and forgot how fruitless it was to even think of pitting her *Awareness* against Draco's.

She forgot everything but her bruised pride and his endless mockery in the face of her anger. Paying little heed to the frisson of warning that played its way up her spine, or the wild rush of blood roaring in her ears, she threw her hands out in front of her and let loose a burning wave of power.

An electric burst of lightning raced in bright tendrils from each of her fingertips, the tiny streams of white-hot energy coalescing in the center of her palms to form a solid beam of power that blazed out from her hands. The beam of silver lightning hit Draco squarely in his chest and flung him backwards several feet. In a protective gesture, Draco also flung out his own hands and caught the full force of her power surge with a blast of his own.

A golden beam of energy flowed forth from Draco's hands and streamed to meet down the middle of Rayven's silver one. Rayven skidded backwards and was forced to dig in her heels to avoid stumbling. She "pushed" harder with her mind, her anger and frustrations feeding the fire raging within her. She didn't stop to think about how easy it was for her to demonstrate such a violent display of power, she only thought about making Draco regret his taunting of her.

Silver threads of electricity whipped out from where the two energies met in the middle of a long stream, and raced down the golden length of Draco's energy burst to spill over his hands. A deafening sound like thunder sounded around them, and a strong wind whipped at their hair. He reciprocated her move and golden fire swallowed her hands as well. The golden light warmed her skin, and was a sensation just shy of burning pain, but Rayven refused to back down before him. She threw the full weight of her body and mind behind the power flooding from her outstretched palms. She screamed as stray flashes of lightning arced and raced between them outside of the concentrated beam of their dueling energies. The lightning flashed high and bright into the darkened sky, illuminating the field below.

Abruptly Draco's golden light was extinguished and Rayven's power once again connected with his chest. Draco flew backwards, rolled twice from the force of the blow, and then lay still upon the ground, smoke rising from his chest. Rayven's power blinked out, as if turned off with the flip of a switch, and she collapsed in a boneless swoon onto the dusty ground. The sudden twilight stillness was broken only by the sound of their harsh breathing.

Onca was struck dumb by the display. He'd never seen such an awesome exhibition of pure power. He'd heard of such things, brightly visual displays of power known as royal duels. He'd always believed that royal duels were a myth. No Aware could create a physical manifestation of pure power like that and wield it against another of their own kind—none that he knew of at any rate.

Only the purest and most ancient bloodlines were reputed to hold the secrets of such power, but so far as Onca knew, no one had ever bore witness to such a display in living memory. That his eyes were deceiving him had occurred to him numerous times throughout the blinding battle, but as bright spots danced in his sight he could not help but believe in the reality of what had just happened.

He'd actually been witness to a royal duel. It was the stuff of legends.

When his lungs had started to cooperate again, Onca was uncertain whom to go to first. He chose Draco, as he seemed the one more the worse for wear. As he reached his side, he saw that Draco had regained consciousness. If, in fact, Draco had ever really lost consciousness, which Onca doubted after seeing his friend's newest display of strength. He'd probably just been knocked breathless by the blow from Rayven's lightning bolt.

A charred hole steamed from Draco's flowing black shirt, but his skin was unmarred. His silver eyes seemed dazed for a moment as he looked up at Onca.

"Did you see that?" he breathed with a look of wonder.

"I did. Are you well? Can you stand?" Onca asked, reaching for Draco's hand.

Draco chuckled unsteadily and rose stiffly. "I think I'll be recovered in a moment. I don't think Rayven really meant to hurt me or I would not be talking to you right now. I think she just wanted to bruise my ego a little bit."

Onca helped to dust off Draco's shoulders, secretly looking for more injuries, doubtful that Draco could have escaped such a battle unscathed. There were none. Perhaps Draco was right that Rayven had merely been toying with him, though Onca would have thought otherwise from the sheer violence of Rayven's attack. He couldn't deny that Draco seemed lucky in his escape from serious harm.

"Well, if that was her intention, then she succeeded admirably," he said.

"She has killed in such a manner before. I have seen it in her memories. She killed one of the General's men, in mere seconds, with this show of power. If she had meant me true harm, I fear she would have felled me with her first blow."

The two men slowly approached Rayven as she lay on the ground. Her face was pressed to the earth and her breath was shuddering her entire frame.

"Do not weep, Highness," Onca said. He hated the sight of a woman's tears, and could not bear the thought that his Empress suffered because of her lapse in control.

Rayven didn't answer.

Draco bent down to her and gently turned her over to face them. She wasn't crying. She looked dazed and confused—her eyes glazed and shocked. Draco chuckled and gathered her into his arms. She went willingly, burying her face in the masculine fragrance of his shoulder and neck.

"Are you hurt, *a grifa*?"

Rayven let out one last shuddering breath against him, and her tremors subsided as Draco's warmth seeped in to her suddenly freezing body.

"Why do you keep calling me that? What does it mean?"

Draco was taken aback by the calmness of her voice and her unexpected question. "It is in our ancient language. It means my little beloved one. Answer my question, *a grifa*, are you hurt anywhere?"

Rayven tried not to let the meaning of the endearment thrill her too much, and she pulled back and looked at Draco's charred shirt with a pounding heart. His unblemished chest was highlighted in the silver light of the moon, and she rubbed her hand over it to be sure he was uninjured. He sucked in a breath at her touch and gathered her closer against him.

"I'm great. Just peachy keen. Couldn't be better," she said with a tinge of self-mockery. "I see you're none the worse for wear."

"I thank you for not maiming me, Highness."

"Yeah," a strained chuckle escaped her lips. "I guess you need those glorious pecs to woo all the ladies, huh? We wouldn't want you to be scarred or anything."

Draco couldn't help smiling over her derisive tone. He enjoyed seeing these small flashes of jealousy from her. It said much of her growing attachment to him. He liked knowing that she found the image of him with other women distasteful. He also liked knowing that she found his "pecs" glorious, even if she hadn't meant her words as a compliment.

"No, Highness, my conquests shall remain relatively effortless thanks to your kind thoughts for my welfare."

Rayven snorted, refusing to comment on his baiting words.

"Are you over your upset now?"

Rayven tensed in his arms. She hated how nonchalant he sounded over the whole situation, while she was still reeling from the shock. The strength of her power had more than surprised her, and here he was acting as if it were a common occurrence for him to be attacked in such a manner. She hadn't even bruised him…well, at least she'd bruised him in advance during training that day. Maybe she would neglect to work on her landing techniques for the next few days, just to make up for her disappointment. True, she hadn't wanted to seriously injure him, but a few black and blue spots would have done a lot to salvage her bruised pride.

"Yes, I'm over my upset," she said in a regal tone, her chin lifting slightly.

"Good. I think you look a bit tired. Why not take the rest of the evening for yourself and try to work some of the soreness out of your muscles?"

"That's all I ever wanted," she said defensively.

"Well, all you had to do was ask me, *a grifa*. I am ever ready to see to your comforts. You should have taken a break earlier today, and then you wouldn't have become so tired. You push yourself too hard, Highness."

Rayven gritted her teeth and socked him solidly in the stomach with her clenched fist. Life was so unfair...he didn't even grunt.

Chapter Eighteen

Rayven limped into the Gathering Tree over an hour later, looking ready to collapse. Her hair was still wet from her dip in the stream and dripping down her back to her waist. During her first week of training, Draco had shown her how to dry her hair using her powers over Air and Wind, but she had been too weary to even try it after her bath tonight. Her body was sagging with fatigue, and every step sent waves of pain throughout each of her muscle groups.

Upon seeing her entrance, the group of Aware who had already gathered around the feasting table rose to applaud and cheer her. Obviously the tale of her impressive display of power had already spread through their ranks. Rayven struggled not to blush with embarrassment and tried not to walk too stiffly to her chair. Draco was not yet present, or so the empty seat beside hers attested. He always sat on her left, in a chair identical to hers, at the head of the expansive stone table.

Ursus, who had become her closest friend besides Draco and Onca, came to sit in Draco's empty chair, though she looked ready to bolt from it at any moment.

"Highness, I'm so proud of you! However did you learn to fight a royal duel? I thought they were just wild tales of the days of old. I do so wish I had seen it for myself."

"Ursus, I've told you time and again to call me Rayven. All this royal deference is hard enough to take, but it is especially discomfiting coming from those who I would call friend. To answer your question—I have no idea what you're talking about. Explain to me what a royal duel is first, please."

"Highness—*Rayven*—a royal duel is a wondrous and magical phenomenon. Our people have strong psychic powers 'tis true, but we cannot fight against one of our own kind using our *Awareness*, no matter how strong our abilities are. It's impossible. Almost an evolutionary defense, I guess you might say—to keep any one of us from becoming too corrupt with the strength of our own powers. We have all heard the stories of how the ancient ones of our race were able to display their powers for all to see in such duels for sport. Their *Awareness* was exponentially stronger than ours is now.

"Slowly, as time wore on, only the strongest among our ancestors were able to showcase their powers in such a manner, and after that, only those with the most ancient and pure bloodlines—the younger bloodlines lost much of their potency as it was slowly bred out of them over time.

"In times gone by we were not often called upon to use our powers in battle, so it was said our strongest members would gather at tournaments and have royal duels, to prove their strengths and abilities, which offered much entertainment for all to see.

"We had always believed these stories of ancient tournaments being performed before audiences to be myths—or exaggerations of the truth. We suspected they were fables that our parents told to us as youths to entice us into studying more diligently in our training so that we might one day grow as powerful as our ancestors supposedly were. No one has even heard of such a thing as a royal duel being fought for thousands of years."

Rayven tried to meet Ursus' excited gaze, but she found she could not, and looked away. She didn't know what to say, but in the face of such unbridled excitement Rayven felt guilt unlike any she'd ever known.

She knew that what had happened between she and Draco out on the training field had not been as uncommon an occurrence as Ursus seemed to think. How could it be? Draco hadn't even batted an eyelash when she'd unleashed her rage upon him. He had in fact met her blow for blow, and come away unscathed but for a ruined shirt. Perhaps Ursus and many of the other people here were not accustomed to such raw visual displays of power, but Draco and Onca had certainly seemed nonchalant about the whole thing.

"Oh." Rayven knew she sounded less than eloquent, but she didn't know what else to say.

"Do you think you and Draco might show us your newfound powers on the training field tomorrow?"

"Not yet, Ursus," Draco's black velvet voice poured over them as he appeared behind Rayven in a warm puff of wind. "As a matter of fact, I do not think it is wise to have an audience out on the training fields anymore. With this new development of the Empress' powers, it is best that she not be distracted by a crowd."

Rayven turned back to face Draco, a denial forming on her lips, taking exception to his arrogant tone. When she saw him, however, all thoughts fled from her mind, as always seemed to be the case whenever he was near her. Her breath fell outward on a sigh, as she drunk in the sight of him.

He had bathed, and donned new midnight-black, leather-like trousers that hugged him like a second skin, and showed off his powerful thighs and calves beautifully. He was wearing a flowing silver shirt with flaring bell sleeves that were gathered with a wide cuff at his wrists.

He had left his shirt unlaced and his great muscular chest seemed dark behind the brightness of his shirt. His hair fell in a hematite curtain down his back to his waist, and a long lock had fallen forward over his shoulder to dangle temptingly near his navel. He looked like a pirate. He looked like wild and forbidden fruit—he looked like dangerous sex.

He seemed to know exactly what she was thinking, and he ran his eyes down the length of her body, scorching her exposed skin in a molten silver burn. She was wearing a scarlet *evansai* bustier with a matching skirt that fell to her ankles and was slit up both sides to the waistband. Underneath the transparent fabric of her skirt she was wearing a matching scarlet thong, which she knew was more than visible to Draco's hungry stare.

She hadn't given it much thought before she'd left her *Bito*, but now she realized that she'd never dared to appear quite so scantily clad before around Draco, at least not since her nude arrival on the beach a few weeks past.

Normally she chose to wear the thicker and less transparent garments that Ursus had supplied her with. Tonight she had simply been too weary to worry about her modesty and had carelessly grabbed the first garment at hand in her clothing trunk. Now, as Draco's eyes roved ravenously over her tingling breasts and exposed thighs, she wished she'd been more careful with her choice of attire. She couldn't easily control her blushes when Draco stared at her like some hungry wolf, as he was doing now. His intense regard did strange and thrilling things to her libido that she didn't like thinking about.

Ursus jumped up from her perch in Draco's chair and assumed her seat farther down the table. Draco reached out to caress a damp tendril of Rayven's hair before he sat down.

"You are radiant tonight, Empress."

"No, I'm dog-tired tonight, and I look as weary as I feel."

"You are always a vision of loveliness, whether you are tired or not."

"No, I'm not, Draco, and quit trying to win my good graces. I'm still very angry with you for taunting me, and until I get some rest I'm probably not going to forgive you either."

Draco leaned closer to her, and whispered in her ear, "If I got down on my knees before you, would you forgive me? Simply command me and it shall be as you wish."

Rayven's flesh tingled where his tuft of warm breath caressed her skin. She heard the sexual innuendo in his voice and pulled away from him to flash him a warning look. She was tired of his seemingly endless attempts at flirting with her. He was constantly touching her hair or her skin and whispering thinly veiled sexual comments into her ear. If she didn't know any better she would think he was seriously trying to catch her off-guard and seduce her.

Looking about her at all the ethereally beautiful women around the feasting table—those that weren't already mated and even now riding upon the hardened shafts of their mates as mated couples were wont to do almost every moment of every day—Rayven disbelieved that Draco would choose to lavish attention on her for any other reason besides teasing her. He could have his pick of any woman there, and she knew her beauty paled in comparison to theirs.

"Quit doing that, Draco. I'm tired of playing these silly games with you."

"Then let us forfeit the rules, *a grifa*, I am ever ready to move on to more serious play."

Rayven's eyes flared, shocked, as Draco's hand dropped to the exposed skin of her leg and pushed his way under the material of her skirt to wrap his large hand around her inner thigh. His skin burned her and he squeezed gently, his fingers spanning outward and coming close to the band of her thong at the apex of her thighs. A strange yearning swept through her at his touch, but she refused to be bullied by her passions for this man.

Rayven shoved at his hand, trying desperately not to attract the attention of the other diners. It seemed that her struggles, thus far, were going unnoticed by her people, for which her modesty was eternally grateful. She glared angrily into his burning eyes.

"Stop it this instant," she hissed.

Draco's eyes burned a trail down from her eyes to linger at her lips, breasts and mons.

"I think it is time you realized that I will not obey your every summons, tiny one—Empress or no. I think it is time you know just how dangerous a game it is that you play with me." And so saying, Draco jerked Rayven from her seat to place her squarely on his lap, with her legs spread wide over his powerful thighs.

Rayven choked on an outraged gasp and squirmed against his hold. He held her firm and even dared to move one hand down to her waist in order to pull her more firmly against his rock-hard erection. Once she was pulled against him as tightly as he could manage, he threw both arms around her to cage her and his voice sounded deeply in her ear as he spoke.

"Your flimsy *evansai* clothing cannot shield you from me, *a grifa.* I can feel your pussy lips wet and hot against my cock—even through my own clothing." He ground his hips against her for emphasis, and Rayven almost swooned at the exquisite friction of his movements.

Looking around, mortification and pure lust warring dangerously within her, Rayven noticed that the surrounding people were pointedly ignoring her struggles with Draco. She wondered fleetingly if they would come to her aid should she command it.

She promptly discarded the idea, sure that her people would side with Draco, were she to protest too vehemently over something they accepted as commonplace at their dinner table. They would probably be thrilled that Draco wished to mate with her, thinking there might be a chance of a child between them—after all, their main goal these years in exile was to encourage procreation.

Draco had the upper hand with her people, no matter her position among them, she knew. And, a tiny voice inside her whispered, she didn't want to test Draco too much…he might stop his wondrous attentions…and she wasn't sure she ever wanted him to.

Draco's hand came down between her legs and dove underneath her clothing. He pulled aside the thong she wore, and speared his fingers through the tight curls that shielded her labia. Rayven let loose a shuddering sigh as he petted her there, a tingling, flooding warmth overtaking her and making her cease her struggles against him. She lay limply back against his chest and he growled his appreciation in her ear. To reward her for her surrender, he parted the lips of her labia and dipped his finger in the wet heat of her. She could feel an answering gush of fluid drip out over his digit and he rubbed the new wetness all around the flesh of her pussy.

Draco brought his other hand down to join the first, not having to hold her secure against him any longer. He expertly found the hardened nubbin of her clit between her pussy lips. He rubbed her clit expertly with one hand, while the other hand thrust two fingers into her flooded vagina.

Draco almost groaned aloud his lust when he felt how incredibly tight her channel was around this small penetration of her. He'd never known a woman so small or so tight, so wet or so hot. He wanted to loosen the laces of his clothing and thrust his turgidly swollen cock into her pussy, and fuck her until she screamed for mercy. Instead, Draco gritted his teeth and held onto what little self-control he had left. He thrust his fingers into her more deeply, and manipulated her plump little clit in such a way that he knew her orgasm would be upon her the soonest.

Rayven keened softly in her throat, uncaring now if she was drawing any attention from the other diners around her as sparks flew before her tightly closed eyes. She threw her head back and rotated her hips helplessly against Draco's hands. She felt his large fingers scrape against some hidden and magical place deep within her pussy, and shuddered almost violently when his other hand began to pinch and pull at her. Never in her life had she felt so out of control, so crazed with arousal and lust. Rayven tried and failed to stave off the swift approach of her orgasm.

Draco felt the first pulsating quivers deep within her dripping vagina, and he thrust his fingers in and out of her in an effort to heighten her pleasure. He caressed her clit furiously, and suddenly her orgasm was upon her. Draco pulled one hand free from her to turn her face forcefully to his so that he might taste the cries of passion she could no longer contain with his hungry lips.

He speared his tongue into her mouth and, in a similar rhythm, thrust his fingers into her clenching cunt, feeling the tight spasms of her muscles and reveling in the knowledge that it was he and no other that had brought her to such a gloriously forceful release.

When her tremors against his hand began to subside he pulled his fingers from her pussy with an audibly wet slurping sound, and set her gently from him, back to her original seat by his side.

"God," Rayven said shakily. She righted her clothes awkwardly as she came back to herself, down from the glorious heights into which Draco had so expertly thrown her. Out of the corner of her dazed eyes she saw Draco bring his sopping wet fingers to his mouth, as he sucked and licked the evidence of her orgasm from them. She felt an answering clenching of her lower muscles as she saw how clearly he seemed to enjoy the taste of her passion, and she averted her eyes from the sight in an effort to erase the image from her memory.

"D-Draco…please, don't do that again."

Draco tilted her head up and around to once again meet his gaze. His eyes were deep pools of molten starlight, full of dangerous passions—anger among them. "Do not think to deny that I pleasured you thoroughly, Highness. I felt you coming against my fingers…and I know for a certainty that it was the best you'd ever had. Why must you fight against it, should I choose to help you find release again?"

"I'm not used to such public displays, Draco—not like you and your people so obviously are. Yes, I admit that I enjoyed it." Rayven tried to sound emotionless about it, falling back on her ability to look at almost every situation from an intellectual viewpoint. "You played my body like an instrument and it is a testament to your skills as a lover, I'm sure. But I'm not an exhibitionist…and you didn't do that to show you cared for me as a lover. Quite the opposite. You did it to prove a point—that you have power over me. Well, you've proven it…are you happy with your success? Now I can feel properly chastised, as well as mortified that you taught me the lesson in such a public place."

"Our people think nothing of such displays. If anything, they encourage it. We are a sensual people who often indulge in the act of sex…you know this. Why be embarrassed by it? It did nothing to undermine your position amongst us—in fact, several at this table are doing far more with each other than you and I just did."

"Whatever, Draco. I'm too tired to get into this discussion with you. But I beg of you—" how Rayven hated those words, "—if you feel the need to teach me a lesson in the future. Do it when we are not in front of our people."

"As you wish, Highness. I had forgotten how prudish your adoptive world is, and how you are unused to such acts of passionate abandon. I let my temper and my passions get the better of me. But if it is an apology you are looking for from me, you will not get it. I enjoyed it. You enjoyed it. Let us leave it at that."

Rayven glanced down at Draco's lap and saw the rigid bulge of his cock beneath the leather of his pants. She wasn't sure how much he'd enjoyed it if he was still so hard, but she was too weary to argue further with him on the matter. She *had* enjoyed it, no matter that it had embarrassed her, and no one had even seemed to notice their actions or their conversation. With a languorous feeling of satiation still swimming warmly through her veins, she couldn't stay mad at him for too long over it. She would let the matter drop, as he seemed inclined to do. She turned back to her meal and concentrated on forgetting how wonderful Draco's hands had felt upon her body.

Draco breathed deeply of her scent and tried to calm his ardor. Seeing Rayven dressed so scantily had almost undone him. He'd seen her nude before, when they'd met on the shore the day of her arrival, but this was something altogether new and tempting. Seeing her with her breasts, firm and lush, cupped lovingly by their satin curtain, her lusciously long legs peeking out of her transparent skirt, and her femininity barely covered by a teasing scrap of scarlet had made him reel under an onslaught of pure animalistic lust. He'd barely been able to control the urge to throw her over his shoulder and retire to her *Bito*...to ensure that she learned every lesson he wished to teach her.

He barely reined in his aggressive passions and pulled a deep breath into his lungs. His heart rate had yet to slow, the tightness of his trousers was growing more and more uncomfortable and his heavy erection throbbed demandingly. He tried with great effort to cool the burning fire in his veins, but fantasies of throwing her legs over his shoulders and having his way with her sweet body were bombarding his every other thought.

He knew his frustrations would only get worse before they could be appeased, and it didn't help that she looked so delectable. He could think of naught else but claiming her over and over again in their bed feathers. He growled low in his throat and downed a full goblet of *tearwine* before slamming the drinking vessel down upon the table with resounding force.

"What is wrong with you *now*?" Rayven asked in startlement.

"What do you think is wrong with me, Empress? In concealing attire you are a breathtaking creature, as well you should know, but you sorely tempt my passions when you are dressed thus."

"I'm wearing a lot more than most of the other women here! No one else is staring or groping me."

"Perhaps not, but I am not made of stone, *a grifa*. I still have the taste of you on my tongue—the feel of you on my fingertips and cock, and I cannot help but long for more. You would make a delicious feast for one as hungry as I, were you but willing."

"Quit toying with me like that—*I don't like it.*" Rayven's angrily shouted words at last seemed to catch the attention of the diners and all fell abruptly silent.

Rayven felt her cheeks heat with embarrassment. Why did Draco always make her act like a shrew? He'd been the only person she'd ever met who could make her lose control over her emotions so easily. The fact that her anger seemed to constantly amuse him only served to enrage her more. She couldn't for the life of her understand her reaction to him.

She looked at his too-beautiful face, and saw his lips twitch faintly with a smile. Her embarrassment fled in the path of renewed anger, and she desperately strove not to lose control before the gathering of her people.

She smiled sweetly at him, her glowing eyes anything but amicable, and addressed her people without taking her gaze from Draco's. "Please ignore us, we were just having a friendly little disagreement. I'm sorry I shouted."

"It didn't sound friendly to me, Highness. You fairly bellowed at poor Draco," Setiger teased her with flashing amethyst eyes and a small smile playing about his lips.

"Well, nobody asked you your opinion, Setiger, now did they?" Rayven's voice dripped honey-smooth.

Setiger merely chuckled at her tone and chose not to answer her. He turned to converse with another man at his side, and the sounds of merriment and conversation swelled around the hall once more.

Draco reached out and took Rayven's hand. He brought it to his lips and turned it over to suavely press a hot kiss against her palm.

"Bottle your passions, *a grifa*, and save them for when we are alone." His voice was like deep midnight, dark and dangerous. It poured over her skin like warm silk and left her trembling in its wake.

"I don't have any passions, Draco, and we are definitely not going to ever be alone if you're acting like you are now."

"You will enjoy the coming pleasures I will bring to you, Empress, this I promise you. I will have you trembling and crying out in my arms, as you were just moments ago, and you will love every delicious moment of it. In fact, I wager that you will eagerly beg me for more."

Rayven reeled as Draco's words burned into her mind. She felt the brush of his *Awareness* deep within her subconscious as he sent her image after image of her body entwined with his in various erotic positions. She gasped as she felt the brush of invisible fingers over her nipples, bringing them to aching points beneath the thin bustier she wore.

"Stop doing that! I'm not going to have sex with you, not now, not ever. You're not my type at all." They both knew she was lying, but she couldn't help it, and she rushed on, "You're an asshole over half the time, and all you do is make me angry when I'm around you. Just now I wasn't myself, I've had a very trying and shocking day. I wasn't thinking."

"You're right, Rayven, you weren't thinking—you were feeling. Feelings are often more sincere and powerful than intellect. Perhaps you should think on the implications of that."

Draco's voice had taken on an even more ethereal quality and she heard his words in her mind as well as aloud. His voice seemed to reach deep inside her, to places she'd never felt aware of before. Her body grew warm and tingling. She was suddenly breathless and she felt a pulse of ecstasy wash through her from her womb outward.

She was suddenly acutely aware of his scent, a heady and masculine mixture that smelled of sandalwood and rosemary. It made her feel giddy and intoxicated, and she found it almost impossible to keep from flinging herself wantonly into his arms.

"What are you doing?" she asked softly, swaying slightly in her seat. Her eyes were hooded with desire, and no small amount of alarm. She knew he could see her attraction to him in the depth of her gaze, and she unsuccessfully tried to hide it from him.

Draco smiled down at her wickedly. He knew he was being unfair, using the power of his voice and his pheromones to draw her to him, but he found that he didn't care. He knew they were mates, even if she did not, and he couldn't fight the urge to use his innate preternatural powers over their bond to seduce her.

Only a male's true mate could be bespelled in such a way, and he found his heart glad that he had such power over her. He was careful not to use his full allure, as that would send her into a frenzy of lust, but he could not resist tempting her in such a small way and reveling in his effect upon her.

Reluctantly admitting to himself that now was not the time for his passion play with her, he released his hold on her libido and watched her as she gained control of herself. He ran his hand soothingly down her back in an effort to help her calm the wild urges he knew were still flooding through her body. Her breath released on a shuddering sigh and she sent him a wary look from under her lashes.

"Whatever you did—and I don't care what it was—don't you ever do it again. I may not be as powerful as you, but I promise you I will make you pay for it if you use your powers on me like that again."

Draco merely threw his head back and laughed at her threat. Rayven hated that he never seemed to take her temper seriously, and she vowed that she'd find a way to surprise him someday. Somehow.

"You are overtired, Empress. Eat your meal and seek your rest for the evening. I promise I will not torment you further tonight."

Rayven scowled at his lighthearted tone, but turned to her food as he'd instructed. She was too tired to argue further with him…but she couldn't help smiling over the thought of what she would do to him in retaliation once she had more control over her powers. She couldn't wait.

Chapter Nineteen

The next morning Rayven was awakened from her exhausted slumber by Onca's indigo head poking into her *Bito*.

"Today we are going to take a small break from your normal routine, Highness. It will be more of a physical workout for you, so be sure to wear comfortable attire."

Rayven groaned. If today's training was to be more physical than usual, she wasn't sure how she could endure it.

"What will I be learning today?"

"*Blazesword* fighting."

*****

When Rayven arrived on the training field twenty minutes later, Draco, Onca, Avator and Setiger were already there, awaiting her. She tried not to look too curious when Draco pulled two brightly glowing blades from a black sack held by Avator. Draco handled the two swords reverently and with a show of great respect. He treated them like precious heirlooms, and Rayven was struck with the thought that they probably were. The swords looked like the ones she'd seen in both the General and Onca's memories.

Draco turned to Rayven and with a flourish he handed her one of the blades, handle first. All traces of the passionate satyr of the night before were gone. Rayven sighed when she realized that Draco was in his mentor mode once again. She wasn't sure if she was relieved or disappointed that he seemed inclined to go on as they always had been after last night's events. She let her brooding thoughts pass as she studied the blade in her hand.

Draco's voice caught her attention once more. "These are known as *Blazeswords,* Highness, and are the most ancient weapon of our people. As you can see from their bright glow, the name is appropriate for the look of them, but the name's meaning goes far beyond its aesthetic properties. When wielded properly, a *Blazesword*'s heated blade can cause painful burning wounds that will not heal rapidly or well, no matter what healing techniques are used."

Rayven raised the hilt of the offered *Blazesword* and was pleasantly surprised when she easily hefted its slight weight. It was about four feet in length and its blazing metal blade and haft looked solid enough to weigh much more than it did. She started to expertly flick and twirl the blade about, before a thought occurred to her and brought a wicked smile to play at her mouth.

Draco had never asked her what weapons she knew to wield, and she'd never offered the information. Perhaps, if she played her cards right, she could surprise him a little bit with her blade work. After the past few weeks of seeing him as a stoic and unflinching taskmaster, she looked forward to the opportunity to catch him off-guard.

Her wicked juices bubbling, Rayven clumsily lowered the blade's point into the dust at her feet. She was a skilled student of the saber, foil and epee blades. She'd surprised more than one master instructor with her quickly learned skills and techniques. She'd often heard the saying among her different masters that it took two lifetimes to master the art of the blade. She'd shocked everyone in the know when she'd drawn close to becoming a master in a few short years.

She couldn't wait to see the look on Draco's face when she expertly thrust and parried his every attack. She almost laughed in her glee, and was unable to keep the wicked gleam from her eyes and smile. She was anxious to begin the day's "lesson".

Draco smiled at her unexpectedly, a bit of wickedness on his face as well. With a slight frown she wondered if he was reading her thoughts again. Despite the fact that he'd taught her how to shield her thoughts from others, he always seemed able to breach her mental defenses. And he always seemed to do it at the most inopportune moment.

"I am not as fine a swordsman as Onca, nor I suspect as you are, Rayven—" he ignored her indignant gasp that he'd already foiled her attempts at subterfuge, "—but I am willing to wager that I can still surprise you."

He *had* been reading her thoughts, damn him! She tried not to be too disappointed.

Setiger grinned engagingly at Rayven. "Are you experienced with the *Blazesword* then, Highness?"

"Not exactly—" she tried not to sulk as Draco brandished his blade before her, "—but I have taken instruction with various other blades."

"Really? Do they have many similar weapons on Earth?" Setiger asked.

"Well, their swords are mostly just metal blades with sharp edges for cutting or hacking. They don't use them as a weapon of war anymore though, they have much more destructive firepower now. Sword fighting is more a sport now than a battle skill."

Avator's eyes widened at her words and he couldn't help asking with a harsh tone in his voice, "What kind of destructive firepower are you talking about?"

Not knowing how to explain such a complicated thing as the various methods of mass destruction implemented by the people of her adopted planet, Rayven used one of her newfound mental skills and sent a bombardment of images to the minds of her friends. She showed them the guns, tanks, missiles and bombs often used during times of war on Earth, and each of the men blanched with undisguised horror.

"Don't tell me you've never seen anything like that. After spending only a few short hours amongst the General and his men I won't believe it. They've got weapons unlike anything I've ever dreamed of. Those laser guns are much stronger than any Earth weapon I've ever seen fired, and those headbands they wear are terrifying in the extreme."

Avator grimaced at her mention of the General. "Yes, he has many powerful weapons, but none that would affect the ecosystem of an entire planet such as the Earthlings' atomic power."

Rayven shot her eyes to Onca's and saw him shake his head at her in warning. Obviously the other Aware didn't know the General and his armies had ravaged their homeworld's ecosystem just as thoroughly, as if an entire arsenal of nuclear weapons had been unleashed upon it. Rayven had seen the decimation of Nye in Onca's memories, and it was clear he had not shared these images with anyone else.

Setiger spoke up, his eyes suddenly guarded and wary. "What headbands do you refer to, Highness? I know of their *lascannons*, but I've never heard of these headbands that are used as weapons."

Rayven briefly explained about the platinum-colored metal bands the General's henchmen had worn when they'd first attacked her. When she mentioned the tiny blue stone embedded in the center of the headband, all four men went still and their eyes took on a feral, hunted look. If Rayven didn't know better she'd think they looked as if their souls had departed their bodies, leaving behind grim statues made of unflinching iron. Their eyes glittered brightly with a preternatural quality and their bodies seemed to grow even larger in their already giant frames.

A cold wind blew bitingly at Rayven's cheeks—a spillage of power from the withdrawing men before her. She knew now that despite the usually peaceful and contemplative veneer her people wore, they hid an underlying strength and power underneath it all. She could feel their pain as if it was her own, and it bled from her aching heart to encompass her entire being. She didn't know why her description of the General's strange weapon should affect them so, but she vowed to herself that she would do anything in her power to take the anguished, enraged looks away from her friends' faces. No matter what it took.

Rayven reached out to clasp Draco's hand. It was the first time she'd ever willingly reached out to make comforting, physical contact with another being in her memory. She wanted to offer any comfort she could, so long as it would simply take away the strange look on his face. Her heart was an aching hole within her breast, as she met his bottomless gaze.

"What's wrong?"

Draco seemed incapable of speech, and after two tries Onca was able to find his voice and it was he who answered her question. "They use our *Chama* stones as weapons."

He offered no more explanation and Rayven sent a puzzled look his way.

"What is a *Chama* stone?"

"The blue stones in these headbands you mentioned are our *Chama* stones. The Galactic Armies stole them from us during the Great Massacre, with little regard for their sacred worth to us." Draco's words were gravelly and deep, the musical and entrancing tones missing from his voice as if they had never been.

Avator's lapis eyes were full of raging electric blue sparks, and his voice was just as grating as Draco's. "How *dare* they use our ancestors' *Chamas* for their bloodthirsty pursuits!"

Setiger seemed incapable of speech and a low, menacing growl came from deep within his throat. Rayven had always seen him as the carefree member of Draco's Council and was shocked to see the barely suppressed violence on his face. He looked as if he were battling some internal bloodthirsty beast and was losing. His muscles rippled and moved with a preternatural grace. With his bronze mane flying about him on the strange cold wind and a bestial growl sounding from his throat, he seemed almost leonine to Rayven. He resembled a great jungle cat on the brink of launching a powerful attack upon its prey, and the image unsettled her more than she was willing to admit.

Onca cleared his throat shakily. "When our people choose to die, they let their souls leave their mortal bodies and travel to the land beyond life. They leave behind a piece of themselves so that their descendants will always have their love and wisdom to guide them should the need ever arise. Their physical bodies fade and disappear, leaving behind a *Chama* stone, a tiny seed of captured psychic emanations that is treasured for all time by their descendants."

Rayven glanced away from Setiger and thought on Onca's words. She remembered the tiny blue *Chama* stone she'd been compelled to steal from the General's fortress. At this very moment, it lay in the bottom of her clothing trunk, wrapped reverently in a protective swatch of black *evansai*. She'd never understood, until now, why she'd felt so strongly about saving the stone from the strange room in which she'd found it.

With a growing sense of outraged horror she wondered if the bag from which she'd taken the *Chama* stone had been full of other similar stones. With an aching heart, she suspected this was so. She wished now, with fervent regret, that she'd simply taken the whole bag—snatching it away from the evil intents of the General. She couldn't bear the thought that General Karis might have a sack full of the souls of her dead people carelessly tossed into a dark room in his castle.

Rayven looked deeply into Onca's ruby eyes and realized the five empty holes in his ancestral sword were the settings for his ancestors' *Chama* stones. She could see that he, too, was remembering the great blade he'd retrieved without permission from their homeworld of Nye. She could feel his bitter pain over the thought that General Karis and his men were using the power of his ancestors' spirits to fight their battles.

"*Chama* is the ancient word for soul, isn't it?" Rayven asked Draco, not sure how she knew such a thing, but certain it was so.

Draco squeezed her hand, gone cold and still in his own, and nodded, still not trusting himself to speak. Rayven thought about telling him the room in the General's castle that was probably harboring a bag full of such stones, but only briefly. She couldn't share this kind of horror with him, or any of her other people. She vowed fervently to herself that she would set this terrible wrong to rights no matter what it took. She couldn't bring herself to think of the reaction her people would have, knowing that General Karis was raping the memories of their ancestors in such a way.

"How do these soulstones work?" Rayven asked, trying desperately not to sound too interested.

She fought valiantly to keep her thoughts shielded from them—Draco most of all. If he learned of the plan already taking shape in her mind, he would tie her to him with a leash and not let her leave his side for days. Even though he expected her to one day lead an attack on a galactic-sized army, he still treated her like a fragile child who would break under the weight of too many responsibilities. With a slight frown, she realized that her tantrums the night before had probably only served to enforce this opinion he had of her. For what seemed the millionth time she wished she'd shown a little more self-control in the face of his goading taunts.

"It depends upon the nature of the ancestors' spirits—how the stone may be used," Onca explained. "For example, my father and his father and so on were all members of the Imperial Council. They each had individual strengths, but on the whole they were personal bodyguards to their rulers, as I have been Draco's bodyguard these past years. Because of their roles as warriors, my ancestors' *Chama* stones were set into ancestral weapons, so during battle if guidance or assistance was needed, their descendants could wield the full psychic power of their heritage against any threat or danger." Again Rayven was assaulted by the haunting images of Onca's ancestral sword devoid of its *Chama* stones.

"Other families often use their *Chama* stones in various ways. Some used to place them above the threshold of their homes to bring good fortune and wisdom. Others wore them as settings in jewelry to keep them close by for protection and good luck. Still others merely kept the stones in a sacred place and only took them out to consult with their ancestors' spirits when a great need arose."

"What do you mean by consult?" Rayven asked.

Draco gave Rayven a strange look and she prayed he hadn't caught a whiff of the direction of her thoughts. She strengthened the shield about her thoughts with the hopes that he wouldn't try to break past her defenses. She gave him what she hoped was an innocently curious look, and almost sighed her relief aloud when he seemed satisfied with her offered façade.

Draco answered her question, his shoulders still broad and stiff with suppressed anger over the cause of their discussion. "We use the stones as oracles, mostly. To do this we simply hold a stone in our hand or if the stone is set in an object we at least make physical contact with it and ask our ancestors for help or guidance. We can also just visit with our ancestors on the astral plane, but they are merely shades of the true forms of our bygone loved ones and cannot always interact with us in the ways we would wish."

"If the spirit of an ancestor is sentient enough that we have to ask it for guidance, or help, or whatever, how are the General's men using their powers as weapons so easily? Why don't the souls within the stones simply refuse to work for them?"

"As you said, Rayven, the General's men are using them as jeweled placements in their metal headbands. This places the *Chama* stones directly over their Third Eye, and no matter how strong the soul contained within a *Chama* stone, this position allows the user to filter his or her own psychic energy through the stone as though through an amplifier."

"The Third Eye? Do you mean the hocus-pocus psychic wannabes back on Earth are right about its significance as a great seat of metaphysical power? They believe the area in the middle of the human brain, if used to its fullest potential, can be used to open the connecting link between the physical and spiritual worlds."

"It is a position of great psychic significance, yes. Whenever anything with metaphysical properties is placed over the Third Eye, or the center of the forehead just above and between the eyes, a being's innate psychic powers are amplified exponentially. It's the same for all beings, no matter their origin or heritage. All sentient beings have some form of divine spiritual powers, though some are stronger than others. It is this spiritual power, this innate psychic gift, which binds us to all things and to each living being, keeping us alive and healthy, keeping us whole."

"How do they know to use them this way?"

"It's common knowledge that our ancient ancestors often wore the *Chama* stones for such purposes as the General uses them. They were territorial and did not allow transgressions from their subjects to go unpunished. However, instead of using jewelry to wear the stones, our ancestors assimilated the stones into their flesh so they could not be removed, and would always be close by.

"Many a great Emperor or Empress was said to shine like the stars from the many *Chamas* worn in their skin. As time wore on, and our race gained a reputation for its no-nonsense approach to any threat, rival races and planets left us alone and sought war and power elsewhere."

Rayven tried to imagine the peaceful people she'd grown to love and regard as her brethren as powerful, vengeful beings who would quickly strike out at any threat. Obviously things had changed over the course of their history, or they would never have let things grow as drastic as they had.

"So what happened? Did our people grow complacent in their roles as top dog of the universe, or were they simply unprepared for the force the Galactic Army unleashed upon them?"

Setiger at last seemed to find his voice and he answered her question with a twinge of regret in his voice. "Over the millennia our people's powers have dwindled. Though we are still the most powerful beings, psychically speaking, we are not as great a force to be reckoned with as we once were. In the days of old our people were more ethereal beings than physical ones. As time wore on our people relied more on their physical selves than their spiritual selves and lost much of their psychic strengths in the process."

"So, evolutionarily speaking, we are becoming more and more like regular humans?"

"Not entirely, our genetic makeup is still vastly different from other humanoids. But yes, in a small way the weakening of our psychic gifts is making us more and more like other humanoid beings." Draco sounded weary, as if the conversation had drained him of his seeming never-ending reserve of patience and strength.

"They use the stones to open and travel through intergalactic doorways, much the same as you have taught me to do with my *Awareness*. That's how they were able to reach me on Earth. That's how they were able to strike me down and capture me. But I do not think they can use the stones much beyond what they've already shown. I don't think they've mastered telepathy, telekinesis or mind control, or I would have had a harder time getting away from them."

"Thank the Fates for small favors. However, I think it's only a matter of time before the Galactic Commune begins to uncover some of the *Chama* stones' hidden properties. Once our enemies know the full potential of the stones, then they will surely learn how to use them to their full capacity."

Rayven gently laid her *Blazesword* into the dust at her feet and moved to take Draco's other hand in hers, so that she clasped both of his hands in a firm and steady grip.

"Then we shall have to simply take them back before it is too late," she said fervently.

Draco chuckled, though the sound was humorless and sent a chill down Rayven's spine. "I fear that time is our greatest enemy, my eager queen, and it is already beginning to win out against us. I think we stand little hope of winning a war against the Galactic Communal Army if they learn to use the *Chama* stones against us, and I have no idea how to keep them from doing so."

"We must hurry up Empress Rayven's training then," Avator addressed the group at large.

"We already rush her in her instruction as it is," Draco protested.

"Better to train her fully and hope for the best, than to throw ourselves into a fight that we cannot win with undue haste and an ill-prepared leader." This from Setiger.

"She has already learned much, perhaps it will be enough for the battle to come," Onca interjected, his words hopeful but his voice uncertain.

A heated argument broke out among the men and Rayven was left standing on the outskirts of it as Draco moved away from her to move closer to his friends. He loudly lent his own thoughts to the debate and gesticulated forcefully with his hands, a sure sign of his agitation.

Rayven resented the fact that the impassioned debate was centered solely on her and her readiness to lead her people. She felt insulted that they had such little faith in her growing abilities, and then remembered that she had helped to cultivate this doubt in her skills. She had foolishly vocalized her doubts in her own abilities to lead her people to these men, had in fact lamented her role as Empress to them more than once. She had expected to fail from the first, and her weakness shamed her as nothing else ever had.

Until this moment, she had resented and mourned the fact that she had been born to rule a group of people she'd never even known existed. She had focused on the implausibility of such a thing, and wallowed in her own self-doubt without a care for the insecurity this would cause among her people. In this moment of revelation she hated herself for her cynical approach to the duties she must learn before she assumed the throne of her people. She wished now that she had the chance to start over again, this time with a more mature attitude towards her destiny as Empress of the Aware.

Rayven searched deep inside herself for the power she now knew for a certainty lay dormant there. She let the power take her in a rush that made her skin grow tight over her muscles, as if it would burst under the sudden internal pressure. Her extremities tingled and her heart raced with the sheer force of the power contained within her. Her body thrummed and hummed with her *Awareness*.

For the first time she realized what Draco meant when he spoke of control. He had told her that he would teach her control of her *Awareness*. He hadn't spent the past weeks teaching her new skills as she'd thought—the skills had always been there for her to use. He had merely been teaching her to control the force of them—the intent behind them. He had been helping her to direct her *Awareness* as a conscious intent, as opposed to an instinctive reaction as it had always been for her in times of trouble. She realized that now she had at last learned to call upon her hidden power and keep it contained just beneath the surface, ever ready to release itself at her command. This had been Draco's intent all along.

She looked at the still-arguing men—for the first time she *really* looked. She used her *Awareness* to see into their souls. She could see their inner selves, as if she were looking into clear pools of water at the once hidden wonders that lay beneath. She could see the purity of their natures, the nobility and grace of their spirits. It was a humbling and mystical experience, and her eyes misted with tears at what she had discovered.

She could see Avator's pain and anguish over the loss of his mate, his regret that he'd failed to save her from her horrible fate. She saw his deep devotion to the survival of his people and his ingrained sense of loyalty to her as his Empress.

She could see Setiger's own sense of duty to her and their people, his willingness to give his very life to save them should it be necessary. She could feel his longing for a mate and children, and his deep passionate love for the faceless woman that he wished someday to call his own, as if his emotions were her own.

She saw Onca's deep sorrow over his lost family and friends. She was brokenhearted by his constant self-punishment over not being able to foresee the death of her parents and their people. He felt cursed by his precognitive abilities, and their penchant for failing him during the time of his people's greatest need.

Draco's defenses against her newfound gift were stronger than the other men's and it was a few heartbeats before she could wear down his shields to see into him as clearly as she had his friends. She was almost overwhelmed by what she saw inside him. He was the most powerful of their people, this she already knew, but he had done much in the way of hiding the true strength of his abilities from her—and from the rest of their people.

He could shape shift, and his favorite form was the black hawk of her dreams. She would have been angry that he'd kept this secret from her if she hadn't been awed by his noble motives in keeping her safe from harm. He could use his *Awareness* like a physical weapon, striking pain and madness into the minds of his enemies.

She saw his valiant struggle during the battle of the Great Massacre, how he'd felled many foes with his flashing *Blazesword,* and destroyed many others with the powers of his mind. She saw his despair over the loss of her parents before his duty had forced him to save her and his few remaining people from total slaughter. She saw his own reluctance to lead their people, and knew he had reluctantly but dutifully assumed the role in her absence.

He had longed for her return with an almost physical yearning, and Rayven was forced to turn away from the deeper feelings she sensed he harbored for her. She couldn't understand them, wouldn't understand them, no matter how hard she tried. It was as if he saw his future shining brightly within her eyes, and it wasn't merely the future of the *Aware*'s continued existence, but the future for his personal salvation and redemption.

The emotions she sensed in him seemed too dark and wild to be called love, and she doubted not that he would resent her labeling it so mundane an emotion. She saw an image of herself reflected from him that in no way represented what she knew of herself. He seemed to regard her as some exquisite and untamed flower, a precious and exotic thing to be cherished and protected, but not to be tested lest it wilt and break under too much weight. Rayven found herself resenting his opinion of her, even as it secretly thrilled her.

Rayven quickly turned off the thrumming power within her, and was surprised at how easy it seemed to do so. She could feel the power within her slumbering, but lightly, as if now that she knew of its existence it was unable to cut itself so completely off from her as it had before. She realized in that moment that the more she called on the *Awareness* within her, the less deeply it would be able to hide itself. With enough practice she sensed it would soon flow through her like a raging electrical current that could be turned on and off like a light switch. Ever ready to make itself available with but a small thought from her mind.

The argument had picked up steam between the men while Rayven had been in the thrall of her discovery. She almost smiled as the men who had become her friends yelled and railed at one another. She knew they were volatile personalities to say the least, but was unafraid that they would harm each other in their bellowing tirade.

"I tell you she is not ready! She can't even levitate properly yet," Draco's shouted words broke over her reverie, and Rayven suddenly found herself insulted over their arguments concerning her power.

With wicked glee bubbling within her she called once again upon the power within her and sent Draco flying high into the air.

"Shiiit!"

Rayven almost laughed. It seemed Draco had picked up her colorful vocabulary, which she'd used carelessly and frequently during her long days of training. She ignored his startled protests or the shocked gazes sent her way from Onca, Avator and Setiger. She remembered how Draco had twirled and tossed her in the air the day before, and she did the same to him now with a feeling of triumph in her heart.

"What were you saying about my levitation skills, Draco?" she called out with deceptive sweetness.

"By the Fates, woman, put me down before you drop me!"

Rayven grinned an evil grin, her eyes flashing impishly. "Whatever you say, Draco," she said before she sent him flying towards the ground.

Before Draco could rally his own powers to slow down his descent Rayven brought him to a screeching halt and slowly lowered him the last few inches to the ground with a soft thump. He lost his balance, and Rayven laughingly suspected his knees were weak from his unexpected flight into the air. He fell with a hard thud onto his rear.

Draco looked up at Rayven with stunned eyes. Onca, Avator and Setiger did the same. She schooled her features to look mild and unconcerned, as if she juggled people in such a fashion on a regular basis. She met Draco's beautiful silver stare unflinchingly.

"What?" she asked, her voice oozing innocent concern.

"How did you do that?" Each word was clipped as Draco found his voice.

"What do you mean?"

"Yesterday you couldn't raise me more than six feet off of the ground, and today you send me dozens of feet into the sky. Yesterday you couldn't lower me softly on my feet to save your life, and today you place me gently upon the ground with a smile. What happened between then and now that your control has grown so?" His voice was almost accusatory, as if he suspected her of secretly practicing without him—something he had of course expressly forbidden her to do.

"Today is another day. Perhaps I was just having a bad day yesterday," she said nonchalantly shrugging her shoulders in the vague way she'd seen many Gallic people do.

Draco stood from his slumped seat on the ground, and moved to tower over her. His head shook slowly at her words, and his eyes roved over her body as if she had something to hide.

"That isn't true, Rayven." Uh-oh, he'd used her first name. No titles and no endearments, just her name, and from his dark tone, that meant trouble. "You know it isn't true. What has changed?"

"Perhaps I have changed, Draco. I don't like hearing how doubtful you are of my ability to lead my people." Rayven's voice had taken on a regal tone. Unbeknownst to her she sounded eerily like her father, but those around her easily recognized it and were awed by it.

"I don't like being excluded from conversations that involve me, either. Especially when those conversations are happening right in front of me. If you thought of me as your Empress—your ruler—you would show a bit more respect when in my presence."

Each man around her flushed with embarrassment over his actions. Her reproachful tones chastised them for their careless impertinence, and in that moment she was more their Empress than ever she had been. Each man bowed respectfully to her and apologized for their disrespect. All prostrated themselves before her to beg her forgiveness. All, that is, except for Draco who stood silent and unmoving before her as if he still suspected her of some great trickery.

Rayven bored her eyes into his and tested her powers yet again. She sent a light mental push with her mind and looked into Draco's mind. An image of his thoughts was revealed to her as if a curtain had been drawn back from a stage. As she suspected, he did indeed believe that she had been secretly practicing her skills without him, and the thought both frightened and angered him. He feared for her safety should she attempt such a thing without his knowledge. His fear that she might harm herself without him there to protect her was his reason for forbidding her to practice her skills on her own in the first place. Though she felt touched that he worried over her so, she still resented his doubt of her ability to take care of herself.

"I didn't practice this on my own, Draco." She almost smiled when she saw his eyes widen at her answer to his unasked question. She'd never been able to read his thoughts against his wishes before, and it seemed to alarm him that she'd been able to do so now.

"Turnabout is fair play, Draco. You read my thoughts and I'll read yours. It's only right."

Draco's eyes hardened and he threw up a shield over his thoughts, pushing her from his mind. It was an awesome display of strength and control, but she was glad to find he was unable to completely block his thoughts from her. Though his mind seemed blurry and unfocused to her, she knew if she pushed hard enough she could probably discern his thoughts without too much of an effort on her part. The knowledge thrilled her, and she strove to keep him from her mind so that this new ability of hers would remain her secret.

"Do you swear to me, Highness, that you have not disobeyed my orders and practiced on your own?"

"In the future, Draco, you will not question my word—" Rayven was startled to find how easy it seemed for her to sound like offended royalty, "—but for now I will promise—*on my honor*—that I have not been practicing the use of my powers on my own. When would I have found the time? You only give me a few hours to myself each night, and during that time I'm so tired that all I can do is sleep."

"Then explain how you have learned to control these aspects of your *Awareness* so quickly."

Rayven's lip almost pouted outward before she could stop it. No matter how hard she tried, she didn't think Draco would ever treat her as anything other than a pesky little woman-child, who he sometimes liked to tease and flirt with. She resented it, but was secretly glad she could look forward to having at least one man around her who couldn't be cowed by her imperial tones when she was made ruler in truth.

"I don't know, Draco. I honestly don't. I just got fed up with hearing you talk about me like I'm some insignificant little kid who couldn't possibly shock or surprise you—experienced adult Aware that you are. I had to do something to prove myself, and it just happened that I found a way to do so in that moment. That's all. I promise you."

Draco looked like he wanted to believe her but was still uncertain. Rayven opened her mind to him a little, just enough so that he could sense the truth of her words for himself. She felt the brush of his mind along hers and saw that he at last believed her. She once again shielded her thoughts from his, and pushed him forcibly from her mind in much the same way that he had done earlier. She saw a gleam of something akin to pride flash within the depths of his eyes and then it was gone.

"Now can we please just drop the subject and get on to my training? There's no use in wasting any more time, as it has now been made clear to me just how precious it is to us. Let us begin my *Blazesword* training, shall we?"

Draco's eyes went still and serious, and he nodded in agreement. He went to pick up the discarded *Blazeswords*, and thus Rayven's day of training was at last begun.

Chapter Twenty

Onca flung his sweat-drenched hair out of his eyes and swiftly parried yet another one of Rayven's brilliantly executed attacks. He couldn't remember the last time anyone had come close to besting him with the blade, and was shocked at the level of skill his Empress had attained in her young years. He was over a thousand years old and had studied the art of the blade since he was old enough to hold one in his hand. Rayven was a fledgling—only twenty-eight years old, and yet she was dancing around him as thought she were a master of the sword. He would never have believed her so skilled, had he not seen her fight for himself.

Rayven twirled away from a thrust from Onca's sword before swiftly twirling back at him with a feint and thrust from her own blade. Her swift footsteps barely seemed to connect with the ground—so graceful and light were her movements. It seemed to Onca, and to the other three men who watched on the sidelines, that Rayven didn't rely solely on her eyes to help defend herself from Onca's expert swordsmanship. Instead, she seemed to sense his movements with some extrasensory perception, her blade already moving to block his feints and parries before he'd made the conscious decision to move.

Draco, Avator and Setiger could do nothing but watch the flurry of movement between the two dancing duelists. Rayven and Onca moved with a speed that was difficult to follow with their eyes, even with their preternaturally honed eyesight. For a surety, no normal human would have been able to track their movements without a slow-motion video recording of their fight. Draco had dueled with her first, and had been disarmed less than ten minutes into their fight. Though Draco was not the best of swordsmen among their people, he was by no means the least talented. He'd never been disarmed so swiftly, not even by Onca, who was the best swordfighter among them.

Now, seeing her holding her own against Onca, Draco wondered how she'd kept from laughing when he'd arrogantly assumed he had sword skills to teach her. He should have known—if not from looking into her memories of her sword training on Earth, then from his own memory of how talented with the *Blazesword* her father was—that she would be a formidable sparring opponent. She more than held her own with the ancient weapon—she wielded it as if born to it.

Onca executed a series of attacks, sparks flying from the force of the two blades meeting, and disarmed Rayven in a burst of fluid speed and power. Rayven stumbled and clutched her now-bruised wrist as Onca saluted her with his blade. The fight was over.

Rayven was accustomed to fighting with the saber or foil or Taji Sword, of being hit time and again by these practice blades, especially during her first year of training. Being hit by those blades had normally felt no worse than receiving a firm tap on the shoulder, though in some cases when she'd fought less skilled opponents the blows had left bruises on her skin. Being hit by a *Blazesword* was entirely different, even after Draco had put a safety shield over the sharply honed and burning blade. Onca had only tapped her on the wrist, but the result had been a burning pain up her arm that had forced her to drop the blade into the dust at her feet. She knew her wrist would be black by morning, and though she knew Onca had not meant to harm her, she still felt angered that she'd foolishly lowered her guard and sustained the painful bruise.

Draco came to her side, concern written clearly over his face. "Are you all right, *a grifa*? Does your wrist pain you overmuch?"

Rayven almost rolled her eyes, but stopped herself just in time. She hated seeming delicate in front of Draco, but it seemed she just couldn't shake the image of her fragility from his eyes no matter what she did.

"I'm fine. Just surprised. I'm used to more forgiving practice blades than the heavy blows of the *Blazesword*. I'll get used to practicing with it, and I'll know better next time not to get hit by it." Rayven laughed softly.

Draco shared in her laughter, but insisted on looking at her wrist, which was already discolored and slightly swollen. "Not very many of our women can fight with the *Blazesword*. Their bones are too delicate for the sport. You are quite an impressive swordswoman, Empress. Unlike any I have ever seen come before you."

"I have had many hundreds of years' worth of practice with the blade, Highness. I have never seen one so young as you fight with such skill and finesse. Perhaps one day, after all of our troubles with the Galactic Commune are over, you can teach me some of the movements you used during our duel. I've never seen those styles of fighting before. It was most impressive." Onca's eyes were awed and full of praise as he spoke to her.

Rayven smiled, pleased that she'd held her own against Onca. He'd been the most skilled swordsman she'd ever met in a duel, and she was amazed she'd managed to impress him. Even a little bit.

"You probably wouldn't know some of the styles I used, Onca. They are ancient styles from the Asian warriors of Earth. They fight with more skill, speed and deadly precision than any other culture in the planet's history. I'd love to share the teachings of my masters with you, Onca, but I fear I could never teach you as well as they taught me."

Onca smiled. "Perhaps one day I will venture to Earth and seek out these masters you speak of. I am ever ready to learn new fighting skills."

"I'm surprised there are any that you do not know," Rayven teased.

"Verily 'tis true that I am relieved I was at last able to defeat you at swordplay, Highness. I would be ashamed to think that I was to be a bodyguard for an Empress that could defeat me in battle should she choose to. Though I am not so pleased that it took me nearly an hour to find your weakness, and now I fear I must practice my art more diligently, else I will pale in your shadow as the years pass and your skills grow."

Rayven laughed at his look of mock-horror over the thought of her becoming a better blade master than he.

Draco once again studied the darkening bruise on Rayven's wrist. His hair blew in the warm breeze and tickled across her face with a teasing caress. She smelled his masculine fragrance, breathing it deep and holding it in her lungs. She was always surprised that his nearness affected her so completely that she could think of nothing but him and how much she was attracted to him. It unsettled her, and she feared that over time her reaction to him would only grow more pronounced.

Her uncontrollable attraction to him was something she didn't enjoy dwelling on, because she feared she could never have him as a lover, no matter how much she desired him. She just didn't think that he could actually choose her as a permanent bed partner over the more beautiful and experienced women of their clan, nor did she think she could endure his dominant nature for long enough to establish an intimate relationship with him. It made her uncomfortable to think about letting herself be submissive to him on so primal a level. It aroused her, but daunted her as well, so she simply chose not to dwell on the idea of having Draco as a lover. It would do her no good to pine away for something she most assuredly couldn't have. Right? *Right.*

"We need to bandage you, Highness, to give your wrist some support so that it does not grow weak under the swelling."

Rayven sent him a look of mock disbelief. "You mean you can't just heal me with your powers? I have to wait for Mother Nature to take care of it?"

"No, I cannot, *a grifa*. I am sorry for it. Though our ancient ancestors could perform such feats of healing, most of us have lost the knowledge and skill to do so."

"I think you just want to see me suffer a little."

"There is that added amusement."

Draco grinned sexily and tugged teasingly on the long, fat braid of her hair. Turning he went to gather their weapons with Setiger and Avator. Rayven bit her lip and watched him as he moved. His fluid muscles were poetry in motion, and she had to forcibly drag her eyes from him when she heard Onca clear his throat delicately at her side.

"You watch him with hungry eyes, Highness. I can taste your desire for him on the wind. Why do you not go to him?"

Rayven straightened to her full height, though it did little to diminish Onca's own shadow towering over her. She raised her chin and bestowed her most regal look upon him.

"I will not discuss this with you, Onca. You are my friend, but my feelings are a personal matter for me to dwell on alone."

"Do you not think it is fair that Draco also dwell on these feelings you have, since they appear to concern him?"

"No, I do not. What I feel for him is my concern. I have better things to do than pursue him like some starving hound. I have a war to win, or have you forgotten?"

"That may be so, Highness, but the passion I see in your eyes for Draco is not something that you can long deny. Things are not always as they seem, and perhaps you are denying not only yourself but him as well with your silence."

"I don't care about that right now, Onca. I'm not about to try to gain Draco's amorous attentions when there is a good chance one or both of us may die in the days to come. I could not bear it."

"There is no shame in taking a little happiness for yourself, Highness. Your role among us is one of great duty and responsibility, 'tis true, but you are not expected to alienate yourself from all joy while you train to assume your duties."

Rayven's fists clenched at her sides. What Onca said tempted her beyond any limit she'd ever known, but she couldn't bring herself to admit her growing affection for Draco to herself, let alone to the man in question. She didn't understand herself well enough yet to know what she wanted in her personal life.

She'd never physically been with a man—had never had the time or inclination to do so. She instinctively sensed that when she did give herself to a man it would not be a pale shade of passion or love, but an all-encompassing, soul-shattering experience for her—especially so if Draco were to be her first lover. He'd already done things to her body and heart the likes of which she'd never experienced before, and it tied her closer and closer to him each time he kissed and caressed her.

Sleeping with him would only make her more vulnerable to him. She could not take a chance that might shatter her heart and soul if Draco were to turn away from her or die in the coming battle. It would tear her apart.

"This discussion is over, Onca. I will hear no more on it from you, and I command you, as your Empress and leader, that you do not speak of this with him. Ever."

Onca's ruby eyes flared bright and glowing for a moment before he replied with pronounced deference, "As you wish, Highness. I am yours to command as always."

Rayven almost wanted to say she was sorry for coming across as highhanded as she did, after all, Onca had grown to be her good friend. However, she didn't want to sound indecisive, and felt that apologizing would undermine her precarious position of authority over him and subsequently her people. She could not afford that, so she kept silent and offered no apologies.

"Let us go in and see to your bruises, Highness," Draco called out to her.

Her eyes never left Onca's, but she called out, "Coming!"

Onca's gaze wavered from their unofficial staring contest, and he bowed slightly to her.

"May I escort you in, Highness?"

Rayven smiled. "Absolutely, Chief Counselor."

Onca at last smiled back at her, though his eyes were serious and thoughtful, as if he were looking at her for the first time.

"You will make a great Empress, Highness. I have seen it before, and I see the truth of my vision reflected in your eyes. I am honored to be here with you now. No matter what happens on the morrow, or the days ahead, never forget that I will always be your friend and loyal servant."

Rayven's eyes softened and she reached up to tuck a lock of his indigo hair back behind his eye with a motherly flourish. She looked at him a moment longer before placing both of her hands at his temples and pulling his face down to hers to lay a soft chaste kiss on his brow.

"It is I who am honored to be with you and my people, Onca. I will do all that is within my power to right the wrongs that have been visited upon us. I vow it to you as my loyal servant, my Chief Counselor, and as my friend."

Onca was silent, but Rayven could see that her words affected him on a deeper level than he let on. With her newfound powers she could see into the heart of him at will and know his thoughts and feelings as if they were her own. She knew in that moment that Onca would do anything to keep her and their people safe from harm. No matter the cost to himself or their enemies. He was a warrior, from an ancient line of similar warriors, and his will was strong and loyal. He would serve her well in the coming war, and she found herself deeply grateful for it.

She took Onca's proffered arm and they turned as one to join Draco, Setiger and Avator. There was a brief moment when Draco's eyes had darkened dangerously upon seeing her hand perched upon Onca's arm, but it passed so quickly Rayven was sure she had imagined it. She wondered idly if Draco had seen her kiss upon Onca's brow, and if he had been at all jealous of it. She felt it was best not to think on such things and she pushed it from her mind. Together the group transported themselves to the sanctuary of the *Neffan* Grove.

Chapter Twenty-One

That night, Rayven lay upon her bed feathers and thought about all the things she'd learned about her people's *Chama* stones that day. Her heart ached with the knowledge that her parents' soulstones might be in that darkened room in the General's fortress. She couldn't bear the thought that she'd had the opportunity to grab the bag of stones and had failed to do so. She wondered whose soul occupied the *Chama* stone that was nestled in her clothing trunk, and shied away from the thought that she could have lost it forever in her mad flight from the General and his men.

She had just moved to retrieve the *Chama* stone from her trunk when there was a disturbance outside of the *Bito*. Someone had come to visit.

"Come in," she called.

Draco's head peeked into the opening of her tent.

"Highness, may I speak with you?" he asked, his voice uncharacteristically deferential and uncertain.

"Sure, come on in."

Draco settled himself at the foot of her bed feathers on the dark wooden floor of her *Bito*. Though Rayven had grown accustomed to the smallness of her dwelling, she was startled at how much smaller it now seemed with Draco inside.

"What's wrong?" she asked, her voice quiet, as if they were sharing a secret.

Draco looked at Rayven for a long moment before he sighed and answered.

"Are you unhappy among us?"

"What do you mean? Have I seemed unhappy to you?"

Draco wearily leaned back against the feather-covered wooden wall of her *Bito,* his hematite hair looked almost purple in the reflected light from the *Neffan* tree's feathery leaves. His entrancing silver eyes closed under a thick curtain of black lashes and he was still for a moment.

At last he spoke, his voice rich and thick, closing over her like the black blanket of a starless night.

"I cannot bear the thought that you are not happy to be here among us. I know that you have suffered much in your young life, and I do not want to know that you suffer more because I have brought you here."

"Did you bring me here?" she asked, thinking of the black hawk and her newfound knowledge that Draco and her hawk were the same.

Draco's silver stare met her golden one, and a frisson of *Awareness* ran up her spine. He was so beautiful sitting there in the purple twilight of her *Bito,* his features so achingly perfect and defined, that without his large muscles and broad chest he might appear almost androgynous. Almost.

"What would you say if I admitted to being the sole cause for your presence here? Would you hate me or…?"

Rayven's heart constricted under his haunting silver stare. She wanted to reach out and touch him, to offer whatever comfort he would take from her—anything to take that tinge of sorrow from his eyes. But she feared what would happen to them both if she did.

"I could never hate you, Draco, never that," she whispered, her words husky.

"You did not hate me yesterday when you attacked me?"

Rayven couldn't control the small chuckle that broke forth from her at his almost sulky tone. "No, I didn't hate you, I was just pissed. There's a big difference."

"Then, yes, I admit that I am the reason you are here. You don't understand what I mean but it is the truth."

"I know what you mean, Draco. You've been naughty by not telling me your secret penchant for Halloween dress-up games."

Draco sent her a puzzled look.

"I know you're the black hawk from my dreams. I saw the truth of that within your thoughts this morning, Draco."

Draco was silent for several heartbeats as if he were waiting for her to say more. When she didn't he asked, "You're not enraged over that, Highness?"

"Should I be? Was it to be some great secret? Would you have ever told me?"

"I would have eventually done so, yes. I wanted to keep it a secret for a time because I did not know quite how you would react to it. Only a few of us have the ability to shape shift, so it is not a common occurrence among our people. I used my animal form among you because I sensed that you would not be afraid of me in that manner, as you would certainly have been if I'd first approached you in my human form."

"You were there with me when my foster parents were killed." Her words were more a statement than a question.

"Yes."

"You were there when I tried to commit suicide."

"Yes."

"I should have remembered. You shifted into your human form right before I blacked out."

"Before you died. You *did* die, but I brought you back before it was too late to call you from the other side."

"How can it not be too late after I died? How did you call me back?"

"You had not made the journey to the other side before I called to you, and so you came back to me."

"How could you keep me from dying when I wanted it so badly?"

Draco was silent and he turned his head away from her so she could only make out a small portion of his profile. Her heart thudded anew as she drunk in the almost inhuman grace of his movements.

"I cannot tell you. You are not ready to hear my explanations yet."

Rayven snorted. "What do you mean? That I don't have the mental capacity for such knowledge, or is this some new skill you don't think I'm ready to learn—the power of life over death."

"Things are not as they may seem, Rayven." His voice sounded strained, almost anguished, as if the conversation were hurting him in a way she could not see.

"What is it with you people and your cryptic remarks? Onca said those exact words to me earlier today. Why can't you just answer a direct question with a direct answer?"

Draco suddenly whirled his face back to look at her with angrily blazing silver eyes. "I saw your little meeting with Onca today. I saw you kiss and caress him. Perhaps you should pose these questions to him, as he knows the answers as well as I, though I doubt he will be any more honest with you than I have been. Especially seeing how close you and he have grown."

"What are you talking about?" Rayven couldn't help that her voice had risen in volume.

"Do you desire him? Do you lust for him? After seeing you with him this afternoon, I would not be surprised. But you must remember, Highness, that among our people, sexual affairs do not last long and mean less than nothing. Only a true mating means much to us, and I strongly suspect that you would expect much from a physical relationship with any male. So do not waste your time or your heart on a meaningless affair. Our people mate for life, and our love is always held in reserve for our true mates. You will find no love with Onca, for he is not your mate."

Rayven thought back to the feelings she'd sensed within him that morning. If what she suspected was true—that he was attracted to her, fond of her—then it was obvious that he was jealous over her supposed attachments to his friend. However, she was enough of an independent woman to take exception to his commanding tone. Who was he to dictate where she let her affections lie?

"How do you know Onca isn't my mate? What if I told you he was?" she stubbornly pressed.

"Then I would call you a liar, Rayven."

Rayven gasped and an angry flush crept up her cheeks. "You jerk! If I say Onca is my mate then he is, and there's nothing you can do to gainsay me." She would have laughed at her words if she weren't so incensed. She couldn't believe they were having this conversation. What she felt for Onca was mere friendship, and it paled in comparison to what she felt for Draco. And despite Draco's arrogant and domineering ways, she feared she could easily fall in love with him. It was a frightening realization.

Draco's eyes flared with his own charged emotions, and he moved towards her with barely controlled violence. He gripped her shoulder with a strength she knew would leave bruises on her skin come morning.

"He is not your mate, Rayven, this we both know." Each word was harshly clipped between his clenched teeth.

"Whatever, Draco. Only time will tell, I guess." She tried to sound flippant, but the intense burning look in his eyes almost frightened her and her words died on a quivering note.

"Aye, it will tell, Rayven. In the meanwhile, do not pursue him. It will only bring you pain at the end of it."

"What do you care?"

"I simply do not wish to see you uncomfortable around your Chief Counselor when you realize that you are not true mates, and that your affair is merely an emotionally empty meeting of flesh." For some reason Rayven thought he had almost choked over his last words.

"You speak as if you already think we are lovers."

"Aren't you?"

Rayven suddenly changed tactics, not wanting to hear the pained note in his magical voice—it hurt her too deeply. "Draco, you're not making sense! When would I have had the time to pursue a fling with Onca?"

"You tell me, you're the one who was fawning all over him as though you couldn't keep your hands from him."

"Take that back!"

"Why? It is the truth. This morning you were practically begging him to take you there in the dust!"

"You're totally overreacting! I just kissed him on the forehead, and at best that could be called a sisterly gesture. Though I don't think I owe you any sort of explanation for my actions, I'm telling you now that Onca and I are just friends. Nothing more."

"Do you swear it to me?" Draco's eyes blazed into hers and his brow almost touched hers, he was so close. His disturbingly masculine scent of sandalwood and rosemary washed over her in a burning wave, and she felt dizzy with a sudden onrush of desire.

Rayven saw something in his eyes that both thrilled and terrified her. He seemed desperate to hear that she had no deeper feelings for Onca. It looked as if he would turn into a violent beast if she did not.

"I swear. He's only my friend, and I would not want him to be anything more. I'm not the least bit interested in him beyond the bonds of friendship."

Draco released a shuddering sigh, his beautiful eyes closing for a heartbeat before he grasped her head in desperate hands and he kissed her with burning passion.

Rayven tried not to get sucked under the maelstrom of his kiss, and pulled back from his magical lips. She was drowning in his eyes and in his scent, and had to struggle to form a coherent thought. It was the hardest thing she'd ever had to do in her life.

"I didn't say that so you would feel free to hop into bed with me. I want more from my first sexual experience than simply lust."

Rayven was chagrined to see the primal satisfaction that gleamed from his eyes when she admitted her innocence to him. She was embarrassed to have admitted such a thing to him.

"I, too, want more than your lust, Rayven."

"What *do* you want from me then?" Rayven could have bitten off her tongue for asking. She wasn't sure she wanted to know the answer to her question.

Draco laid his lips against hers once more, this time gently, as if he were afraid to bruise her. He pulled back after a few heartbeats and stroked his hand down the sides of her head and into her hair. She had pulled her waist-length tresses out of her confining braid, to leave them free and flowing about her. She rejoiced that she had done so when he buried his fists in the depths of it, using her hair to hold her head still for his burning gaze.

"Everything. I want everything you have to give…and more."

Rayven's heart almost stopped at his words, and Draco swooped down to kiss her again. His dark hair flowed over their faces like a shroud, and she was enveloped in a raging and passionate darkness that smelled strongly of him.

Draco used his teeth to bite and suckle her pouting bottom lip, stopping just short of causing her pain. His hands stayed buried in her hair to hold her still for his ravishment. He deepened the kiss, thrusting his tongue into the dark, wet warmth of her mouth.

She brought her tongue into play with his, and he growled into the recesses of her mouth. The sound was like that of a wild jungle animal and it played along her insides like a living thing, dancing and writhing in her blood.

Rayven brought her hands up to clutch him to her and she returned his kiss with a passion she'd never felt before. She suckled upon his lips and tongue, so impassioned that she forgot to breathe and was soon seeing black spots before her vision. She pulled back slightly from his lips to catch her breath, and Draco sent his lips skimming down over her jawline and down her throat.

Draco buried his mouth against her throat, burning her flesh with the intensity of his kiss. He sank his teeth into the tender flesh over her throbbing pulse, stopping just before he broke her skin. The small flash of pain only served to heighten her ardor, and she moaned into the night.

Rayven suddenly found herself lowered onto the plush feathers of her bed, with Draco looming above her. Their legs were tangled together, their shuddering breaths mingling, their heartbeats thundering in perfect symphony. Rayven felt the hard bulge of his arousal pressed against her stomach, and she raised her eyes to his as she moved tentatively against him.

Draco looked down at her and drank in the sight of her. He had not come here with the intention of seducing her, but he feared his jealousy had taken hold of him before he could control himself. He felt an almost instinctive and primal urge to lay claim to her body, to bind her to him as his mate in all ways. He tried to control his raging passions, tried to find some anchor in this maelstrom of desire.

Rayven saw an indecisive look come and go in his eyes. She sensed that he was looking for control, for a way to bring a halt to their love play, and she found that she could not bear it if he were to turn away from her now. She'd never come so close to heaven as she did when in his arms, and no matter what the cost to her heart, she found that she did not want for this to end. She wanted to give herself to him in all ways, to love him and to lay with him in the softness of her bed and know him as only a woman can know a man.

Before Draco could find the words to bring their passion to an end, Rayven parted her thighs and brought her legs around his waist to grind her pelvis against him. She raised herself, using his body to climb her way up him, and she laid her mouth against the pulse in his neck in much the same way he had done to her. She brought her teeth to bear upon him and drew his skin into her mouth. She suckled him there as if he was a ripe fruit and she was starving for a taste.

Draco let out a harsh animalistic growl and rubbed his rock-hard erection against her pelvis. The burning friction caused her clit to immediately swell and tingle. She grew damp between her thighs, and was breathless with anticipation of what was to come.

He lowered her once more to the bed feathers and brought his hands to her breasts. She was wearing the same shirt she had worn every night to bed, the white shirt that Draco had given her that first day on the beach. With barely suppressed violence he gathered the edges of her nightshirt and tore them asunder with one swift motion, laying her quivering breasts bare to his hungry gaze.

"You are so beautiful, *Sudontey*, as breathtaking as starlight, as blinding in your passion as the sun. I want to dip my hands in your light, and bathe myself in your heat."

Rayven moaned softly at his words, and writhed against him with desperate abandon. Draco placed his hands once again upon her breasts, lightly running his strong, calloused palms against their aching peaks. He leaned into her and laid his fiery-hot lips against the center of her chest, before trailing his burning wet kiss down to one of her breasts. He plumped the tingling fullness of her up for his mouth and took as much of her breast into his mouth as he was able. He slowly suckled his mouth over her, until he released her with a wet, popping sound. He licked at her nipple teasingly, and she moaned and clutched at his head.

Draco's hands now roamed freely over her body, and when he encountered the white *evansai* thong shielding her innocence, he ripped that asunder in much the same way he had torn her shirt from her body. The sound of the ripping fabric was deafening in the purple bower. With her body now laid bare to his masterful touch, Rayven writhed beneath him and high keening moans sounded in the back of her throat. Draco's mouth now worked feverishly at her breast and his hands caressed her stomach, hips and thighs.

Draco roved his hands ravenously over Rayven's body, coming close to touching the moist flesh of her pussy, but never quite gifting her with the contact that she so craved from his magical hands. Rayven's frustration grew as Draco's lips feathered across her chest and downward to her midriff. She tugged demandingly on his hair but his head still traveled lower and lower, until he was tonguing the small ring piercing her navel. His tongue dipped into her belly button and she keened into the night. Her body was aflame with desire, her blood a roaring river in her veins, her extremities quivering under the onslaught of her newfound passion.

Rayven thrashed underneath Draco, and he brought both of his hands to her hips to hold her steady as his mouth tirelessly played at her belly button ring. Draco had never felt such a whirlwind of passion and arousal take hold of him before, and he vowed to himself that he would bring her to the peak of her release many times before he let her find fulfillment, so that she too could experience this urgent level of desire that he felt for her. He wanted to bind her to him in her passion, and he wanted to bathe himself in her body's arousal before the night was through.

Without warning, there was a small sound at the entrance to Rayven's *Bito*. If the noise had happened less than a second later, Draco would have been too far lost in his mate to hear it. Even though he heard it, Draco was still reluctant to acknowledge the person on the other side. He licked a hot path from Rayven's navel back up to her breasts, throat and at last to her mouth. He kissed her long and lingeringly before he rose up from her quivering body.

"Someone is at the entrance, *Sudontey*. I do not think they will go away until you answer," he whispered softly. His hands still roved over her body—before, they had meant to arouse, now they meant to soothe.

Rayven's eyes were still dazed with her passion, and she tried to bring his head down for another kiss.

Draco laughed softly, his warm breath sweetly fanning across her face. He untangled himself from her arms with no little feeling of regret.

"Who is it?" he called out with a harsh voice, seeing that Rayven was in no condition to call out to her visitor.

"U-Ursus. I'm sorry, Draco—I did not know that Empress Rayven had a visitor. I only came to bring her the newest attire that I have made for her. I-I'll come back later."

Draco poked his head out of the *Bito*'s entrance, careful not to reveal Rayven's nude form still aquiver behind him.

"You may leave the clothing now, Ursus," he said reaching for her bundle.

Draco could see from Ursus' eyes that she had correctly guessed what had been happening on the other side of the feathered flap of Rayven's tent. She sent him a thought with her mind with a slightly embarrassed flush staining her cheeks.

"Have you claimed her as your mate, then?"

"Not yet, Ursus. You and the others are still to keep her role as mate to me a secret amongst yourselves. I still don't know how she would react to such news, and I will not have her turn stubborn on me after the progress I have made to winning her acceptance this night."

Ursus nodded her understanding and bowed to him before she left. Draco knew that his people were anxious to see them mated, but he could not bring himself to risk scaring his mate away by rushing things. He knew by now that Rayven was fiercely independent, and he feared that any mention of a preordained bond between them would be, in her eyes, a threat to that independence. He wanted her happiness in all things, and it would kill him were she to reject him now, after the passionate embraces they had just shared. He could not bear for her to turn away from him, not now.

He turned back into the *Bito*, and lay Ursus' package down beside Rayven's bed. Rayven had a trembling hand pressed over her eyes, but her body still lay glistening and bare before his starving eyes. He'd never seen a more beautiful woman, though her appeal to him went far beyond any of her physical features.

He knew her to be a strong and loyal woman, with a caring heart, and an open mind. He knew that a love shared with her would be a great and mystical thing, something to be experienced with the whole of their two souls and hearts. He wanted that kind of bond with her, not a shallow meeting of flesh in the dark. He wanted all she had to give, and more.

"Rayven, *a grifa*," he crooned to her, using the full mesmerizing power of his voice, and gathering her in his arms.

Rayven's bright golden eyes burned into his, and Draco almost gave in to the raging desires that demanded he take her, here and now. He'd never stared into a more reflective mirror than her bright eyes—upon looking into them he often felt that he could see every flaw and every grace that he possessed reflected back at him from her wondrous gaze. As he looked within them now, for a brief moment, he saw his own great love for her glowing back at him. His heart almost exploded from his chest, and he had to grip his hands upon her to keep from claiming her, as he so desperately wanted to.

"Rayven, now is not the time for our passion, though I wish it were so. I do not wish to ever cause you harm, and I want you to be certain that this is what you would have between us."

Rayven made to speak, and Draco shushed her with a finger upon her lips.

"We will come back to this another time, *a grifa*. For now you must sleep. Sleep and dream sweet, restful dreams..." He used the same sleeping spell that he had used upon her on the beach.

"*Sleep...sleep...sleep*," he crooned to her in her mind.

Rayven looked into Draco's molten silver eyes, and tried to fight his mesmerizing spell over her. Draco's eyes twinkled almost impishly at her when he realized what she was doing. He sent her a hard "push" with his mind, and Rayven let out a small sigh as the awaiting darkness enveloped her in its comforting embrace.

Just as she had every night since she'd met Draco, Rayven dreamt of him.

Chapter Twenty-Two

It was the middle of the night when Rayven jerked herself awake. All was quiet and calm around her but for the wild beating of her heart. She looked around her, her eyes already grown accustomed to the thick darkness, and as she suspected there was no sign of Draco.

"Damn," she muttered to herself. She didn't know if she was relieved or disappointed that Draco had left her, but swearing seemed to make her feel better about it one way or the other.

Strangely enough, though she knew she'd only been asleep for a few hours, she actually felt well rested for the first time in weeks. Her muscles didn't have the constant aching sluggishness that she'd grown accustomed to, and her mind felt clearer than it had for days. Feeling energized, she remembered her initial plans for the evening and moved to open her clothing trunk as she had earlier.

Digging down into the recesses of the trunk, Rayven at last closed her seeking fingers over the *Chama* stone hidden there. With a sense of awe she uncovered the stone from its black *evansai* shroud. She grasped the seed-shaped stone with reverent fingers and held it up to the moonlight that filtered down over her through the *Neffan* feathers. It glittered brightly for a moment, flaring blue, and then was dull once more.

"It's such a tiny thing to be so powerful," she whispered to herself in wonder.

As she looked at the stone, she felt the sum total weight of her duties as Empress to her people. If such a small thing could be brought to bear against her people, if the General learned how to wield the stones to their full potential, then all hope was lost for her race. She couldn't and wouldn't willingly let such a thing happen.

Realizing she was still nude from Draco's passionate visit earlier, Rayven found the darkest and most concealing clothing she could find and donned it hurriedly. She carefully put the *Chama* stone into a small pocket sewn into the lining of her black harem-style pants. She knew it would be safe there and would be easily accessible should she find the need for it.

With iron-willed determination and a hard look in her eyes, Rayven transported herself onto the training field.

* * * * *

By the middle of her second week of training, Draco had taught Rayven how to open intergalactic gateways with the power of her *Awareness*. He had impressed upon her the importance of disguising the psychic signature released when such a wormhole was opened, to evade discovery from enemies. Though it had seemed that she would never learn to do it, at last, as night had drawn down upon them, Rayven had succeeded in opening a "silent gateway", as Onca had labeled them, without help from Draco. She had been so pleased with her accomplishment that she had hugged Draco in her excitement. He had hugged her fiercely back for a moment before letting her go and turning her face up to his with a hand beneath her chin.

"You must never attempt this particular feat without my guidance, do you understand me, Rayven? Never. I do not know if I could find you were you to become lost in the tunnels of time and space."

Rayven had heard Draco make similar comments throughout her training—that she must never use her stronger powers without his presence and guidance—and she'd tried to obey him as much as possible. Today, however, she had learned the terrible price her people would have to pay because she had been careless when given the chance to steal her people's *Chama* stones from the General. Granted, she hadn't known the significance of the compelling force the stones had used upon her when she'd stolen the lone stone that was nestled in the pocket of her trousers. However, she couldn't help the guilt she felt for not having the foresight to steal as many stones as she could when she'd had the chance. Tonight she hoped to make amends for her grievous error.

Rayven reached into her pocket and grasped the *Chama* stone that rested there. She brought forth a swell of power and instinctively opened her mind and heart to the stone.

"Whoever you were in life, whoever you are now, please help me to succeed in what I am about to do. Help me now to help our people, I beg you, please," Rayven spoke to the stone with her mind, uncertain what to expect in the way of a reply.

Rayven felt a swell of power overtake her, and it had not the now-familiar warmth and feel of her own. She knew instinctively that the spirit of the stone was speaking to her. She felt a wave of reassurance and peace overtake her, a feeling of safety and acceptance like none she had ever felt before. All was calm within her, and she knew that the decision to defy Draco was the right one for her to make. No matter how angry it would make him later.

Releasing the stone with a small twinge of reluctance, she brought her hands up before her and let loose her power. A swirling black portal opened up in a raging torrent before her, the swiftness of its arrival almost startling her. She realized with a sense of awe that she was becoming exponentially stronger each time she called upon her *Awareness*. It was thrilling, as well as frightening, and she sought to calm herself once more by reaching into her pocket and brushing her hand over the *Chama* stone.

Rayven felt at once at peace once more. Taking a deep breath, and preparing herself for the cold feel of intergalactic travel, Rayven stepped calmly through the gateway and into the arms of her destiny.

Chapter Twenty-Three

Rayven blinked and found herself standing outside the immense fortress of General Karis. Apparently Draco had been right when he'd warned her during her first conscious flight through the gateway those many days ago that the experience was far less invasive if she didn't fight it. She'd hardly felt the travel at all and it had been swift and painless.

Knowing that she was concealed from most eyes in the darkness and under the low-hanging cloud cover, she didn't concern herself too much with hiding from whoever might be guarding the castle. She kept as silent as possible and crept up to the outer wall of the keep. Though she'd planned something like this to retrieve the *Chama* stones since she'd heard their history that morning, she wasn't certain how she was to go about gaining entry to the fortress of stone before her.

She reached into her pocket once more for her *Chama* stone.

"Help me please, guide me in any way that you can. How can I succeed in doing this?"

A feeling of loving warmth and perhaps a bit of pride resonated up from the stone nestled in her palm. In a flash of insight Rayven knew what she must do.

Taking a deep calming breath Rayven laid her palm against the stone of the General's castle wall and…stepped *through* it.

Not certain what she might find on the other side, Rayven used her power of invisibility, which Draco had taught to her during her first week among her people. She had never been able to do it quite as effortlessly as she did now, and she was coming to the realization that much of her earlier troubles with calling upon her power would no longer be an issue for her to dwell upon. She was gaining strength and skill swiftly as the hours and days went by.

Rayven sent her mind seeking outward, calling with her preternatural voice, searching for some sign of the *Chama* stones. Following her instincts, she turned down a long corridor and ascended the stairway she found nestled in an alcove within it. She was careful not to make a sound, and was grateful for her caution when three armed soldiers walked by her on the stairs. If she'd been less careful one of the men would have plowed into her, but thankfully she'd managed to move out of the way in time to let him pass.

This was the first time she'd ever used her newfound skills away from Draco, and the thought frightened her. She fully realized the danger she would have to face if she were caught, but she felt that the rewards her people would reap upon her success far outweighed the risks. She missed Draco at her side, guiding her and protecting her, but she knew that this was something she'd have to do on her own.

Maintaining her firm control over her state of invisibility Rayven continued her ascent upon the stairs. She relied heavily on her innate preternatural senses to warn her when she was approaching a stray soldier or guard, and stealthily followed where her instincts led her. Flight after flight of stairs fell away under her climbing feet, and before long she wondered to herself at how vast and immense the castle must be. She'd seen for herself how monstrous it was on the outside, but she'd only scratched the surface of its inner depths with her wanderings. She wagered that it was the size of a small Earth city, or larger. She wondered how many people resided within it, and if they would all participate in the coming war against her people. She shied away from the thought and tried once more to concentrate on her current objective.

Almost an hour had passed before Rayven at last felt that strange yet familiar compulsion calling to her from the *Chama* stone room. Moving swiftly and more surely now through the winding corridors of the castle, Rayven sought out the door to the secret room. When she at last found the door, she was almost surprised to find that it looked no different to her than it had when she'd first seen it almost a month ago. It was small and dark, the color of its wood and frame was almost black, and it had a large black iron handle on the face of it. It was no different from any of the other doors that lined the corridors of the castle in appearance, but the secret treasure nestled within made it seem separate and different from the others in a way Rayven couldn't define.

She looked up and down the vast length of the corridor in which she found herself, to assure herself that no one was around to see the door open as if by an invisible hand. Her invisible hand did just that. After testing and finding the door once again locked against her, Rayven used her *Awareness* to trip the lock and she entered the room beyond with a pounding heart.

Rayven swiftly closed the door behind her and allowed her eyes to adjust to the dark. She found herself thankful for her preternatural night vision, and gazed with wide eyes at the contents of the room before her. She hadn't known what to expect upon gaining entrance to this treasure room but she was unprepared for the disappointing mundanity of it.

The room was piled from floor to ceiling with...*junk*. Broken swords and *Kiel* shields lay littered about the room. Old pots and similar-looking cooking appliances were everywhere, ratty furniture and busted light fixtures were tucked here and there among the debris. She'd never seen such excessive squalor before in all her life. Obviously this was used as some kind of storage room, or for some similar purpose.

Rayven's eyes roved about the room until they at last settled on a small table littered with papers and debris. There, in an almost dejected-looking slump, lay the velveteen sack that she'd confiscated her *Chama* stone from. It was larger than she'd thought, about the size of an oversized handbag. She had feared that the room might be crammed full with similar bags and was surprised to find only the one.

She crossed the room and reached out for the bag of stones. She looked within and saw just how many were inside. There were thousands of the tiny glinting blue stones, more than she'd expected to find. It seemed as though all the General's men had scoured the battlefield after the Great Massacre harvesting as many of the stones as they could find. The thought sickened her. What she didn't understand was why, after all that effort, the General had just thrown the sack of stones into an old storage room.

Perhaps, after the General had stolen a few of the stones to be set in the headbands he'd given to his highest officers, he had seen no use for the rest of the stones. Perhaps he didn't trust his own men enough to give each one a stone of their own. Perhaps he didn't know the full power and significance of the stones yet, but was unwilling to simply throw them away somewhere for fear that someone like she would discover them. She suspected that she would never know the real answer to her question. After all, who could ever truly know the mind of a madman?

As she touched the bag she felt a low throb of power emanating from the stones within. She tried to ignore the frisson of pure energy that ran up her arm from the contact, tried not to cry out from the shocking electric feel of it. She tightened the drawstring to the bag of stones, and tied it snugly to the belt that held up her trousers. She tugged and pulled upon it to reassure herself that the ties would hold no matter how much stress or movement she visited upon it.

At last satisfied that she wouldn't lose the bag short of having it cut from her, she turned to the door once more. She sent her senses seeking beyond her and out into the hallway to assure her safety, and cautiously opened the door. The hallway was empty, and Rayven closed the door with a soft click behind her.

Rayven turned back down the corridor, her treasures snug and safe at her waist, and headed towards the nearest exit.

Chapter Twenty-Four

Once outside and underneath the still-dark early dawn sky, Rayven breathed a sigh of relief. She had done it! She had single-handedly infiltrated her enemy's camp and stolen back what they had taken from her and her people. Pride swelled within her breast, and she looked forward to the stunned look on Draco's face when she told him what she'd accomplished this night.

Well…maybe not. There was no telling how angry he was going to be with her for disobeying his orders, and she just didn't think he would care too much that she'd accomplished something great so much as he would dwell on the fact that she'd willingly placed herself in such danger.

Just this small reminder to herself of the position she found herself in sent a thrill of fear through her body. She needed to open her silent gateway as quickly as possible, as dawn would be upon the planet soon, and she could not afford the risk of being seen. She looked around her to be sure that no one was nearby to witness her actions, and moved to open the gateway.

Before Rayven could raise her arms through which to funnel her power and command the portal to open, she heard a faint noise in the night and went abruptly still. Her heart started to pound as she heard the noise again in the stillness of the predawn night. It sounded like the baying of hounds, though it was a much more fearsome and booming noise than she'd ever heard from any Earthly canine. She had only a moment to wonder to herself if she was perhaps close to the General's kennels before she saw them.

From out of the low-hanging fog they raced towards her. A herd of doglike creatures with gleaming eyes and gaping fanged jaws had been set loose upon her, and their human keepers followed not far behind them. The huge alien dogs had leathery black skin not unlike that of a Vietnamese potbelly pig she'd seen once at a pet store. They had sparse hairs that looked like thick gristle, yellow and orange eyes that glowed like tiny electric lights, and from their razor-sharp teeth dripped thickly glistening saliva. Rayven had never seen a more ugly and more terrifying group of animals in her life.

"Alarm! Alarm! To arms, it is the Aware," the men behind the hellhounds cried.

Rayven heard a loud siren sound into the night, and she knew she'd been discovered. The dogs could smell her scent despite her invisibility, and from the looks of things the dogs had been on patrol for just such an occurrence. Rayven turned to run, careful to keep her form in its invisible state.

Rayven was afraid to open the gateway now that the alarm had been raised. She did not know if the General's men could track her destination through the portal, but she was not willing to take the chance and expose the location of her people. She would have been willing to open the portal to another world—one far from Hostis lest the men pursuing her follow and endanger her people. But she was also afraid of getting lost in the vastness of space, as Draco had warned her was a distinct possibility were she to bounce willy-nilly through portals from planet to planet. She felt it best to try and outrun her pursuers for now, if she could. She would try to open a portal to Hostis when she was certain that it was safe to do so.

Rayven ran swiftly through the morning coolness. The sky overhead was already lightening to a faintly glowing green, and Rayven saw the planet's small blue sun peek out over the horizon. She knew that with the rising sun, her humanoid pursuers would have the advantage of seeing and tracking her footsteps in the dew-drenched grass. The thought was too frightening for her to dwell on, and she pushed it from her mind. If she thought on such matters as that for too long, she knew that she was apt to falter in her terror and lose any chance of escape she might still have.

Rayven tried to lighten her footfalls on the ground, hoping not to leave too clear a trace of her path of flight for her pursuers to find. Her feet barely made contact with the ground, and she sped up her pace. She heard the braying of the hounds still hot on her trail and for one terrifying moment she wondered if they might actually be more adept at hunting her than the Earth canines she was accustomed to. She hoped with all of her being that this was not the case, but feared her hopes were in vain. The hellhounds were gaining on her.

Rayven looked ahead into the horizon, and saw a grove of concealing trees waiting a mile in the distance before her. She sped up her already racing feet, and made for the forest. She wondered idly how far she'd run over the open ground between the trees and the castle, and knew she'd already covered at least a mile since her desperate flight began. With this knowledge, her body reminded her how overworked it had been these past weeks, and she developed a painful cramp in her side and legs.

Rayven's breath was starting to ravage her lungs, and her heart was pounding from her exertion. She tried to resist the urge to glance behind her at her pursuers but found she could not. She looked and saw the hellhounds had gained even more ground and were only a few yards behind her, and behind them more men had joined the chase. At least fifty soldiers ran behind the dogs, and Rayven knew that if she didn't reach the forest soon they would overtake her.

The thought of getting too close to the monstrous-looking hellhounds almost made her heart stop in fear. She looked away and raced as fast as she could to the shelter of the trees. The wind stung her face as she ran, and sweat dripped down her brow to cloud her vision. The bag of *Chama* stones thumped almost painfully against her thigh, though it strangely made no noise as she fled. The only remaining calm in Rayven's mind was ever curious and eager to assimilate information, and it wondered absently if the *Chama* stones were keeping quiet deliberately for her sake. She suspected this was the case.

Rayven at last came to the edge of the forest, and was amazed at the height of the darkly green trees. It seemed that everything on this particular planet was on a grander scale than what she'd grown accustomed to on Earth. The trees towered hundreds of feet into the air. Though the trees of the *Neffan* grove on Hostis stood several thousand feet, they seemed smaller in comparison to these trees. While the *Neffan* trees looked beautiful and welcoming, these trees were dark and menacing, which made them look more towering in their shorter yet more forbidding height.

Just as Rayven was about to enter the safety of the dark forest she was knocked to her knees by a solid thud in the middle of her back. She lost her control on her invisibility, as well as the ability to breathe. Her back was a burning, aching thing where the hellhound had hit her. Another hound came upon her and snapped its vile jaws at her in warning when she tried to regain her feet.

She at last caught her breath, and cautiously tried once more to stand, but the dogs that gathered now around her would have none of it. Their hot fetid breath blew over her, and their sharp teeth snapped dangerously close to her face. She was surprised at how well trained the dogs were, because despite their obvious hunger to rend and tear at her flesh, they held back. She looked into the bright eyes of the nearest hound and what she saw there terrified her more than she would ever dare to admit. She knew that if she were lucky enough to live through this confrontation she would have nightmares of these hellhounds for the rest of her life.

The sickly sweet smell of old death emanated in suffocating waves from the dogs, and Rayven couldn't resist the panicky urge to crawl away from them. One of the dogs charged directly before her face and growled at her. Rayven's higher brain functions scrambled themselves and she found herself baring her own teeth and growling back at the dog. Shockingly it seemed as though her animalistic regression momentarily frightened the dogs, and they each backed off long enough to let Rayven gain her feet.

Knowing that Earth canines could sometimes be unsettled by direct eye contact, and hoping that these dogs were also susceptible to this tactic, Rayven was careful not to pull her stare away from the largest hound before her. Obviously this was the alpha male of the pack, and Rayven focused all of her energy on controlling her fear before the monstrous beast.

One of the smaller hounds nipped at her hand and Rayven backhanded it brutally, never taking her eyes from the alpha hound. The alpha's grisly hackles rose and it growled at her again. Rayven once more growled back. The low animalistic sounds coming from her throat sounded alien to her, but she was thankful for it when the alpha slowly backed down before her.

Rayven slowly broke her gaze from the hounds and looked up to see her swiftly approaching hunters. They were each armed with their *lascannons*, and encased in translucent pink *Kiel* armor. When they were close enough to hear her call out she tried to find her voice, in the faint hopes that she might be able to reason with them.

"I mean you no harm! I only came for something the General stole from me, something that is mine by right. I will harm none of you if you let me go peacefully."

One of the soldiers stopped about fifty feet from her and pointed his *lascannon* squarely at her chest.

"Surrender and you will be unharmed."

Rayven almost snorted but managed to resist the urge.

"If I surrender, your General will either rape or execute me, or both. I'd rather die here in a fair fight. Lay down your weapons and I promise to harm none of you. However I must warn you that if you try to kill me I stand a good chance of killing quite a few of you before you take me down." Rayven hoped she sounded surer than she felt about the truth behind her threat.

"Don't try to play games with us, little alien. I've got you in my sights and it'll only take a second to snuff you out. You have no choice but to surrender."

"Why are you doing this? You're blindly following the orders of a madman! I am the last of my kind, because you systematically hunted and killed my entire race. Why? My people never threatened yours, so what's your excuse?"

"We follow the orders of our leader. We owe our allegiance to him."

"Why? What you've done to my people is murder, plain and simple. Are you not ashamed that you've committed mass murder for the sake of politics?"

"Your people were a danger to all we held dear. It was a pleasure to see them stamped out."

Rayven felt some of her fear drain away into anger, and barely checked the urge to attack him physically. She reached slowly into her pocket to grasp the *Chama* stone, and felt an instant peace and calmness overtake her raging emotions.

"Keep your hands where I can see them!"

Rayven's eyes heated to a glowing gold, and the soldier backed up a step. She slowly removed her hand from her pocket, the *Chama* stone nestled safely and secretly between two of her fingers.

"Be calm," she said, not wanting the now-visibly nervous soldier to accidentally shoot her before she had her say.

"You are all being lied to by General Karis, soldier. My people were never a danger to yours. We were a peace-loving race who liked to keep to ourselves. Your General was jealous of their power and obsessed with lust for my mother, Empress Delphi. When my mother refused to wed him, he went crazy and concocted a story that the Aware were a threat to all humanoids. He attacked my people without cause, this I swear to you. You have all been brainwashed into fearing and hating my people. There is no reason for your prejudice, no reason at all."

Rayven saw the uncertain glances exchanged between some of the men, and hoped welled within her breast. Perhaps some of the General's men could be reasoned with. Then again, perhaps not.

The leading solder again came forward a step, cautiously, as if he were afraid she would move to attack him. "It doesn't matter now, though, does it, woman? All of your people are dead, and if the General is half as vicious as you say he is then you will join them soon enough. Now come forward, slowly, with your hands above your head."

Rayven let her power seep into her tentatively and looked into the hearts of the men before her. She knew that some of them were merely following orders, trying to be loyal to their leader General Karis. But the man before her and a few in the group were happy, even eager, to see her captured and killed. They hated her with a prejudice that was unfounded, but deadly serious all the same. They didn't know her as a person, and they didn't know the true nature of her people, and yet they still chose to think of her as some alien monster not fit to live. She felt like an inferior animal in the face of their deep hatred. She grieved that such persecution was possible among so advanced a race as they obviously were.

Her body still tingling with her *Awareness*, Rayven slowly raised her arms as the soldier had instructed her. As she raised the hand holding her *Chama* stone to her face she was struck with the wild compulsion to hold the stone before her third eye as she'd seen the General's men do with their headbands. She pressed the stone to her forehead, with a motion that looked to the soldiers like she might be wiping sweat from her brow.

They didn't appear to suspect her of subterfuge, a blessing for which she was immensely grateful. She didn't know what she intended to do with the stone, but she trusted her instincts to guide her. They'd never failed her before, and she didn't expect them to now.

Chapter Twenty-Five

Rayven felt the *Chama* stone slip from between her fingers to make contact with the skin of her forehead, one heartbeat before all hell broke loose.

A blinding and excruciating pain racked her brain and made her double over from the force of it. Rayven clawed at the burning, tearing ache that ate at her forehead. In that moment she could think of nothing beyond the agony running rampant through her head, not the soldiers before her, not the hounds still yipping and growling at her, nothing at all.

The sticky, hot feel of blood welled underneath her fingers and gushed down her face. Rayven's trembling fingers felt the *Chama* stone sink wetly into the skin of her forehead, just over her third eye. She dug at it in a panic, but the stone would not budge from its newfound seat in her flesh. Her face was awash in the crimson river of blood that spilled from the wound caused by the stone, and though Rayven knew that head wounds were prone to bleed profusely, she feared that her wound was not dire enough to account for such a shocking bloodletting. The hot, wet stickiness flowed freely down her face and neck, flooding her eyes and mouth with its salty sting.

Though she couldn't see them, blinded as she was by a river of blood, the General's men stood shocked before her. Their training and purpose was forgotten as they stared dumbfounded at the sight before them. They saw the raging river of blood wash down Rayven's face to spill down her front and onto the ground where it gathered in a crimson pool. The scent of her blood excited the hounds, and several of the men were forced to hold the dogs back to keep them from frenziedly attacking.

Rayven's knees gave out under her and she fell to the forest floor. Her hands shook as she tried to wipe the blood from her eyes, and she whimpered like a wounded animal. The pain in her head was dulling to a less excruciating torment, and she was able to think clearly for a short moment. She felt her body begin to tingle unpleasantly, and she was uncomfortably aware of the feel of the earth beneath her, the wind teasing at her hair, and the trees whispering overhead. In that moment of clarity she could feel the planet move beneath her and the lazy flight of the clouded heavens above her head.

She felt a throb through her body, and with a pop that sounded audibly in her thudding ears, she felt her power gush unchecked through her body. Her skin seemed tight, like a blister about to burst. The force of the current within her brought her shooting to her feet as though invisible strings had pulled her body upright. The alien grace of her movement startled the already nervous soldiers, and many of them leveled their weapons upon her once more.

Rayven experienced a burning sensation along her skin, and looked down at herself, her movements slow and dreamy. Blood still dripped freely from her head, but she didn't notice it now. She merely looked down at her body, as if it were a thing separate from her. Before her dreamy eyes, her skin slowly took on a white-hot glow, which grew to a blinding intensity within a few heartbeats. The wind around her began to blow more forcefully, and her hair started to whip wildly around her from the force of it.

"Back down, alien, or I will open fire!"

Rayven wanted to tell the frightened soldier who had called out to the command that she would back down if only she knew how, but she couldn't find her voice. Her power raged through her with a strength she'd never imagined was possible. Her body felt as though it was on fire, and her skin felt flayed by the violence of it. The blood roared in her veins, and the *Chama* stone firmly embedded in her forehead began to hum against her skull.

Rayven felt it a moment before it happened. It seemed to her that her insides were spilling outward, turning her inside out. With a slight tremble of her muscles, Rayven's power unleashed itself upon her enemies, laying waste to all that was before her.

Rayven found her voice on a scream. She screamed on and on, never stopping to catch her breath, and her power raged from her until she felt split asunder. She was blinded by it. All she could see was a white-hot light before her, a blazing fire that had no beginning and no end. She tried closing her eyes against it, but even behind her lids all was a white, blinding haze.

Rayven *became* her power. She lost the memory of her physical form and became pure energy, a never-ending raging torrent of it. Her sense of self was taken from her in a rush, and all that was left in its wake was her unleashed power. Rayven lost herself within the white-hot blaze and she knew no more.

* * * * *

Draco bolted upright in his bed feathers, sweat dripping freely down his brow. His heart was racing within his chest, and his skin thrummed with his *Awareness*. Something was terribly wrong. He could sense it, and the knowledge was like a niggling itch in the back of his mind. He sent his power outward, seeking the cause of his distress.

His heart almost stopped beating within his chest, and he chokingly cried out a word into the dawn stillness. The sound of his cry still echoed in the air around him as he frantically teleported from his *Bito*.

"Rayven!"

Chapter Twenty-Six

Rayven... Rayven... Rayven...

Echoes of a soft voice broke across the quiet stillness. Soft, brief, flashes of light tattooed images onto her eyes in the darkness. Rayven fought to stay in the welcome silent darkness. She feared her awakening, and what lay in wait for her there, beyond the still land of her unconsciousness.

Rayven... Rayven... Rayven...

That echoing voice again. It sounded closer, clearer now. She struggled to ignore the insistent call to wakefulness.

"Rayven," a voice sounded clear and deep by her ear.

Rayven jerked awake. Her hair was a dark curtain over her face, blinding her eyes. She sat up slowly. Tentatively. She plunged her fingers in her hair, sweeping it away from her face, and looked around her. Her eyes widened in shock.

She lay sprawled upon a fur rug thrown over a stone floor. Directly in front of her a fire burned cheery and bright. She looked around to find herself in a large chamber, decadently furnished with rich, warm color, and elegant, plush textures. There was a sound at her shoulder and she whirled around.

A giant of a man stood looming over her, dressed all in black, his loose attire resembling a monk's robes, only more stylish and elegant. He was very tall, perhaps even taller than Draco—and she knew he was at least seven and a half feet in height. The man before her had outrageously broad shoulders, and a hulking, muscular build. It surprised her, however, that his obvious brute strength in no way detracted from his grace or elegance of movement. His skin was dark bronze, as if he spent much of his time outdoors.

Rayven slowly roved her eyes over his body, starting with the shiny toes of his boots and working her way up his large torso, up and up, until her eyes settled on his face. He had a strong masculine face, with a strong jaw, a sharp blade of a nose, and flaring black brows. His eyes were amethyst, though much lighter in color and intensity than Setiger's amethyst eyes. His hair was a glossy onyx river that reached past his buttocks, and flowed around him like a waterfall. With a startling flash of recognition, she knew who he was.

"*Father*," she breathed in wonder.

The man smiled and knelt beside her with a graceful movement.

"You recognize me then, daughter." He smiled tenderly at her, his eyes a deep gazing river flowing into her own.

"How can this be? Am I dead?"

Emperor Thibetanus laughed at her stunned words, a joyful, carefree sound that wrapped Rayven in a feeling of comfort and safety.

"No, Rayven. You are merely visiting me here, on the astral plane."

"How?"

"You called to me and I came. You have my stone upon your brow now, so that I will be with you always should you need me."

Rayven reached up to her forehead and felt the *Chama* stone still embedded there. Her skin had healed around it, and it sat upon her third eye as if she were born with it there.

"The *Chama* stone I found is yours? It's no wonder that it called to me so, then. I thought it was killing me, though, when it drove itself into my skin."

Thibetanus' eyes twinkled. He reached out and softly ran his fingertips over the stone upon her brow. It hummed and tingled when he touched it.

"No. It's been countless millennia since one of our people were able to assimilate a *Chama* stone into their flesh as you just did. However, I'm not entirely surprised that it was an unpleasant experience. Why else would our people have lost the interest in sporting the stones in such a manner, if not because the pain was too great to do it?"

Rayven realized that her father was right. She would never willingly go through that kind of pain again, no matter what great power she might gain from a *Chama* stone by doing so. No amount of power was worth the price of that kind pain to her. It was no wonder that their ancestors had felt the same way.

"What has happened to me? Am I really here with you in person, or am I just here in spirit?"

"Your spirit is here on the astral plane, but your physical body is still unconscious on the forest floor of Varood. Do not fret," he hurried to say, as Rayven's face became panicked, "all is well for now. You single-handedly destroyed fifty-two men and twenty Vampa hounds. They are gone without a trace. Your body may rest safely for now."

"I couldn't control the power that flowed through me; instead it took control of me. I couldn't stop it!"

Rayven's father put his arms around her and gathered her close to him. He set her before him, her back against his chest, his arms a solid cage around the front of her.

"Shush, be still, my *usuloon*—child of my heart. All will be well," he crooned to her then in a language she did not know, but the tone of his words sent a warm feeling of peace into her heart.

He spoke again so that she understood him. "All will be well, I promise you. You must simply learn to harness this new strength you possess, which will not be hard for you at all. The worst of the power spillage is over for now, and it won't take hold of you so forcefully again."

The two were quiet for a time, and Rayven allowed her father to comfort her in his strong embrace. Thibetanus rocked her to and fro, his large hand dwarfing her head as he stroked her hair back away from her eyes.

After a time Rayven whispered, "Why did you not strike out against the General when you had the chance? I saw him as he stood before you on the battlefield, and you did nothing to stop him from killing you."

Thibetanus sighed, his breath ruffling her hair.

"I could not have killed General Karis. My powers were being used elsewhere, to protect those people who escaped with Draco from being detected. I was also protecting others who were fleeing, though I do not think they succeeded in escaping as Draco did. I was shielding your whereabouts from detection, and keeping you safe from any threats you might encounter on your new world.

"Though even if I were doing none of these things, and I had been strong enough to smite down the General, his men would have still laid me low soon after. There were too many of his soldiers for me to destroy them all."

Rayven felt tears seep into her eyes, and her breath came out of her in a harsh sob. "Why didn't you just follow me then? Why didn't you flee when you had the chance?"

"Do you think the General would have let us go? He would have hunted us down, no matter how far we managed to run. I did what I had to do to save as many Aware as was possible."

Rayven's tears burned a hot trail down her cheeks. She couldn't remember the last time she'd cried like this, her tears escaping her eyes and her breath caught behind the aching lump in her chest and throat. She couldn't remember if she'd even cried at all since the death of her foster parents that fateful night over ten years ago. She bowed her head and let the tears fall, her sorrow choking her heart like a vise.

"I was so alone," she whispered brokenly.

"I'm sorry, *usuloon,*" her father whispered back fervently, his arms tightening protectively around her, "you have no idea how much." Thibetanus stroked her hair and rocked her slowly in his arms. Rayven clutched at his arms, his chest pressed comfortingly at her back. She squeezed her eyes shut against the burning sting of her tears.

"Do you blame me for your unhappiness, Rayven?"

"No. I've been angry knowing that you just stood there and let the General kill you, but I understand now why you did it. Being a leader of people whose survival is dependent on you is not an easy thing, and I believe you did the best you could to put their safety before your own. You nobly sacrificed your life that your people might live. I just can't help being selfish and wishing that you and Mother had just left when you could, to be with me on Earth. I'm shamed by my weakness, but I still cannot change the way I feel."

"There is no shame in being selfish now and again. But you are right about the weight of duty a leader must bear for his or her people. You are only now learning just how heavy that burden can be, and I'm sorry to say that you have much to learn yet. But do not despair, my daughter. You have a family now. Your people are your family, and they love you as fiercely as any blood family ever could. You have a mate by your side, and I know that he loves you with a passion that will never fade or die out. In time you will have children of your own, and to them you can be the parent that you always dreamed of having for yourself."

"I don't have a mate," Rayven said shakily, stubbornly refusing to let thoughts of Draco intrude.

Thibetanus turned her in his arms to face him. He looked hard into her eyes.

"Are you so certain that you do not? Look inside your heart, Rayven. If you look hard enough, you will find the true answer, and your heart can find its peace."

Rayven looked into the amethyst eyes of her father, and despite her discomfort with the topic being discussed, she trusted that he spoke the truth. She would dwell on that later, however, as more pressing thoughts intruded upon her.

"Why are you here with me?"

"You called to me."

"How? I don't know how I did it."

"It doesn't matter. When you need me most, you will be able to call on me. Sometimes you will only need the aid of my power, and it will be there for you. Sometimes you will need the comfort of my voice and you will hear it. Still other times you will be lost and in need of guidance or support, in which case you will visit me here on the astral plane where I will wait for you to come. It doesn't matter how, it only matters that it will be so."

"What *is* it with our people? Can't we ever answer a direct question with a direct answer? I swear you and Draco are two peas in a pod!"

Emperor Thibetanus laughed, a deep and booming sound. "Draco has ever been like a son to me. You would do well to dwell on the implications of that."

"You see? Listen to yourself."

"Are you over your grief, *usuloon*?"

"Yes. I'm sorry I broke down like that in front of you. I didn't imagine that if I ever actually got to meet my parents, I'd just freak out and cry like a baby. I'm sorry, but I couldn't help it. I'm scared of all the things that have been happening to me. I'm scared that I won't make a good Empress, I'm scared that I'm going to get the remainder of our people killed in a war I have no business instigating, and I'm scared of being alone if I survive the coming slaughter. I'm sorry if you're ashamed of my weakness."

Rayven's father rose to his feet, drawing her up with him. He took firm hold of her shoulders and stared earnestly into her eyes.

"You could never shame me, daughter. I have watched over you from the land beyond life, and I am proud of the woman you have become. Nothing could ever change that. You have been given a terrible burden, the duty to protect our people and triumph over our enemies. I would be surprised if you did not feel a bit of uncertainty or bitterness over this fact. I wish I could take this responsibility from you, but the Fates have decreed it otherwise."

Rayven straightened her shoulders under her father's hands. She felt his power flow through her, filling her with a renewed feeling of strength and purpose.

"I'll do my best to help our people, Father. I don't want to fail them, or you."

"You will make a great Empress, daughter. You just have to believe in yourself, and the rest will follow."

"I'm ready to go back now."

"Goodbye for now, daughter, until we meet once more."

Rayven was swallowed up once more by the waiting darkness.

Chapter Twenty-Seven

Draco used his matebond with Rayven to hone in on her location and transported himself instantly to her side. When his silent gateway closed behind him, he looked around wonderingly at the scene that lay before him.

At his feet, Rayven lay curled in the middle of an enormous crater, asleep or unconscious, he couldn't tell which. Smoke rose from the blackened rim of the crater, curling black and acrid around them. There wasn't a sound to be heard in the dawn stillness, not the call of a bird or the whisper of the wind through the trees. All was silent.

Draco felt a low thrum of residual power emanate from Rayven's still form. Had *she* been the cause of this brutally desolate scene of destruction? Was it possible? Draco knelt at her side and reached out to turn her over towards him, and felt a shock of electric current race from her body and into his hands. He stumbled backwards, and stared from his tingling hands to Rayven, and back again. He'd never felt such a shock of barely contained *Awareness* before, it had zinged and thrummed in a torrent of pure energy from her body to his, leaving his brain stunned as if from a physical blow.

Draco's heart swelled with wonder and pride, as he realized that it had indeed been Rayven who had scarred this crater into the earth, laying waste to all that stood in the path of her power, obliterating all before her as if they had never been. If what he suspected was truth, Rayven had learned to harness her power in a way he'd never imagined, and the thought awed and amazed him. He wondered what kind of threat she had faced that would cause this magnitude of retaliatory violence from her. He was almost certain that he didn't really want to know.

He moved back to Rayven's side, and reached for her once more, though this time he was prepared for the zing of power that rippled through him at the contact. Rayven rolled over limply into his arms, her body thrumming and humming with suppressed power. Her hair was a tangle across her face, and Draco used his shaking hands to pull it back away from her brow.

He gasped raggedly and almost dropped her at the sight that met his eyes.

From the top of her head almost to her knees she was stained crimson with dried blood. Her clothes were stiff with it and stuck to her skin like glue. Draco could smell the sweet coppery scent of it, and wondered for a surreal and dizzy moment what kind of weapon could have possibly caused an injury that had bled so freely, yet left no wound to find.

The hair at the crown of Rayven's head had turned a brilliant white, leaving a blazing streak about an inch thick through her tresses. Nowhere else had her hair been discolored, and the white streak was a gleaming brilliance against her black and ruby mane. It was a psychic brand, just as her ruby streaks had been. A physical byproduct of the release of an immense amount of psychic energy. And that wasn't the only physical thing that had changed about her.

There, in the center of her bloodstained forehead, in a position just over her third eye, lay a darkly shining blue stone. A *Chama* stone was embedded within her flesh, like a tiny piercing jewel. It would be startlingly dark against her fair golden skin after she washed the blood away. Draco moved to brush his hand over the stone, and felt it throb with suppressed power. It wouldn't budge from its position in her flesh, and Draco knew with a certainty that it never would. Somehow Rayven had found a *Chama* stone, and had assimilated it into her flesh, as their legendary ancestors had done in days of old. He would never have believed it possible, if he hadn't seen it with his own eyes.

He checked her pulse, fearful for one terrifying second that she was dead. He breathed a harsh sigh of relief when he felt it beat strong and steady against his fingers. He shook her gently, and called out to her softly, trying to wake her from her eerie stillness.

"Rayven, wake up! Please, *a grifa,* open those bright beautiful eyes of yours, so I know that you're all right."

He called again, and again, his voice growing ragged, almost frantic as the minutes wore on and she didn't respond. He shook her more forcefully, lolling her head about on her limp neck.

"Damn it, woman, do you have to disobey my every order? Quit being so stubborn and wake up!"

Rayven swam up from the deep, calm waters of unconsciousness. Her body was racked with pain, and she moaned from the force of it. Her head throbbed and she reached up to soothe the ache with her hand. The *Chama* stone nestled in the flesh of her forehead felt warm and tingly under her fingertips. She came awake with a jolt, her blazing gold eyes flaring open to clash with molten silver ones.

"Where am I?" Her voice sounded scratchy, like she'd been shouting and had strained her vocal cords.

Draco let loose a relieved rush of air from his lungs, his feeling of panic fading before an onslaught of fright-induced anger.

"Why don't you tell me, Rayven? You're the one who's recently taken to interplanetary travel in the dead of night."

Rayven blearily looked at him, surprised that her eyes were even functional after all the blood that had poured into them earlier. Her body was stiff and achy, her head pounded in a fierce rhythm, and she felt drained emotionally and physically. She didn't think she could take a lecture from Draco right then.

"Stop yelling, Draco. I can hear you just fine from where I'm sitting." She moved away from his fierce hold and winced at the movement. "Oomph, I'm sore."

"I'm not surprised by that, considering the blast of power you were forced to expend. From the size of this crater it was quite a show."

Rayven got her first good look at the area surrounding her, and what she saw frightened and amazed her.

"I did all *that*?"

"I assume so. You've blown a hole the size of a large house into the forest floor." He tried to laugh but the noise that came from his throat sounded mirthless and forced at best. "Are you all right?"

"Yeah, just a few bumps and bruises. I'll be fine, but we should probably leave as soon as possible. I don't know how long I've lain here, and the General's men are bound to come looking for their missing compatriots."

"What happened?"

"I assume General Karis has had men patrolling the area, waiting for me to return. I was run to ground by these hellish-looking dogs…Vampa hounds, I think they're called." Rayven remembered the name her father had called them by.

"You let loose this type of destructive force because of a few dogs and their keepers?"

"No. There were about fifty men…about twenty hounds. They were going to shoot me—I didn't have much choice but to fight back. I just let it get a little out of hand, that's all. I tried to use the *Chama* stone the way I had seen the General's men use them. I just planned to hold the stone over my third eye and funnel my energy through it, but obviously the stone had other plans. It embedded itself in my skin, as you can see."

Draco reached out to touch the stone once more, and felt it hum against his fingers. "Does it hurt?"

"My flesh feels bruised…achy. But it's not as bad as it was, not by a long shot."

"How did you find it? Is that why you came here?"

Rayven debated on telling him the whole story, but decided it would take too much time and said so. She rose, letting Draco help her to her feet, and laughed shakily.

"Let's get away from here. I don't want to get caught unawares by any more of the General's henchmen. I'll tell the whole story to everyone at once. This concerns all of us, so I want all of our people to hear what I have to say."

Draco gave her a strange, thoughtful look.

"What?" she asked.

"Nothing. You just seem…different. Different beyond your new physical appearance I mean," he said pulling her white hair down for her to see. Rayven didn't even spare more than a glance at it, and didn't seem too surprised by it.

"I think I am different. Just how much different is yet to be seen."

"That's cryptic," he said almost teasingly. "Should I be concerned?"

Rayven smiled at him. She moved to stand closer to him and rose up on the tips of her toes. Even standing on point as she was, her head didn't reach past his rib cage. She snorted, and opened herself to her power. Her body rose up off the ground with a graceful motion, and she placed a kiss softly on his lips, before she lowered herself back to the ground. She almost laughed at Draco's stunned expression.

"How did you…?"

Rayven gave him a sly look from beneath a fringe of black lashes. "I'm learning new things all the time, it seems."

Rayven did laugh at his newest disgruntled expression. If Draco could ever be called adorable, now was the time. He almost looked as though he was pouting over the fact that she'd learned a new trick without his teaching it to her.

"Let's go home," she said.

"Yes, let's."

Before Draco could call forth a tunnel, Rayven beat him to the punch. She stepped through the silent gateway she'd called forth, her tinkling laughter lingering after her to tease at Draco's ears.

"Showoff," he murmured with a grin, before he, too, entered the swirling black tunnel. He couldn't wait to hear her story, and hoped it was a good one, or else he might just have to throw her over his knees in truth as he'd threatened to. His earlier anger was forgotten, but he knew it would flare like a lit taper if he wasn't careful. He would just have to wait and see if Rayven needed to be punished, or rewarded for her foolish bravery.

Chapter Twenty-Eight

Rayven laid the heavy sack of *Chama* stones upon the great table in the Gathering Tree. She loosened the drawstring to reveal the treasures inside, and was pleased to hear the awed and disbelieving gasps of her people.

"They were just laying there in a storage room. Anybody could have picked them up or tossed them out. These were all that I found, and I don't think there were anymore there—except for the ones that were set into the headbands on the General's officers. It's just a hunch, but I don't think there are any missing but those few."

Onca reaching a shaking hand towards the bag before fisting his fingers and pulling back slightly.

"How did you do this, Highness?"

"I told you, Onca. I snuck into the General's castle to get them. After you guys talked about them yesterday morning, I remembered that while escaping from the General's stronghold I'd been compelled to take one from that room. I didn't know the significance of that until I heard your tale."

"And you've had this stone with you the whole time you've been among us, and we never even knew." Onca's crimson eyes strayed uneasily up to the gleaming blue stone in her forehead.

"Well, how would you have known about it? I didn't tell anyone."

Setiger shifted in his chair with a suppressed violence. "We should have sensed its presence."

"Why? It's my father's stone, wouldn't that make it mine to sense?"

"Yes, but he was our Emperor. I just can't believe that we didn't feel *something*."

Rayven almost rolled her eyes at Setiger's plaintive tone. He sounded almost upset that he'd been left out of the all the excitement of the morning.

"Well, the question I have now is, what are we going to do with these?" Rayven said to the room at large.

"We will each sense out the *Chamas* of our families and friends and see that they are used in a fashion that is most suitable to the spirit found within," Draco said.

Rayven looked at Draco with a smile on her face as their people moved to the bag and began searching through it excitedly. Draco smiled back at her and held out his hand. Rayven took it willingly.

"Are you still mad at me for going off this morning without your permission?"

Draco raised a hand to toy with her white lock of hair. His eyes blazed with a barely suppressed violence. "I don't know. I don't like the thought that you were in danger and I was not there to help you."

"I've been in danger before, Draco. I don't need you to save me all the time."

Draco tugged her hair and brought her forward to kiss the top of her head. "I still don't like it."

"I promised you that I wouldn't do anything like it again, or that I'd at least ask you first."

"You promised me before today that you would not use your power without me. How am I to trust you now?"

"I never promised you anything—you just told me not to and then assumed that I would do as you ordered. No, let me finish," she rushed on as he began to speak. "I felt that it was the right thing to do, that this was my wrong to right. I've promised now to always consult you first before doing anything like this again. I will keep that promise."

"My orders are not given lightly. You could have been killed, with none of us the wiser."

"I told you I was sorry to worry you. I won't grovel for your forgiveness—all I did was break one of your rules—you've millions more for me to abide by."

Draco let out a harsh breath, and clutched her shoulders in desperate hands. "I…I was worried. I was afraid I wouldn't be there to save you…when you needed me most." His voice was thick, the words sounded as though they were strangling him.

Rayven's heart melted. "I'm sorry you were worried. Will you forgive me—*not* for breaking a so-called promise I never even made—" she smiled, her eyes soft, "—but for not thinking of how you might feel?"

Draco was silent for a moment. Then, with a devilish twinkle in his eyes he said, "Well, I'm sure I can think of some way for you to make it up to me."

Rayven's eyes widened just before she laughed. All through the day he'd been teasing her like that, with a barely veiled sexual innuendo behind each of his words. He was being much more sexually aggressive than normal and she was surprised to find that she liked this new facet to their relationship, and tried to play along with him.

"You won't spank me, will you?" she asked with a smile.

Draco merely smiled his wicked smile, dark promises shining in his silver eyes, before he turned and strode away.

"I was only kidding," she called out, laughing. When Draco continued without a backward glance, Rayven couldn't help shivering with anticipation.

* * * * *

Rayven walked happily down the pathway to her *Bito*. Draco had told her to seek her bed feathers, to rest her bruised and tired muscles while she could. When Rayven had naïvely asked if he was planning on resuming her training that evening when she awoke, he had sent her a sizzling look and murmured softly into her ear.

"I had training of a different sort in mind, and I do not want your sore muscles to interfere with my instruction, *Sudontey*."

Rayven's sore muscles had almost melted at the tone in his voice, and heat pooled low in her belly as her eyes met the wolfish look in his. For the first time since they'd met, she'd been more than happy to follow his orders.

As she caught sight of her small tent, she heard someone call out behind her.

"Highness, wait," Ursus called again, running to catch up to her.

Rayven smiled at her friend. "What's up?" she asked, knowing how much Ursus enjoyed hearing Earth slang.

Ursus was almost breathless when she came to a halt before her. Her cheeks were flushed and her eyes were bright.

"I just wanted to thank you, Rayven, for bringing our stones back to us."

Rayven reached out to hug her friend, though she only reached to her breasts and she felt like a child doing so. "It was my pleasure and duty to do so, Ursus."

Ursus held out her hand to reveal three blue stones nestled there.

"These are my parents and little brother. They were each killed in the Great Massacre. I never thought to see them again, but tonight I will visit with each of them, and tell them of your great courage in bringing them home to me."

Rayven's eyes misted with tears, and she found that she was surprisingly comfortable with showing emotion in front of her friend. She smiled mistily, and saw that Ursus was also weeping.

"I'm happy to have brought you some measure of comfort, Ursus. For the first time I feel like I've made a difference here and I'm glad for it."

Ursus' dark eyes widened behind her tears. "Oh but, Rayven, you've already done so much for us. You've brought us hope for the future. You've taught us new ways to prepare our food, more efficient ways to dye our clothing, and you've begun to teach our women how to fight with our fists."

Rayven blushed, embarrassed by Ursus' gushing praise.

"I just told you how to recognize different herbs to use for seasoning, I barely mentioned the possibilities of achieving a stronger pigment if you allowed the berries you used in your dyes to ferment, and I only spend a few moments each morning after we bathe showing you and the other women judo positions. That's just kid's stuff."

"Well, it's not kid's stuff to us. You always have a kind word for one of us, you remembered all of our names after only meeting us once, the children love you, the men are loyal to you, and the women have been happier since your arrival than they've ever been before."

"But that wasn't anything big, it was just me being me."

"Exactly. Your presence among us has been more beneficial than you know. Though I am more than grateful that you retrieved our *Chama* stones, I want you to know that you needn't have done it just to prove yourself to us. You are young—a fledgling in your power, and still we can all see the greatness within you. From your first day among us, you have gained in strength and skill—and not just on the training field. You seem more at peace with yourself, and more relaxed around other people."

Rayven's eyes were thoughtful, and Ursus was moved to add, "You are too doubtful of yourself, Rayven. You are a great Aware, but you do not believe it fully yet. Once you lose your self-doubt, and believe in your abilities, nothing will be able to hold you back from your destiny. Nothing."

Rayven smiled at her friend. "Are you becoming a seer like Onca?"

Ursus laughed, a wicked gleam in her eyes. "You'd be surprised at what talents I have, Highness."

The two friends laughed together joyfully before hugging once more and parting ways. With a weary but happy smile on her face Rayven threw herself onto her bed feathers and fell instantly asleep.

* * * * *

It was nightfall when Rayven felt warm lips press against the nape of her neck. She moaned softly in her sleep, trembling as they laid a burning trail along her neck to her spine, and slowly down her back. She stretched her body in a lazy feline movement as two large hands trailed down her sides before moving to cup her breasts beneath her. She sighed and murmured sleepily as teeth bit teasingly at the flesh of her buttocks and a cool waterfall of hair fell over her back.

Strong hands suddenly lifted her and turned her over, and she came fully awake to see Draco looming over her in the darkness. He had already divested her of her clothing, but he remained fully dressed in his usual loosened shirt and breeches. His heavily muscled chest peeked out at her from behind the gaping ties on his shirt, and Rayven reached up with both hands to stroke his naked skin. Draco's breath hissed out at the contact of her cool hands upon his heated flesh, and she smiled at his reaction.

Draco jerked her upright in a motion that sent her tumbling against him. He took both of her hands in his and he drew them to the lacings at the front of his shirt. He forced her to grasp her fists in the loose material, cupping his much larger hands over hers and holding them tight. Draco waited until she met his eyes, and a frisson of power leapt between their clashing eyes. He tightened his hold on her fists even more and ripped open his shirt using both of their hands. The material tore cleanly away with a loud rending sound.

"I-I thought *evansai* was supposed to be strong. Nearly indestructible."

"I am stronger."

"Oh," she breathed on a sigh.

With a dangerous look in his eyes, Draco cupped Rayven's head and held it up for his kiss. His lips, teeth and tongue played hotly at her mouth for a moment before he lowered her once more to the bed. He swept his hands teasingly down the front of her body, letting them come to rest upon her pubic bone. He firmly pressed the heel of his hand in a circular motion onto her flesh, and a wave of ecstasy washed through her.

Draco fell on her with a wild passion, his hair flowing out over the both of them like a cool wave of silk. His lips and teeth pulled at her breasts, nibbling and suckling the sensitive flesh, before settling on her plump nipples, one after the other. His mouth was wet and hot, branding her with each suckling kiss. All the while, Draco's hands roved over her body, leaving no curve unexplored, no part of her body a stranger to his expert touch.

Rayven moaned and writhed beneath him, her skin aflame with raging desire. She felt Draco slip a well-muscled thigh between her legs and, with his encouraging hands tugging at her hips, she rode him with wanton abandon. She ground her pussy against him, leaving his trousers wet with the evidence of her body's arousal.

After several moments Draco stilled her movements and held her tightly in his arms before rising up above her to meet her eyes with his own. Rayven was almost startled to see the glowing, animal-eye shine that reflected back from his silver gaze, but she knew instinctively that her own eyes were aglow with a similar fire. She met his gaze steadily, putting all of her secret feelings and yearnings behind the force of her stare.

"Is this truly what you want, *Sudontey*? If you have doubts, best you make them known to me now, because after we are joined there will be no going back to your empty, virginal bed."

Not having the words to express how she felt, Rayven instead rose up to kiss him upon the mouth. She sent a hot wave of her power flowing from her body to his, as her lips moved sensuously upon his. Draco gasped with pleasure into the recesses of her mouth, and returned her kiss with an almost bruising force. His tongue dueled hotly with hers, and his teeth bit at her lips. Her mouth tingled and a low pulse thrummed pleasantly at her breasts and pussy.

Draco dragged his lips from hers, and his hands tore at the fastenings of his trousers. Rayven blinked and suddenly he was nude. Her eyes roved over his body, taking in his familiar, well-beloved face, his wide shoulders, muscular chest, and trim waist. Fighting the urge to blush, Rayven allowed her eyes to stray lower and her breath caught in the back of her throat. From what she could see, Draco's height wasn't the only overly large thing about him. Rayven whimpered, the sound almost akin to panic, as she wondered just how in the world she was supposed to accept *that* part of him into her body.

Draco's velvet voice sounded in a husky chuckle, "Trust me, *Sudontey*, we will fit. We were made to fit each other, like sword in sheath, or hand in glove."

Rayven smiled, and tried not to swoon at the images his words seared into her brain. Rayven inhaled and caught his masculine scent on the night wind.

"I love the way you smell, Draco," she felt compelled to tell him, on a breathy sigh.

Her lover merely smiled, his teeth blazing white against his night-shadowed face. He bent his dark head and kissed her, a soft, heated brush of lips. His breath flowed into her mouth, and she gave it back to him on a sigh. He ran his knowing hands down her body, pausing to knead her flesh in all the right places.

Draco's voice entranced and enthralled her as he began softly speaking in her ear, the words a language she didn't fully understand, but the passion behind them all too clear. He switched to English and told her all the things he wanted to do to her before the night drew to an end. He told her how beautiful she was to him, how powerful and aroused she made him feel. He told her how sweet he knew her pussy would taste, and how thirsty he was for a draught of her liquid heat. His voice brushed against her skin like silk and velvet, dark and dangerous. It thrilled and tormented her, bringing her passions to a raging boil. Rayven cried out incoherently into the deep night, and still the music of his voice played on.

Rayven felt Draco move down her body as his hands spread her legs wide, and before she knew what he intended he bent his sleek dark head to her. Rayven keened loudly into the darkness, her hands coming to clutch themselves in his silky hair. Draco's tongue lapped lazily at her, burning her, branding her, and bringing forth a flood of moisture from deep within her. His lips and teeth played lightly against her swollen, tingling clit. He spread her labia wide with his fingers, and buried his face into her sopping wet flesh, devouring her like a starving beast.

Rayven's head thrashed wildly about the feathers of her bed, her back arching, pressing her wet flesh more forcefully into his fiery-hot kiss. His mouth turned voracious upon her, and he bit, licked and suckled her, his head moving rapidly to and fro between her legs. Draco thrust a long finger into her dripping channel—curving like a hook within her and scraping over her G-spot with expert ease. After only two fierce thrusts and scrapes of his finger deep within her, Rayven came on a burst of quivering ecstasy, her cries of fulfillment echoing around them.

Just as Rayven sank down from the heights of her orgasm, Draco renewed his fervent kisses upon her silken wetness, thrusting another long finger into her to join the one already nestled inside her. He sucked and bit at her clit, making wet slurping noises as he fed on her. Draco used the length and breadth of his tongue to lap at her from where his fingers thrust within her to her clit, licking her in one long swipe, and then repeating the process over and over, savoring her. This sent Rayven racing back into the heavens, riding the waves of another delicious release. Over and over he threw her up over pleasure's peak, each time stretching her pulsing channel with the addition of another finger, until she cried desperately out for him to stop.

She felt herself stretched tautly over four of his fingers, the pleasure-pain of it almost sending her over another peak and into yet another violent orgasm. She fought against it, trying to regain some of her lost control. She tried and failed to calm her ragged breathing, and her skin burned from her passionate exertions. Draco gently flexed his fingers within her, and she helplessly surrendered herself fully, losing herself to ecstasy once more.

This time, when Rayven came back to reality, it was to find Draco positioning the purple head of his cock between her drenched folds. She tensed, and his eyes flew up from his guiding hand to meet hers.

"I'll be gentle, *Sudontey*. Trust me."

Though he had not phrased his whispered words as a question, Rayven nodded her acceptance of them anyway. She brought her hands up to clutch at his broad shoulders, her nails digging lightly into his flesh. She felt that if he didn't enter her soon she would die, and she moved eagerly against his cock.

Draco began to enter her, and though he had stretched her virgin's flesh with his fingers, his erection was much larger than she expected it to feel. Her body squeezed tightly against Draco's invading girth, denying him entrance in an instinctive, panicked movement.

"I took your virgin's membrane with my fingers," he said darkly. "You will not feel pain from our joining, *a grifa*, so relax and let me inside." His voice played over her in an almost mesmerizing manner.

In the back of Rayven's mind she suddenly realized that he had been using his voice on her like an erotic weapon throughout their love play. She had always assumed that his voice was naturally beautiful and sensual, but now she suspected that he used some secret power to make his voice even more appealing to her than it would be on others.

"Are you bespelling me with your voice, Draco?"

Draco almost groaned at the inquiring note in her voice. She didn't seem at all displeased that he might be doing so, but she sounded incredibly curious about it nonetheless. If he weren't already grasping at the last vestiges of his control he would have found the situation hilarious.

"Don't let that analytical brain of yours take all the magic out of the moment, *Sudontey*," he teased her, deliberately saturating his tone with his *Awareness*, unleashing the full power of his voice upon her.

Rayven reeled under the dark force of power in his voice, and yet *another* orgasm raked its exquisite claws down her body. She felt every muscle tremble and pulse, and Draco used the opportunity to enter her body on a forceful thrust. He filled her. And filled her. And filled her deeper still.

"Take all of me, *Sudontey*, take everything I have to give you."

He filled her relentlessly until he came to rest at last against her belly, his cock now fully embedded in her, stretching her body tautly, filling her deepest recesses. His heavy, tight sac rested against her buttocks, and he squirmed against her to join even more tightly with her. There wasn't even the space of a breath between their two bodies, and Draco almost lost what was left of his self-control when Rayven's cunt shivered in milking tremors around his burning cock. She was wrapped so tightly around him that it was almost painful. The hot liquid that dripped down from where he lay buried in her pussy and farther onto his balls was so erotic that it almost caused him to shoot his load into her right then and there. He'd never had a woman so wet and tight in his life.

Rayven cried out and her body clenched against his invasion. She could actually feel the walls of her channel as they pulsed with liquid warmth around his thick shaft, the pleasurable feel of her movements almost undoing them both. She felt split open, like a ripe fruit in the hot sun. She felt a gush of liquid wash down her pussy and ass, and onto the bedclothes beneath them. She squirmed against him, trying to entice him into the thrusting motions she so desperately craved. Her swollen clit brushed against him, and she almost swooned with the pleasure of it. Draco groaned in response as her flesh greedily gulped at his.

"You feel like hot, wet *evansai*, my heart. You're so tight I can't breathe. I've never felt such pleasure." His voice was ragged and his teeth were clenched with his obvious effort to control his raging passions.

Rayven grew lightheaded as his voice once again played over her. His scent, sandalwood and rosemary, was stronger now than ever before. She breathed him in as if he were a drug and she were a junkie who'd long been denied a fix. Rayven opened her closed eyes, and blearily tried to focus upon him, dizzy with the scent of him.

"Pheromones," she breathed in wonder. Even in the throes of ecstasy, she couldn't turn off her ever-inquisitive brain.

Draco lightly chuckled, but stopped as it caused his deeply buried shaft to jerk within her. Rayven moaned, and he didn't know if it was from pain at his movements or from pleasure. Sweat beaded upon his brow, and he tried to control the wild urge to thrust with animalistic abandon into her tight sheath. He wanted to fuck her—there was no softer word for the things he wanted to do to her. But he knew she was still too tender from his rending of her virginity, and that he would have to wait before he ravished her in the way he wanted most.

Draco kissed his mate, drinking from her lips like a man dying of thirst. Rayven moved instinctively against him, and he moaned into her mouth with the pleasure of it. He thrust silkily in and out of her—once, twice—and had to force himself to lie still once more. He did not want to cause her injury.

Rayven felt the hot length of him swell unbelievably larger within her, and the pleasure of it almost split her asunder. She wrapped her legs tightly around his waist and ground up forcefully against him, eager for the friction her movements produced. She looked at Draco's face, and drank in the look of exquisite torment written across his features. Her heart swelled within her breast and she knew for a certainty that she would never love anyone as deeply as she loved this man.

"You don't have to be gentle with me anymore, Draco. Make me yours in every way. Let loose your passion."

After hearing her words, Draco fell upon her like a madman. He thrust forcefully into her, his shaft pumping in and out of her drenched cunt with exquisite abandon. His balls slapped audibly against her ass, and his powerful thrusts scooted her away from him. He pulled her back against him forcefully, jarring both of their bodies with the harsh impact. Immediately, Draco paused.

"Did I hurt you, baby?" he asked worriedly.

When Rayven could find her voice she gasped out her reply. "God no, Draco. Don't stop. Fuck me. Ride me as hard as you want—I love it!"

Draco smiled a wolfish smile, before his face grimaced and he resumed his violent thrusts within her. He held her steady with his large hands at her buttocks, and he raised her up against him as he rose on his knees, bending her back like a bow. Rayven's arms flung out over her head and she keened into the night. Draco's cock sank deep within her before pulling almost out, and sinking back once more. Her breasts jiggled with their movements and Draco bowed over her body to nip and tug at her nipples, bringing their bodies impossibly closer.

Rayven felt the wave of her orgasm a moment before it washed over her, drowning her, pulling her into its deep current with an almost punishing force. She screamed aloud as a wave of near agonizing pleasure consumed her flesh. She felt full and completed when she felt the pulsing movements of her pussy tighten around his huge cock—penetrated in every way possible.

Draco felt the walls of her tunnel clench like a vise around his shaft, and he was lost to the siren lure of her sweet body. With a hoarse shout, he felt the burning, pulsing throb of his own orgasm wash through him, and he followed her across the precipice. His body thrust and strained against hers, sweat glistening on his skin.

He felt gush after gush of his glistening seed flooding her womb, drenching her with his essence and spilling out between their joined bodies to stain the bedclothes—flooding the room with the scent of rosemary and sandalwood. He'd never felt such a violently satisfying orgasm. Pulse after pulse shook his frame, and he shuddered over her with the onslaught of it.

Their wild cries sounded long into the night, until at last they lay spent and at rest, held protectively within each other's embrace—completed at last.

Chapter Twenty-Nine

The dream swept through Rayven's sleeping body with a biting cold wind. She moaned softly in her sleep, and thrashed about upon the bed, desperate to escape the nightmare.

She tightly grasped the hilt of the sword in her hand. The sword of her five fathers – five direct ancestral forefathers who had all owned the sword once upon a time. Five dark blue soulstones glittered dangerously in the hilt under her strong hands, one for each of her warrior ancestors. The sword's blade was a blaze of blue-white fire spilling out over her hands, and illuminating the faces of her enemies before her.

All around her the men who were her enemies advanced upon her. She had no care for the danger she was in. In fact she welcomed it. If she could not slay her enemies as she wished, then she welcomed the peace that death would bring her. She was tired of the endless struggle to survive, weary to her soul from it. She was almost eager to taste of Death's immortal kiss…but first she would aid her people in this last small way – by thinning out the numbers of General Karis' army.

Not a word of challenge was spoken – no quarter sought or given, from her advancing enemies. With a flurry of movement, battle was at last engaged. With an almost magical series of movements she whirled among the throng of her attackers, lashing out lightning-quick with her Blazesword, *and felling all who dared venture too close. She at last came to rest, twirling her sword gracefully and skillfully between her hands. More than twenty bodies lie scattered upon the ground, their blood splattered about their fallen forms.*

With a burst of preternatural speed she moved farther into the General's keep, searching for more enemies to gift with a deadly kiss from her sword. She didn't have to search for long.

Another cluster of men came at her, weapons at the ready. Before their lascannons *could fire, and before their blades could slice through the air, she attacked. She slaughtered them all, her movements far too swift to be detected by her enemies' inferior humanoid sight. Her sword dripped crimson with blood, its previous white blaze now tinted pink beneath the precious liquid. She felt the awesome hum of power emanating from the soulstones beneath her grip upon the sword's hilt, and stretched her lips in a dark smile.*

Over and over, as she sped through the corridors of the General's keep, she met foe after foe after foe. Each newcomer fell beneath the whirling maelstrom that was her sword's twinkling blade in a torrent of blood and gore. It was almost too easy – the humanoid soldiers were no match for her masterful blade work. She found it ironic that she had come here looking for a warrior's death in battle, only to find babes with weapons that were no challenge to her great skill and therefore held no threat to her life.

More soldiers rushed to engage her in swordplay now, though these men and women were garbed in the horrific Kiel *armor-plated uniforms that she remembered first seeing during the Great Massacre. She felt her* Awareness, *the preternatural flair that gave her swordplay its razor's edge, grow dim and weak within her. The* Chama *stones beneath her palm ceased their humming, and she grew dizzy as her power fled her.*

However, even without her Awareness *to aid her, she was an expert with the blade. She was far more skilled than anyone could ever guess, including her Empress and her closest friend. She had found no real use for her talents before now, but she had practiced diligently these past twenty-eight years of exile. She had pushed herself relentlessly, striving for perfection with her blade, in hopes that one day she would have just such an opportunity as this to test her skills.*

She whirled in a flurry to attack the soldiers. Her blade flashed, biting into the armor of her opponents, slicing through it and into the flesh beneath. Though her blade skills were still extraordinary without the aid of her Awareness, *the same could not be said of her other skills. Though she felled dozens more of her attackers, she did not sense the presence of a new swarm of soldiers approach at her back. Her extrasensory perception was almost like a dead thing within her, muffled and subdued by the presence of so much* Kiel *around her. She didn't see the newcomers, didn't sense their armed approach beyond her line of vision. She didn't witness one of the soldiers raise a* lascannon *to fire upon her.*

With a hot blaze of pain eating its way through her back, she sank to her knees before her foes, and slipped into blessed oblivion…

Rayven shot bolt upright in her bed with a wordless cry. She was trembling with the lingering memory of the dream, sweating and panting. With a sudden, startling clarity, she realized why the dream had seemed so real to her.

"Draco! Draco, wake up." She frantically shook the nude form of her sleeping lover beside her.

Draco came awake instantly, his eyes clear and alert.

"What is it, *Sudontey*? What is the matter?"

"It's Onca…he's been captured."

*****

"How did this happen?" The cry sounded again and again amongst the ranks of the hastily gathered Aware.

After Draco, Avator and Setiger had searched the treetop city for Onca, finding no trace of him, Rayven had called an emergency assembly of her people to share with them her dream of Onca and its implications to the fate of her people. Draco stood by her side before the gathering of her people, her bastion of strength during the ensuing uproar of panic and unrest.

Rayven let them argue and debate amongst themselves for no more than a moment before calling for silence in her most regal tone.

"We will not let this circumstance bring us to too much grief. While it is unfortunate that this has happened, it has changed nothing. It has merely forced our hand, and our battle for freedom will have to come sooner than we planned."

"But we are not ready yet, Highness. We have had no time to prepare," this panicked statement came from a woman within the crowd.

"Be calm, Ney."

Rayven sent a warm wave of calming energy out over the crowd, instantly bringing quiet peace to the room. She was no longer so surprised by how easy it was becoming to direct her power in such ways, and was pleased to see the results of her efforts.

"We have had almost three decades to prepare. A few more months would make little difference to our plans. We've also had unexpected good fortune with our newly found *Chama* stones. There's no time like the present to take action against the Galactic Commune, and Onca's desperate actions have made this even more apparent."

"I still can't believe he did something so foolish," cried Setiger.

"Do not judge Onca too harshly, Setiger. Though I believe Onca planned this type of single-handed attack long before now, I do not think he expected to be taken prisoner. I think he expected no less than death at the hands of our enemies."

"Now he has placed us all in danger! General Karis is sure to torture him into spilling our secrets, and he will bring his armies here to destroy us." Avator pounded his fist upon the stone table before him in angry frustration.

Rayven sent her power seeking outside of herself, the *Chama* stone thrumming with energy against her skull. She sought and found Onca, looking through his eyes at the scene that lay before him. She felt it when Onca recognized her presence within his mind, and she sent him waves of comfort and reassurance, as she used his eyes to assess the situation. After a few moments, she left him, leaving him with the promise that she would be there to rescue him soon.

Rayven's people saw her eyes go flat with a faraway stare. The stone in her forehead flashed a bright blue before it dimmed, and was still. Draco laid his hand softly upon her arm and called to her.

Rayven came back to herself with a soft sigh, and she looked at Draco with bright tears in her golden eyes. "Onca has been tortured almost beyond endurance. His body is racked with pain and injury. The torture did not wring the truth from him, but the General has promised to use some strange device upon him that will delve his mind and discover our secrets. I don't know what this device is because Onca himself does not, but I fear that the General indeed has such a thing if he threatens the use of it."

"What are we to do, Highness?" Avator asked firmly, and for once Rayven felt like a true ruler.

"We save Onca, before they kill him or break his mind. It no longer matters if the General finds our whereabouts—he was going to eventually anyway, whether we told him willingly or no. All that matters now is saving Onca's life and bringing him home to us."

"How are we to do that, Empress Rayven?" Ursus asked her from the throng of the crowd.

For one terrifying moment Rayven didn't know how to answer her, but then the stone in her head sent a pulse of power through her body and she spoke without consciously realizing what she had to say.

"I have a plan," she said, suddenly realizing with no small amount of surprise that her words were true.

The group of gathered Aware drew close to one another, and Rayven shared with them her newly hatched plan. Almost an hour later, when all the kinks had been worked out, and everyone knew their roles in the play that was to follow, Rayven had at last assumed the mantle of duty to which she'd been born.

Her people looked to her expectantly, waiting for her next order. When it came, she did what she'd been destined to do all along. She led them.

Chapter Thirty

Ysault Dimensional Plane
Ampilon Star System
Planet Varood

The tall, willowy woman was dressed in the dark blue uniform most commonly used by a Galactic Communal Soldier. Her shoulders were straight and sure. Her blonde hair was cropped close about her ears in a stylish bob, and her serious brown eyes stared straight ahead of her as she walked purposefully down the corridor. She looked sure of herself, confident, and attracted little notice as she passed by several soldiers on her way to her destination.

The woman came to a halt before a door, which was being guarded by an armed solder standing at attention before it. "I've come to speak with the prisoner," she said in a dry, no-nonsense tone of voice.

The guard looked at her, startled. "I was told the prisoner was to receive no visitors. Do you have a security clearance pass?"

"General Karis sent me personally. Do I really need a pass?"

"I can't let you through without a pass, ma'am, I don't care who sent you."

The tall blonde woman's dark eyes roved alertly around the corridor, warily, as if reassuring herself that they were alone, before returning her eyes to his.

Suddenly a wave of vertigo shook the guard, his mind feeling like it had turned to gelatin within his skull.

"You've just seen my security clearance, Soldier, now let me pass."

At once he saluted smartly to the woman before him and moved to retrieve the keys to the locked door from his pocket. He unlocked the door and respectfully opened it for her to enter. Before he closed the door behind her she turned back to look at him with a level stare.

"You will not remember this, Soldier. You have not seen me." Her lips didn't seem to move around the words, but he heard her loud and clear within his mind.

With a start the guard looked around him. His hand was on the handle of the now-closed door to the Aware prisoner's cell, and he couldn't remember why this was so. He had no reason to open the door, would, in fact, be punished severely by his superiors if they knew he'd made any move to do so. The soldier listened intently for any sounds within the cell, and when he heard nothing beyond the door he once again resumed his post before it. He let the odd occurrence slip from his mind.

* * * * *

Rayven looked at the door as it closed behind her. She couldn't believe how easy it had been to take control of the soldier's mind like that. She almost giggled with glee over the confused look she knew was even now spread across the guard's face. With a long, calming breath, she turned back to the dark recesses of the room.

There, chained upright against a *Kiel* slab propped against the wall, his bloodied wrists encased in *Kiel* handcuffs, slumped Onca. Rushing to his side, and ignoring his nude state, Rayven tenderly pushed his dark hair, stringy with dried blood and sweat, away from his torn face. She almost cried out at what she saw there.

Onca's face looked as though it had been split open with a dull knife down his left temple and cheek. His nose was obviously broken, his eyes black and swollen, his lips torn and bloodied. His body was in no better shape, and Rayven feared he'd have many broken bones under the bruised and swollen flesh that dotted his muscular form. Fearful that the guard outside the door might hear her were she to speak aloud, Rayven spoke directly to his mind.

"Onca, my poor friend, are you conscious? Can you hear me?"

Onca slowly raised his head and stared blearily into her eyes. Remembering her disguise, Rayven used shaking fingers to squeeze the concealing brown contacts from the gold blaze of her eyes. Her wig and prosthetic nose, and the latex patch covering her *Chama* stone followed. She left her high-heeled boots on, in case they needed to flee on foot.

"Highness," Onca breathed on a ragged sigh, his voice almost too faint for her to hear. He tried to smile and blood spilled from his torn lips in a trickling river of crimson down his chin.

"Don't move. I've come to get you out of here," she said.

"No. I have failed you, my queen. I have failed our people. The General knows of our existence now. He knows where we hide. Leave me. Save our people, and yourself."

Rayven tried to shush him, afraid the guard might hear his ragged whispering. She sensed that he was too weak to speak with her telepathically, and sent him fortifying waves of her own strength. As she did so, she moved to the cuffs confining his wrists.

"You cannot use your powers to open these cuffs, Highness. They are *Kiel*, and we cannot—" his words were cut off abruptly when Rayven pushed with her mind and easily opened the locks of the cuffs.

Rayven smiled at his look of shock. "Apparently *Kiel*'s debilitating properties do not matter much where I'm concerned."

The bonds at his wrists fell away, and Onca slumped against her, almost knocking her to the floor. Rayven called upon her inner reserves of strength and supported as much of his weight as she could. He moaned when she put one of his arms around her shoulders, his own shoulder protesting because it was out of joint. Rayven listened carefully for any sounds of alarm beyond the door, but none came. She moved to his other side and put that arm around her shoulders, putting her own arm around his waist and supported him steadily against her hip.

"I'm going to teleport us out of here, Onca. Be as quiet as you can. I'm afraid to open a doorway in such a small room, or I would do so, but it's best if we sneak out of here and do it outside. I don't know how a silent gateway would function in this small space, and I don't want to have to test it just now."

"Why are you risking yourself like this, Empress? I have betrayed you, betrayed our people. I deserve to be punished for my weakness, leave me here."

"Onca, I'm only going to say this once. I forgive you for this fiasco you have caused, I know that you didn't for one moment entertain the notion that the General's men would attempt to capture you before they tried to kill you. I know that you longed for death, as I, too, have felt the terrible desperation that can lead one on that path of self-destruction. I respect the fact that you wished to serve some purpose before you died, which is why you launched an attack on our people's enemies, and I'm sorry that you were so brutally punished for it. What's done is done and cannot be changed. Neither I, nor our people, bear you any ill will for what has happened."

"But I have revealed our whereabouts to the General and his infernal mind-reading machine. I did not do it willingly, but the damage is the same either way. How can you forgive me so easily?"

"You are my friend, my seer, my bodyguard and my Chief Counselor. It is because of all of these facts and more. You have not endangered our people beyond hope. Even now, Draco and many of our strongest people are on Earth, visiting a business associate of mine in order to purchase weapons that will aid us in the coming confrontation. All will be well, you'll see. Now, come on, and help me get us out of here."

Rayven opened the doorway to her inner power, and teleported them both to the edge of the forest outside the castle. She laid Onca gently on the ground at her feet and looked around cautiously to ensure that no one had spotted them from the castle. She listened for the braying of the Vampa hounds, but heard nothing in the distance.

"How did you know where I had gone, Highness?"

"I dreamed I was you during your attack—everything you did, I did with you."

"How? You are not my mate, and should be unable to walk within my mind like that."

Rayven remembered suddenly how easy it was for Draco to walk within her mind. As much as it warmed her heart to know that he was her mate—her soul mate, it also frightened her. Knowing how important they were to each other, how deeply involved their destinies were, only made it more difficult for her to focus on the coming battle. What if she were to lose him? How could she ever hope to live without him now that she'd known his love?

She forced her thoughts back to the task at hand. "I don't know, Onca. It just happened. I think a lot of the normal rules pertaining to our people just don't apply where I'm concerned. Look at the *Kiel* for example. It doesn't affect me the way it does you. And look at the way I assimilated my father's *Chama* stone into my skin. I don't think the why of it matters too much anymore."

Onca nodded wearily in agreement, his blackened eyes almost swollen shut.

"Why did you sneak through the castle wearing a disguise? Why didn't you just teleport to my side?" Onca asked in a weary, pain-flooded voice.

"I was afraid that I might pop in when you weren't alone. With all the people occupying the keep it was hard for me to hone in on the location of your cell to see how safe it was for me to teleport there. It was just easier for me to infiltrate their fortress incognito. Besides, I promised Draco I would be as cautious as I was able. He almost didn't let me come alone to get you like I had planned. I had to pull rank on him in front of everyone to make him give me permission."

Onca let out a soft, weak laugh. "I bet he hated that."

"Oh yeah. If we'd been alone it would never have worked. He's more stubborn than anyone I've ever met, but he knew better than to openly defy me. It would have undermined my authority in front of our people, and he would never willingly do that to me. I knew this, which is why I didn't wait to discuss it privately with him."

"It's scary sometimes, the way your mind works."

Rayven merely grinned at his words, saying nothing.

Raising her arms high before her, Rayven called forth a portal. While the vortex whipped at the wind around them she went and helped Onca to his feet once more. She was careful of his injures, but forceful in her movements. She was eager to get him home so that he could rest and heal properly. Holding him protectively against her, and supporting most of his weight, she dragged him with her into the swirling black void.

Chapter Thirty-One

Ysault Dimensional Plane
Sord Star System
Planet Hostis

The next twenty-four hours were hectic for Rayven and her people. A few hours after she arrived with Onca and put him in a deep healing sleep, Draco had returned with his group from Earth, heavily laden with firearms and incendiary devices. Before they'd parted ways, Rayven had given Draco instructions on how to access her many different bank accounts, giving him carte blanche to buy whatever they needed. She'd given him instructions to buy necessary supplies and ammo, but beyond that she'd left him to his own devices.

He'd succeeded brilliantly in his task, purchasing the kind of arsenal that was sure to impress the soldiers of the Galactic Army, right before the majority of them were blown to bits, of course.

Rayven had those among them with sewing skills working tirelessly on crafting *evansai* headbands with *Chama* stones sewn securely into the linings for their people to wear. Avator and Setiger were busy supervising a makeshift smithy, where those people who were possessed of their own weapons came to have their ancestral soulstones set into their swords, knives, and bows. Rayven called those with small children before her for a meeting.

"I wish to send your children to Earth for safekeeping during the battle. I have a house in Greece, which no one knows about, and they'll be safe there for a time. I can send one or all of you there with them to help keep them safe. I'll leave the choice up to you, but I am adamant about getting these young ones out of here before the battle begins. I do not want them harmed if it can be avoided."

The women nodded in agreement, and one of the women spoke from the tiny group.

"Let Mala go with them, Highness. She is breeding and in a delicate stage of her pregnancy. The rest of us have already discussed this and wish to remain and fight beside you and our people."

Rayven looked to Mala, a tall silver-haired woman whose elfin face looked no older than eighteen. She was fair and beautiful beyond belief, just as all of their women were.

"Is this what you want? I do not know when, or even if, I will ever be able to call you back to us after this."

Mala nodded, her eyes sad. "My mate Lema is staying here to fight, but he insists that I flee to safety to protect our unborn child. I do this with a heavy heart, but the children and their survival are more important than my own selfish need to stay here with my mate. If we lose the war, at least our children will have survived, and I will not be alone with them by my side."

Rayven nodded, knowing it hurt Mala to be separated from her mate, but respecting her for the selfless sacrifice in devoting what could end up being the rest of her life to the children of her friends. Wasting no time, she sent Mala to fetch the children and what supplies she would need. Less than an hour later she sent them to her safe house on Earth through a silent gateway, with instructions on how to access her bank accounts should the need arise.

As night fell upon the planet, Rayven and her people were still scrambling to make ready for the battle that was sure to come. Rayven was showing a large group of men how to use various different types of automatic and semiautomatic weapons. She was more than pleased with how effortlessly they seemed to learn by her examples. She found herself thankful that her species as a whole seemed predisposed to possessing advanced learning skills, and higher brain functions. For the first time in her life she didn't feel like a sideshow freak because of her skills.

Without warning Rayven's sight dimmed and swam dizzyingly as she received a clear vision of General Karis shouting through a loudspeaker to a large army of armed soldiers. Her heart almost fell to her feet with fright, before she came back to herself with a jolt. Ignoring the concerned looks of the men gathered around her, Rayven dropped the Uzi she had been holding and immediately ran in search of Draco.

She found him at the forge with Setiger and Avator, helping them to set *Chama* stones into a stack of weapons. She ran frantically into his suddenly outstretched arms.

"What is it, *a grifa*? I can taste the bitter tang of your fear on my tongue."

"He's coming."

Draco grasped her shoulders, meeting her eyes with an urgency she'd never witnessed from him before.

"Are you certain, *a grifa*? So soon?"

"Yes. I saw him, I saw his army. He's coming here."

"How long do we have?"

"I'm not sure. Maybe an hour."

Draco was silent for a moment before saying softly to her, his words too faint for any of the surrounding people to hear, "I had hoped for more time."

"So did I, I'm sorry. We need to hurry. Can we be ready in an hour?"

Draco laughed, a dark and humorless sound, his eyes were cold and hard.

"We'll have to be."

* * * * *

Half an hour later, all of the Aware were gathered once more in the great hall of the Gathering Tree with an arsenal of armor, guns, and various other weaponry adorning each and every one of them. The exceptionally tall men and women were armed to the teeth, and looking pissed enough to use every last bullet, arrow and grenade. It was a frightening sight to behold.

"I feel like I'm on the set of an Arnold Schwarzenegger movie," Rayven muttered to herself, finding no humor in the situation.

Rayven had decked herself out in her usual grand style. When it came to fitting as many weapons as possible to her small frame, she was a marvel and always had been. She wore black combat boots that reached her shins, a plain black-handled dagger was tucked within each one. She wore soft black pants that allowed her free and easy movement. Strapped to each thigh was a black-gripped Browning P-35 "Hi-Power" handgun, securely fastened but easily accessible should she need it.

She wore a belt at her waist, which sported a fully loaded 9mm Beretta pistol in a holster on each hip. Over a black tank top she wore a lightweight Kevlar vest with a row of pockets down the front of it specifically designed to hold small silver throwing knives, which she'd found useful to have close at hand in several different situations over the course of her bizarre life. Across her chest, hanging from a shoulder strap was a mini-Uzi.

Held securely within spring-loaded projectile releases on each arm were two Glock handguns. If she were to raise her arms just a few inches above her head, the strap on each elbow would pull back to release the guns, thrusting them into her hands with a lightning-quick movement. She wore a loose shirt with wide cuffs to hide them, should the deception be necessary, though she doubted it would matter. She'd pulled her hair back in a tight braid away from her face, and nestled within its thickness were small, sharp, lock-picking tools. She wanted to be prepared for every eventuality, unwilling to rely solely on her *Awareness*, should she find herself captured by the enemy.

When she said she was "packing"...she really meant it.

Draco was decked out in similar fashion, Rayven having helped him don his small arsenal herself. His hair was pulled back away from his face and fastened at his nape, revealing his strong masculine features. She'd never seen him look so gorgeous. Or dangerous. She went to his side, wanting to spend these few moments before their battle as close to him as she could.

"*Sudontey*, you are beautiful, even armed to the teeth as you are."

"I've been meaning to ask you what that means. *Sudontey*."

Draco looked uncomfortable for a moment, and if Rayven didn't know any better she would have sworn that he blushed under the golden bronze of his skin.

"Must we speak of this now, my love? Can it not wait until later?"

Rayven looked at him suspiciously, her left eyebrow cocked questioningly over her brow.

"There's no time like the present. Hell, there may not even be a later. So spill it, what does that word mean, and why are you hesitant to tell me? I don't think it's derogatory…at least I hope it's not." She smiled.

"*Sudontey* is a word from our ancient tongue. It means…wife of my heart…or…mate of my heart."

Rayven was silent and drank him deeply with her eyes. She remembered the words her father had spoken to her on the astral plane just a few short days ago when he'd mentioned the existence of her mate, and she'd stubbornly denied the truth of his words. She thought of all the times she turned away from the knowledge, even ignoring it. Why she'd ever tried to fight this tie to Draco, she didn't know. She knew now that they had been fated from the start.

Rayven knew she loved Draco, and she knew that he loved her in return. Now she knew that their feelings for one another were more than just that pale emotion. Love? No, it was so much more mystical and all-encompassing than that. She knew that he was the other half of her heart, her soul—that elusive something she'd been searching for unknowingly her whole life. For her, there could be no other love, no other lover, not ever. She knew, too, that it was the same for him.

She reached up to hold his face in her hands, and gazed deeply into his mesmerizing silver eyes.

"I love you, mate of my heart. I always will."

"*Zudontey*. The word for your male counterpart is *Zudontey*," he said with a ragged catch in his melodious voice, his eyes drinking her in like a man dying of thirst.

"I love you, *Zudontey*, more than I ever dreamed possible," she said, tears beginning to sparkle in her eyes.

"And I love you, *Sudontey*. I always have," he said before he gathered her in his arms for a soul-shattering kiss.

Though it was more than uncomfortable, almost painful, to embrace someone while sporting a small arsenal strapped to your body, it was even more so when both participants were thus armed. Rayven didn't care—she clutched at him fiercely and returned his kiss with equal fervor. She poured all the love, fear and desperation she was feeling into her kiss, and felt a strange sense of peace when he reciprocated in kind.

When they broke apart, Draco raised a shaking hand to stroke her cheek.

"No matter what happens, I will be with you always. If Fate should choose for me to die in this battle or any other, I will wait for you in the land beyond for all eternity."

"Don't talk that way. You'll live. You have to, for me and for our people. But if it's a vow you want from me I'll give it gladly and freely. If Fate should choose for me to die in this battle or any other, I will wait for you in the land beyond for all eternity."

They stood there for a long moment, the two of them, staring into each other's love-filled eyes as if they could do so forever more. Alas it was not to be, and before long reality intruded upon them.

The stone in Rayven's head began to thrum, and a sense of danger and warning swept through her body like wildfire. She almost lost her breath, and didn't even feel Draco's arms catch her to keep her from falling beneath the barrage of *Awareness* that took her in a heated rush. The strange attack lasted no more than a few seconds, but it was long enough for her people to gather closer around her. When she came back to herself, her eyes had gone flat and hard, and those who knew her best almost did not recognize the dangerous look they saw written on her face.

"They're coming. Make ready."

Five of the men went to find their posts along the outskirts of the *Neffan* grove. Draco had purchased several sniper rifles for this occasion, and these men were assigned to them. With them, two women also turned to leave; their assigned tasks were to use their newly acquired grenade and missile launchers at their enemies from the secrecy of the trees. Those men and women who remained behind were assigned to engage in battle out on the training field, where they would meet General Karis and his massive army. As one, the entire remaining group of Aware teleported to the fields beyond the grove, where their preparations of the day were awaiting them and the arrival of their enemies.

Chapter Thirty-Two

The training field was a barren stretch of sandy earth and dry grasses, just as it always was, but today it looked much different to Rayven and her people. Rayven stood at the head of the group of her gathered people. She looked at each of them in turn, trying to send them waves of reassurance and confidence, even though her own heart shuddered in fear. Surrounding her, towering over her, were the grim forms of Draco, Avator and Setiger. Even in the face of their possible decimation, the men looked strong and brave, and it gave her a small measure of comfort.

All of her people, every man and woman, stood tall and noble, their eyes and hair gleaming like jewels. They were beauty and grace personified, almost too blinding, too ethereal to gaze upon. Despite the obvious dangers, her people were willing to fight down to the last one—for their right to exist, for the continuation of their species, and for their right to be free. Rayven felt her heart swell with pride for them, and was glad to be with them now, whether their fate was total destruction or glorious victory.

Rayven felt the gathering darkness within her *Awareness*, the ever-present knowledge within her mind of the General and his movements. It took her in a cold rush, bringing with it the faint smell of old death. It would not be long now before their enemies arrived.

With a sudden whirl of wind, Onca appeared at her side, his face still bruised and torn, but the vicious slice down his cheek was stitched closed. His *Blazesword* was held drawn in his hand.

"You should be resting, or at most, hidden with the snipers. You'll only get yourself needlessly killed in your weakened condition."

"I will fight at your side, Highness. I can do no other."

Rayven wanted to argue, but she could see by the dark and stubborn look on his face that it would do her no good and only waste precious time. She smiled and nodded. Onca and Draco nodded to each other, and she knew with a sense of relief that at least there was no dissention among the friends over Onca's actions from the past twenty-four hours. It warmed her heart, and lifted a weight from her shoulders that she hadn't known was even there. If they were all doomed to die today, Rayven didn't want her last hours spent as a mediator between the men.

She turned and spoke to her people, needing to express her feelings to them before their time ran out.

"People of the Aware, our time is now. We die or we triumph, only the Fates can know which, but we will fight for what is right. We gather here, as a family, to face our enemies with might and justice on our side. No matter what comes to pass in these next moments, I want all of you to know how proud I am to be among you. You have all become my friends, my clan, my family, and my heart is gladdened by it.

"My father told me that a leader's duty is often a heavy burden, but I think in this moment that this statement is untrue. My duty to you is an honor and a privilege, and I am proud to be your Empress. I will give my all to live up to your expectations, and lead you to freedom this day, this I swear."

Her voice died on a sudden burst of wind. Rayven and her people straightened and turned as one to witness the opening of a vast black portal. Draco reached down and took Rayven's hand.

"Believe in yourself, *a grifa,* do not fight what you are. Just follow the plans we've set before us, and trust your power to do the rest. Call upon the elements of nature to aid you as we discussed. We will lend our power to each call until we have no more strength. We will follow as you lead."

Rayven nodded and squeezed his hand tightly in reply. The dark stone over her third eye heated and vibrated with suppressed power, and Rayven heard the whisper of her father's voice in her mind.

"Be strong, daughter."

Rayven's shoulders straightened, and she felt a thrum of her power wash through her. She calmed her mind, making her thoughts still and fade into the dark, tranquil pool of her subconscious. She pushed all worry from her mind and heart, and stood proudly as she faced the arrival of her enemy.

Out from the thundering blackness they came in a rush of fury. Hundreds of soldiers came pouring in a flood, wearing *Kiel* armor over their uniforms and firing their *lascannons*. Rayven's people fired their weapons in retaliation, mowing down row after row of Galactic soldiers with a barrage of bullets.

Las blasts struck out in a fury of explosive light, surrounding and infiltrating the ranks of the Aware. Rayven saw an Aware woman struck by *las-shot*, and almost shouted with relief when the woman's Kevlar vest deflected the blow. Rayven had hoped that the vests would serve such a purpose, and thankfully they now helped to even the odds just a little in their favor. Rayven felt a blast whiz by her shoulder and she calmly raised the mini-Uzi already in her hand to let loose a hail of bullets upon the nearest Galactic soldier, advancing farther into the fray as she did so.

Rayven lost sight of her people as she moved deeper into the sea of Galactic soldiers. Her destination lay ahead—the still-open gateway from which more and more soldiers streamed through. Her goal was to get close enough to the gateway to collapse it, trapping the advancing army in the tunnels of time and space, killing any who were unlucky enough to be caught within. Unfortunately, soldiers kept getting in her way, slowing her progress as she met each one and killed them.

She would have simply transported closer to the gateway, but there was too much chaos to attempt such a dangerous maneuver. Transporting so close to a raging gateway might result in catastrophe, one wrong move and she could be hurtled through time and space with no defense against any enemy that might be waiting on the other side of the portal.

Frustrated by her slow progress, she let loose a pulse of power, and her enemies fell dead before her, their bodies flying outward like the parting of the proverbial Red Sea, clearing a path for her to move through freely. *Kiel* armor was no protection against her onslaught of deadly power and raining bullets, something for which she was immensely grateful. With the Uzi in one hand, and her Hi-Power in the other, Rayven visited justice upon her enemies.

Rayven opened up a mental pathway to her people.

"Release the first wave of power!"

Rayven's command echoed in the minds of her people and as one they sent a pulse of energy to their Empress. Overhead clouds gathered blackly and thunder rolled. Rayven opened her *Awareness* to accept the rush of her people's wave of combined energy. It flooded her body in a rush of fire. Rayven closed her eyes and sent her power flaring outward.

"I call upon the power of Earth! Come forth and give us aid," she cried aloud and with her mind.

With a roar the ground beneath the fighting armies' feet rumbled and roiled. The earth before Rayven's feet flew upward and outward, sending the soldiers around her spilling to the ground. Great chasms opened, screaming and flaming like the gaping maw of hell, and soldiers by the hundreds were swallowed whole by the greedy earth. The land beneath Rayven and each Aware were the only islands of calm, as all around them the ground shook and belched beneath their enemies.

Rayven moved forward and was almost surprised to find that wherever her footfalls landed the earth became calm, letting her pass freely and unhindered. She shared this information with her people, using their now-opened psychic channel, and felt their acceptance of this phenomenon—it was no less than they had expected. Rayven broke into a loping run, firing her weapons at any soldiers who dared to come too near to her.

The hellish earthquake began to calm, and the intensity of the battle was resumed as more and more soldiers swarmed to attack. Rayven's guns were drained of bullets, and before she could reload or reach for another weapon she was met by an armored soldier wielding a *Blazesword.* Without pausing in her stride, Rayven brutally drove the muzzle of her Hi-Power into the man's throat, crushing his windpipe.

Whirling and dodging his widely swinging sword, she used her gun like a club upon his face and neck. She dropped her guns, freeing her hands, and spun in a blur of movement to come behind him. She took hold of his head between her hands and wrenched his neck with a strength that snapped his vertebrae with a sickening crunch. As the soldier fell to her feet, Rayven drew her Berettas with a flourish, and resumed her trek through the battlefield. Her time for regret over the carnage would come later, she knew, but for now she had to focus on the battle that raged around her.

Hoping her people had been given enough time to recuperate from their release of power, she called on them once more.

"*Release the second wave,*" she cried as more and more opponents moved to engage her.

Rayven felt her people's answering wave of *Awareness* take her, and welcomed the rush of energy into her a greedy gulp. She added her own power to the fray and sent it outward in a dizzying rush.

"I call upon the power of Air! Come forth and give us aid!"

A typhoon of raging wind swept out over the battlefield, raising dust and debris high into the night sky. All along the battlefield soldiers were lifted from their feet and sucked into the raging heavens until they disappeared into the atmosphere.

Only the Aware were safe from the unrelenting force of the hellish wind, free to fight those soldiers who were lucky enough to escape the hurricane raging all around them.

Rayven pushed her way through the flailing bodies of Galactic soldiers, firing into them without mercy. Rayven sensed a menacing presence at her back and turned to fire point-blank into the face of an oncoming opponent. The woman's face disintegrated under the tearing force of the bullets, leaving a husk of gore behind. Pushing the image from her mind, and fighting the urge to scream at the horror of her own actions, she turned back to run once more for the open gateway.

Chapter Thirty-Three

When at last Rayven reached close enough to the tunnel to focus her will upon it, she slowed and tried to gather her scattered wits. She felt the stone at her brow burn as she called upon her *Awareness*. Rayven holstered her weapons and threw out her arms, hoping that the physical movement would help her focus her power. She released a torrent of white-hot power in a stunning visual burst. Tendrils of electricity raced from her outstretched hands, curling and locking about the rim of the portal.

Rayven had never succeeded in closing a portal that had been opened by someone else. While training her in the ways of calling a silent gateway, Draco had told her that manipulating a tunnel that was not one's own was difficult in the extreme. He'd instructed her to try and close a tunnel that he'd opened and she'd never been able to do so. After half a day of trying, Rayven had given up on ever learning the skill.

Now, however, she knew that failure was not an option. Her people depended on her to close the doorway and stop the seemingly never-ending invasion of Galactic Soldiers. She hoped that there were many soldiers to be trapped within the tunnels of time and space. She didn't want to think about what might happen if the General recouped his losses and opened yet another portal after she closed this one.

As Rayven concentrated on closing the interplanetary doorway, she felt a burst of searing pain eat at her thigh, and almost lost her concentration. She didn't have to risk a glance down at herself to know she'd been hit by *las-shot*. The laser burst, burned and ate at her flesh, flooding her with pain. She tried to rally her failing strength and sent a new burst of energy into the portal.

Wind raged, thunder boomed, and Rayven lit up the surrounding area with the bright light of her power. Rayven pushed and strained, a mental and physical struggle, against the portal. The portal refused to close, and with a startlingly clear vision, Rayven realized why. She could "see" with her mind, through the vast distance of the portal and through to the other side. Rayven recognized three of the men who had been sent to fetch her from Earth. They stood around the portal, blue light racing from the *Chama* stones upon their brows, holding the gateway open with a stunning show of combined force.

Rayven was enraged that the men dared to use her people's sacred soulstones in such a manner against them. She let her anger fuel her power, and lost herself to the flood of *Awareness* that followed.

A pulse of blue energy streamed forth from her father's *Chama* stone and raced through the tunnel with unimaginable speed. Rayven pushed and pulled with her *Awareness* at the edges of the tunnel all the while, struggling to close the doorway even as more soldiers streamed forth from it. She didn't know how many people had passed through the tunnel already, and wasn't sure she ever wanted to find out. From the looks of things, her people were even more grievously outnumbered than they'd expected to be.

The racing stream of power emanating from her *Chama* stone raced through the tunnel, at last reaching through to the other side. The electric blue wave struck out against the three men who struggled against Rayven's efforts to close their gateway. Rayven "saw" with her mind the scene that unfolded, as her father's *Awareness* blasted into their bodies, sending them flying through the air. She couldn't countenance the thought of letting one precious stone remain within the clutches of her enemies, and with a thought she removed the silver bands from their broken bodies and brought the ill-used *Chama* stones back through the tunnel, sending them crashing to the ground at her feet.

Without the men on the other side of the tunnel fighting against her, Rayven's power flowed in a torrent and brought the portal closed with a deafening boom. Rayven stumbled from the shock of it, and ceased to funnel her power through her hands. She'd done it! The portal was closed. Rayven hoped fervently that there was no one on the other side of it that had a *Chama* stone capable of reopening the doorway. She didn't want to have to go through all that again.

Rayven's thigh burned and ached. She looked down and saw a blackened, bleeding furrow in her exposed flesh. She'd only been grazed by a *las-shot* from the look of it, but the pain of the wound was still intense nonetheless. She had to forcibly push the pain from her mind, lest it cloud her mind beyond anything but the need to ease the ache.

"You!"

Rayven's head jerked around towards the forceful cry. Her eyes widened as she saw the General's second-in-command approach her from the still-whirling wind and dust.

"You," he cried again, leveling a *lascannon* at her. "You're the cause of all this trouble, little Aware. I'm going to enjoy seeing you bleed."

She threw her arms up in a frantic jerk, sending the Glock handguns hidden in her shirtsleeves flying into her hands. Even with her preternatural speed, she was too tired, and too slow. She didn't even fire one round before the Lieutenant fired *las-shot* into her chest and stomach. The force of the blow sent her flying backwards, her feet shooting out from under her. She landed with a bone-jarring thud on her back. Through some miracle she didn't lose her grip on her guns, but the blow left her helpless—stunned.

Her vest had deflected the blows, but only barely. The Lieutenant had fired at close range, and the *las-shot* had eaten almost clean through the body armor to her flesh beneath. She tried to catch her breath and gather her scattered wits, but the Lieutenant stopped her with a heavy boot pressed to her chest. She was so tired and breathless that she couldn't think clearly, let alone strike out at him with her power, and for a terrifying moment she was forced to look up at him helplessly.

Lieutenant Devon leveled his *lascannon* at her face, his face a mask of hatred and dark satisfaction.

"Say hello to Death for me, little Aware."

Rayven found her voice.

"Why don't you greet him yourself, asshole?" she said before swinging her gun up in a movement too quick for his eyes to see. She shot him cleanly through the forehead right above the *Chama* stone headband he was wearing.

The Lieutenant looked at her for a stunned moment, a look of almost comical surprise on his face. He opened his mouth as if to speak and blood flooded from his mouth down onto his chin. His eyes glazed and he fell to the ground, pinning her body beneath his deadweight, his blood soaking her in a red gush.

Pain radiated in excruciating waves throughout Rayven's body as he fell upon her bruised chest, and she fell with a sigh into the swirling dark of her unconsciousness.

* * * * *

Draco sent his *Blazesword* slicing into the flesh of yet another opponent. Bodies littered the ground around him in bloody heaps, and still more and more soldiers came to meet the bite of his flashing sword. He sent a group of attackers flying backwards with a pulse of energy, crushing their skeletons with the force of his power. He whirled and danced in a flurry of preternatural speed, his sword singing through the air as he moved.

He'd long ago used up his supply of bullets, and had taken the *Blazesword* from the clutches of a fallen foe. Though the guns had proven a superb weapon against the *Kiel*-armored soldiers, he much preferred the heft of the blade within his hand. He had been unable to use his *Awareness* against the debilitating *Kiel* worn by the soldiers, until Rayven had opened her mind and connected to the mental pathway of their people. Amazingly it seemed that some of Rayven's immunity to *Kiel* was imparted to the Aware while she was connected telepathically to them. It was quite a useful skill to have, as the soldiers relied heavily on the armor's protection against their *Awareness.*

Suddenly Draco faltered, and he felt his connection with Rayven cut off as if by a switch. He reached for her and found only empty blackness. His heart stopped within his chest and he let loose and anguished cry that could be heard clearly throughout the battlefield. He fell to his knees and gasped into the dust. Within his mind Draco heard the anguished cries of his brethren as they realized the cause of his torment.

"The Empress has fallen! Empress Rayven is lost to us!"

The cry sounded through their telepathic connection, rising with the volume of their combined anguish and despair. In that moment the surviving Aware faltered, and many of their numbers fell under the renewed strength of the Galactic Army.

Draco wrapped his arms around himself, heedless to the animalistic cries of anguish escaping his lips as he sought desperately with his mind for some sign of Rayven's living presence. He perceived a vision of her lying dead under the body of a Galactic soldier, blood covering her still form. He cried his sorrow and torment into the night once more.

In his preoccupation Draco didn't see the soldier approach behind him. He likely would not have cared had he noticed, nor made a move to protect himself. His heart was broken and his spirit was unwilling to go on without his mate by his side. He didn't see the soldier brandish his sword with evil glee, but he felt the hot kiss of the *Blazesword* as it thrust into his body, piercing his already shattered heart. The soldier pulled the sword from Draco's body with a wet, sucking sound, and moved on to fight the other faltering Aware.

Draco looked down at his chest, his movements slow and dreamlike. He saw the dark red stain of his lifeblood seep down from the wound through his heart and smiled almost serenely. He was almost relieved to have his pain over Rayven's loss ended so quickly. He welcomed death gladly, and the chance to meet his mate in the land beyond life. He closed his eyes and lay down in the dust to wait for the cold embrace of death to close upon him.

"I'm coming, *Sudontey*. Wait for me as you promised." His voice was a lingering whisper released into the raging night.

Chapter Thirty-Four

Rayven felt a burning rush of fire in her veins and she awoke with a start, her heart pounding. She tried to move under the deadweight of Lieutenant Devon, her clothes wet with his blood. She felt the despondency of her people gnaw at her soul with tearing jaws. In an instant she knew why their spirits had flagged, and sent them waves of reassurance to convince them that she was alive and well. When she realized that Draco's presence in their psychic link had dimmed and weakened, she teleported to his side immediately.

Draco's body lay prone in the dust, his blood thick on the ground beneath him, seeming almost black in the darkness. Rayven cried out and dropped to his side, pulling his head onto her lap and crooning to him softly.

"*Zudontey*, my love, I'm here."

"I thought you were dead, *a grifa*." He coughed so hard that his whole body shuddered against her. Thick dark blood spilled from his mouth and Rayven held him closer to her as he bled his life away on the ground.

"Don't die, Draco, don't leave me. I cannot bear it." Her throat was choked by her tears. Her heart thudded with fear and panic, as she tried to stem the flow of blood with her hands upon his chest. With every beat of his great heart he lost more of his precious blood, and it pulsed out like a crimson river over her hands.

"I love you, my stubborn Empress. How I have longed these many years to tell you so. My world was empty before you came—silent and cold. I've never been so happy as when I first held you in my arms that day upon the beach. I will take the memory of you with me to the other side, and rejoice in the wonder of the time we've shared together."

"Don't do this—" Rayven's tears burned her cheeks and fell onto his face, "—You have to fight against it, Draco. You'll heal—you have to heal. *Please, please don't give up.*" Her despair was a painful, choking vise around her heart and soul.

Draco brought a blood-soaked hand up to her face, and his eyelids fluttered, his lashes beating against his cheeks as he fought to keep his gaze locked to hers.

"No! No! Goddamn it, I won't let you leave me," she screamed down into his face. "I love you, I love you…I've always loved you," her voice died away as her choking sobs robbed her of her ability to speak.

Rayven sent a plea outward to the astral plane. She begged the powers that be for the strength to save her dying mate. All that met her fervent cries was a dark and empty silence. Her heart stuttered in her chest. She couldn't let Draco die in her arms. She could not face life without him. He was her soul, her heart, her everything. She searched desperately for an answer, some clue, as to how she could save her mate from death.

"So, Rayven, it has come to this."

Rayven stiffened as General Karis' voice poured over her. She resisted the urge to ignore him…but her duty to her people weighed heavily upon her shoulders. If Draco were to die, then she would soon join him and gladly—but not before she had laid asunder all the enemies that had played a hand in robbing her of her mate. She laid Draco's head gently in the dust and rose, turning to meet the evil countenance of the General of the Galactic Commune.

"Not too fast, my dear. As you can see I've got a *lascannon* aimed at you, and I wouldn't want to see who was the fastest on the draw so to speak."

Rayven looked into his cold green eyes. He was wearing a gold band around his head, sporting a *Chama* stone over his third eye. Rayven instinctively realized whose soul the stone contained.

"You dare to use my mother's *Chama* stone against my people?"

General Karis flashed her an evil smile, which made her flesh crawl. His eyes sparkled with a mad light. "I see you recognize my stone. It makes my revenge so much sweeter, to know you realize just whose spirit is about to crush you and your pathetic army. You've fought the good fight, considering how outnumbered you are, but the tide has turned in my favor, and victory is a sweet flavor on my tongue."

"Why are you doing this?" Her voice was calm, but weary.

"Because I can. Because I like to see the once mighty Aware reduced to ashes strewn about a battlefield. Because I couldn't have your mother, and would see her dead before I saw her in your father's arms. Take your pick, it's all the same to me."

"You're insane."

"Believe what you want, but pretty soon you'll be dead, and I'll be alive. Insane or not, I win."

"Fuck you."

General Karis' eyes burned with a mad rage upon hearing her words.

"Die then, little Aware," he said just before he let loose a pulse of blue light shooting straight at her.

Rayven didn't think, didn't even hesitate. She raised her hand calmly before her and caught the flow of energy within her palm. There was no pain, and no discomfort. The blue wave of power felt warm, almost welcoming, and Rayven could feel the presence of her mother within its bright illumination. Rayven let the blue light seep slowly up her arm, and farther, until her body was encased in a soft blue glow.

General Karis roared his rage and fired his *lascannon* into the shining star that was Empress Rayven. The blast merely seeped into the light and infused it with an even brighter fire. He fired again and again, each *las-shot* following the course of the first—infusing Rayven's bright aura with a growing strength.

"H-How can this be?" stuttered the General. He clawed at the golden band encircling his head, but it would not budge, and he could not stem the flow of power that leapt from his *Chama* stone to Rayven.

Rayven didn't respond, wasn't even sure she could if she had wanted to. She opened her heart and let her inner power fully unfurl itself within her. She was blinded by a blue-white fire and her skin felt ready to erupt from the force of the energy she contained within her.

She reached out with her power, over the world, over time and space. She felt the sudden, startling presence of a thousand other Aware. Her lost brethren had heard her call and lent their power to hers across the vast distance separating them. She bound the power of their *Awareness* with her own, the force of it almost splitting her in twain. She raised her arms and face to the heavens and lost herself in the glorious blaze.

*****

Everyone on the battlefield ceased their struggles and watched as a swirling typhoon, a blue-white funnel of energy, began to rage around Rayven's glowing form. What few Aware remained standing, went still and lent their power selflessly to the whirling storm that held their Empress, leaving themselves exposed to any who wished to attack. But no one attacked, as all eyes remained glued on the blinding display in the middle of the battlefield.

The funnel cloud around Rayven widened and brightened. It rose thousands of feet into the air, illuminating the world as if the sun had risen above it. No one could separate the blinding light of the energy storm from Rayven's form now. It was as if they had become one, Rayven's physical self all but forgotten, to be replaced by pure swirling energy. Wind railed and screamed down upon the onlookers, raising a wall of sand into the atmosphere to commingle with the energy storm, which gained in intensity and ferocity.

As one, the Aware let loose a scream which echoed out over the battlefield, to the heavens beyond. The sound was deafening, even over the roar of the storm. Twenty-eight years of anguish fueled the force of the scream. The memory of a million lost brothers, sisters, parents and mates was shared with the cry, bringing low all that heard it. Every soldier on the battlefield was struck to their knees, their eardrums bursting with the force of the noise. The noise swelled impossibly louder, the power of it a tangible, physical thing.

The energy storm that enveloped Rayven pulsed outward once, twice, three times. A second elapsed, the calm before the storm. Then, with a deafening explosion, the storm of *Awareness* released itself fully, bursting like a giant dam, and laying waste to all that stood before it. The planet was engulfed in a blue-white flame.

Every man and woman in the Galactic Army was torn asunder in the midst of the explosion of power. Sand and wind whipped the skin from their skeletons, whittling their bones to dust. The force of the storm was so great, yet the Aware were unharmed by it. Soldiers fell into dust upon the ground, and still all the Aware felt was a hot breeze breathe over their flesh.

The maelstrom of Rayven's power only a few seconds, but it was more than long enough. With an audible whoosh, the energy storm receded, imploding in upon itself, until it drew back into the form of Empress Rayven. All eyes were blinded by flashing spots, but Rayven's form stayed clearly visible to the onlookers, as if her image had been tattooed onto their eyes. The sudden silence was deafening, as all waited breathlessly for what was to come next.

* * * * *

Rayven came back to herself with a start. She looked around with widened eyes at the scene that lay before her.

The battlefield lay empty. No trace of the General or his great army remained. Not one *lascannon*, not one fragment of *Kiel* armor, or swatch of clothing littered the barren field. It was as if the battle had never taken place. The only thing that broke the scene was the still image of her people, standing and staring at her expectantly.

Rayven looked away and searched for Draco. He lay still in the dust, his face ashen. With a sob she fell at his side once more, her surroundings fading from her consciousness. She shook his still form, calling to him with a voice that sounded strained, as if from misuse.

"Draco, Draco." Harsh sobs tore at her chest when he didn't answer or stir.

A blue twinkling caught the edge of her vision, and Rayven turned, eyes awash with tears, to find her mother's *Chama* stone resting on the ground beside her. The golden band was gone, decimated along with the General and his men. The stone winked up at her almost pleasantly, and she reached blindly for it. Not fighting the compulsion that washed over her, her heart dead from the rending loss of her mate, she closed her hand over the stone.

Searing, blinding pain raced from her palm and up her arm. The agony took her body in a drowning flood, leaving her gasping hoarsely. Sticky, hot blood poured freely from her hand as the stone burrowed itself into the flesh of her left palm. Rayven held the tortured limb up before her disbelieving eyes. She saw the flesh of her palm open like a mouth and bite down with bloodied lips upon the *Chama* stone. She felt a frisson of *Awareness* wash down from her father's stone in her forehead to commingle with a similar rush released from her mother's. The two powers met and held, infusing her with the strength to fight the overwhelming pain that tore through her.

Rayven felt a stirring in her mind, and heard her mother's voice speak softly to her.

"My daughter, I'm so proud of you. You have triumphed over our enemies. Be not sad at the pain of your fallen mate. Use my power to call him back to you. Bring him back and heal his wounds, *usuloon*."

Rayven didn't hesitate. She laid her bloodied left hand upon Draco's chest and sent a flood of power into his body. A pulse of soft blue light encased his quiet form, bathing the area surrounding him. An electric spillage of energy leapt and arced between Rayven and her mate, before spiraling up into the night sky. With a powerful pulsing throb, the light faded away a few seconds later. Nothing happened for several moments, and Rayven almost gave up hope that her power could call him back to her from the cold embrace of death.

All of a sudden, Draco's chest rose and fell, and his heartbeat sounded faintly in the quiet night. Rayven cried out in surprise, then laughed joyfully, her tears of relief and happiness spilling unchecked down her cheeks. She turned him towards her and cradled him once more on her lap. Draco opened his silver eyes, and Rayven had never been so happy to see anyone come awake in her entire life.

"Did I miss anything, *a grifa*?" he asked with a smile on his face.

Rayven laughed. "Not much, my love. Merely the decimation of an army."

"Is that all?" His look was teasing, and full of love for her.

Rayven bent over and laid her lips to his. They each tasted the salty wetness of her tears as she kissed him. She opened her mind to him fully, unreservedly, and gave him all of her love. He reciprocated, and she knew that all would be well between them and that he was truly healed. She could have held him that way forever, but she had her people to see to, and reluctantly pulled away from him after a few precious moments.

"Can you stand?" she asked softly.

Draco nodded and moved to do so, waving her offered hand away—stubbornly preferring to rise unaided. He was shocked and surprised at how easy it was to do so. He expected to feel at least a little pain after his brush with death, but he felt almost refreshed—as if he'd had but slept a restful sleep.

His last clear memories had been of his spirit rising to the astral plane, unfettered, and eager for the cold peace of death. He'd seen from a distance the image of Rayven's amazing display of power, but it had been as a dream. Looking about him now, at the battlefield empty of all enemies, he accepted the reality of what he'd seen.

"You did all this," he breathed in awe.

Rayven's dazed eyes met his. "I think so," she laughed nervously.

Rayven felt her mother's presence within her, and she moved instinctively to the nearest body of a fallen Aware. She laid her healing hands upon the man and a pulse of blue light encased him. A great heat plucked at her nerves and ate up her vision, and blindly she reached out to the next body beside her. She touched him and he was awash in a blue glow from her hand.

Following the compulsion that drove her, she moved on to the next body, and the next, and the next, stumbling and groping her way down the length of the battlefield. Draco came to her side and helped to support her when she would have fallen, and all the while she kept touching her hands to shoulders and chests and foreheads. She visited every fallen Aware, wounded, dying, or dead, and healed them with the power of her touch. Soon, all around the battlefield, men and women who had seemed dead or wounded beyond hope rose up from their deathbeds on the dusty ground.

As the blue heat receded from her vision, it took the last of her strength with it, and she slumped wearily against Draco. She lost the support of her own legs and Draco caught her as she fell, picking her up high against his strong and newly healed chest. She gave in to her suddenly overwhelming weariness, to the gathering dark that ate at her vision and swallowed the world. She fell asleep in his arms.

Chapter Thirty-Five

Rayven awoke to sunlight spilling warmly down through the purple branches of her *Bito*. She felt energized and well-rested—a feeling she'd almost forgotten over the past month—and wondered for a moment how long she'd slept. Her hand brushed along a bandage at her thigh, and with a rush she remembered the events that had transpired before she'd fallen asleep.

She must have made some sound because at that moment Draco's hematite head poked into her tent, as if he'd been waiting for her to awaken.

"You're awake, *Sudontey*," he said with a smile.

"Is everyone all right?"

"More than all right. We didn't lose a single one of our people during the battle, thanks to you and your healing touch."

Rayven looked down at her left hand and the *Chama* stone that lay twinkling there. "Truly?"

Draco nodded, looking happier than she'd ever seen him. His features were almost boyish from his joyous expression.

"Your touch bridged death itself and brought back those who had been lost to us. Those who were wounded were healed instantly when you laid your hands upon them. It was miraculous."

"What time is it?"

"It's past midday, but you have been sleeping almost three days now. You were very tired after expending so much energy."

Rayven started in surprise at his words.

"Three days!"

He nodded.

"Have you heard anything concerning the Galactic Commune? Do we need to fear reprisal for killing their leader?"

"Setiger just arrived from Varood with news. It seems the Galactic Commune is no more, collapsed without their army and leader. The planets that fell directly under Communal rule have each established temporary governments to rule them while the dust settles. It seems we're not the only group of people who were glad to be rid of the General and his armies."

"So we're in the clear? Free to come and go as we please without fear of being hunted down?"

Draco nodded and Rayven squealed excitedly, launching herself into his arms.

Draco laughed and hugged her fiercely against him.

"Are you ready to rise, *a grifa*?" he asked. "I will accompany you to the stream for a bath if you would like."

Rayven met the suddenly wicked gleam in his eyes with her own, and felt heat pool low in her belly. She gave him a blinding smile.

"Absolutely."

* * * * *

Rayven dunked her head under the cool water, washing the soap from her hair. When she surfaced, Draco dove from a rocky outcropping above her, causing her to laugh even as she sputtered from the wave of water that sluiced over her.

The bathing stream was really more of a large lagoon. It was nestled in a rocky outcropping, underneath a small waterfall that stood about thirty feet from the water below. Thick green foliage dotted the rocky landscape along the water's edge, giving the lagoon a closed-in feel. The water was blue, just as all water was on Hostis, and it cleansed the skin better than any shower or bath Rayven had ever had on Earth.

Draco broke through the surface of the water a few feet away and swam gracefully to meet her.

"You are beautiful beyond words, Sudontey, with your hair a wild, wet tangle around you," he said, reaching to gather her against him.

Rayven felt the demanding swell of his engorged cock brush against her stomach in the water. The blue liquid lapped gently at her breasts, just barely concealing her swollen nipples from his heated gaze. Draco reached down and brushed his hands over her full breasts, his fingers teasing at their erect crests. The tips of his fingers slowly circled the tight nubs, sending waves of exquisite pleasure coursing through her.

She gasped out his name on a wave of longing, and arched her breasts into his burning palms.

He coiled his arm around her narrow waist, raising her above the water and dipping his sleek head to her, taking her plump nipple into the hot, wet recesses of his mouth. He suckled hungrily, feeding on her like a man too-long denied.

Draco felt her tremble as he suckled her. He heard the gasping cries that escaped her throat, and the wanton noises moved him.

"Rayven...Rayven..." he panted against her flesh, his breath fanning over her hotly.

He moved to bring his powerful thighs tightly between her legs, wrapping her ankles around him with urgent, guiding hands. She bobbed in the water, her burning hot pussy brushing against his thick, hard cock. He sent the tips of his fingers scoring down her back and felt the answering spasm of her nails digging into the flesh of his shoulders. She shuddered against him and he brought his teeth gently to bear against her sensitive nipples. He released his hold on her with a wet, popping sound and moved his lips up to hers.

He kissed her with every ounce of passion he possessed, thrusting his tongue into the honeyed warmth of her mouth, licking at her teeth and the roof of her mouth. Rayven moaned into his kiss and returned it with equal fervor. He moved his hands down her back to cup her beneath her buttocks, bringing her more forcefully against him, and rubbing his cock sensually against her silky-wet pussy.

Rayven cried out at the heated feel of him between her legs. She shimmied against him with wanton abandon. She clutched at his shoulders and kissed him wildly, tasting him, drowning in the pleasure he gave to her. Her stabbing nipples brushed against the heated flesh of his muscled chest, sending waves of pleasure from her breasts to her mons on a heated rush.

"I can't take any more," she cried out against his mouth, her body writhing against him.

Draco chuckled and moved his hand between their bodies to press his thumb against her swollen clit. He deliberately sent waves of his scent flowing over her, knowing it would drive her wild. With an erotic movement of his fingers, he sent her plunging over the edge of orgasmic bliss. She screamed against his mouth, the hot pulsing flesh of her pussy trembling against his hands, drenching him in a burning wetness that felt far silkier and thicker than the water that surrounded them.

While her body still trembled from the aftermath of ecstasy, Draco positioned the head of his cock against her and thrust into her tight, wet sheath. He felt her close around him like a tight fist and threw back his head on a pleasure-filled groan.

"You feel like heaven, mate of my heart," he said to her, his voice tight with need.

Rayven bent her head to his neck and took his flesh in her mouth, closing her lips and teeth over his pulse hungrily. She suckled him there and felt him grow impossibly larger within her. He thrust forcefully in and out of her, rocking her erotically against him, knocking against the deepest recesses of her feminine core.

Her breasts bobbed in the water with their rocking movements, sending waves splashing out around them. She felt a wave of heat consume her and she moaned, moving her hips in a circular motion against him, sending ripples of pleasure through them both.

Suddenly Draco stilled, his nostrils flaring as if scenting something on the wind. His eyes were closed, but they opened now and his eyes clashed with hers. "You are fertile, *Sudontey*. I can smell the scent of your ripeness like the most fragrant of perfumes."

"You can smell that?" she asked, shocked, even as she pulsed and throbbed around his invading shaft, her body rippling pleasurably around him.

"You smell like a flower, heady and intoxicating. Your body is eager to accept my seed, and I find myself just as eager to gift you with it. What say you? Will you bear my babe or no?" His words were harsh, gritted out from behind clenched teeth as he strove to find some semblance of control.

"You would ask me, give me the decision, even though we desperately need to replenish our population?"

"I cannot impregnate you without your permission, my love. The choice is yours alone, and though it would please me more than anything else to know you carry our child's spirit beneath your heart, I will not fault you if you choose to wait. Much has happened in your life in a short span of time and I would not burden you with a pregnancy if you do not wish it."

Rayven's eyes filled with tears, and she thought of holding the spirit of their child between them, of gifting it with a physical being. A small boy that looked like his father, or a girl who would be just as stubborn as she was—the start of a family between them. She felt her heart swell with the thought.

Rayven rose up, bringing her lips to his in a soul-shattering kiss. "I love you, Draco. Give me your baby, our son or daughter. Give me this piece of you."

Draco pulled her to him tightly, unleashing a violent storm of passion between them. He kissed her mouth heatedly, almost bruising her with his lips, as he drove his body into hers over and over again. They bobbed in the water, oblivious to the splashes and waves they were making with their abandoned movements. Draco sent his pheromones bathing over her skin, releasing sizzling electric currents of his *Awareness* flowing from his body into hers.

"Oh, oh, Draco, yes!" she cried out brokenly against his mouth.

Draco drank in her cries greedily and gave her back his own, groaning and growling into her mouth as the force of his passion swept through him. "Come on, baby, let it come. I want to feel you milk me of my seed, I want you to make me drench you with it."

At his words, Rayven came against him with a heated wet throb, the muscles of her channel gripping and squeezing spasmodically around his thrusting shaft.

"Give me a child, Rayven," he cried brokenly as he flooded her with his glistening semen, his seed flooding through her on a rush of heated warmth.

They both cried out with the force of their passion, their voices rising and echoing into the sky above them.

Epilogue

Ysault Dimensional Plane
Sord Star System
Planet Hostis, Home of the Aware
Three months later

"These are the coordinates of each of our missing people, over seventeen hundred accounted for and ready to be brought home. As you know, those who have the power to open a gateway have already begun to arrive on their own, but there are many others who cannot achieve this and they must be fetched from their places of exile with your help."

Onca looked at the parchment Empress Rayven had given him. His face still bore the scars of his time spent among the General's men, but it in no way detracted from his handsome, masculine appeal. It merely served to make his face appear manlier, almost rugged. He turned to Rayven with a surprised look on his face.

"This shows that some of our people are on the planet Earth. That's where you were exiled, Highness."

"Yeah, isn't that just too nutty," quipped Ursus, ever eager to use Earth slang when she was afforded the opportunity to do so.

Rayven laughed. "I think you should go there, Ursus. Onca has been assigned to go alone, but I think you'd have fun accompanying him. You could take a few days and tour, eat the local fare, buy the local gear."

Ursus' jaw dropped, before she squealed with excitement and launched herself at Rayven, almost knocking the smaller woman down with the force of her embrace.

Onca's eyes rolled heavenward. "I can't believe I volunteered to do this."

Rayven pulled herself breathlessly from Ursus' hug to give him a cheeky grin. "You asked for it, Onca. Now where was I? Oh yes, Setiger, you are to travel to the planet Hevin, and Avator, you are to go to Tremor. And I think you'll be pleasantly surprised by what you find on Tremor, Avator. In fact I'm certain you won't believe your eyes, when you see what's waiting there for you."

"What do you mean, Highness?"

"You'll see soon enough."

Draco laughed at her words. He knew that Avator's mate, Lamiya, was exiled on Tremor Moon, having escaped there with a group of thirty others who had managed to open a silent gateway during the Great Massacre. Rayven had told him the story, and many others concerning their lost brethren. It pleased him to no end that he hadn't been the only one strong enough to escape the battle through a gateway—it relieved some of the guilt he bore for having failed to save more of their people. However, Avator knew nothing of Lamiya's survival, and it seemed that Rayven wanted it to be a surprise for him.

"It would appear that our Empress has taken on some of our more annoying traits. She's becoming more and more cryptic as the days pass," Draco said, flashing a grin to his perplexed brother.

Rayven rolled her eyes and once again addressed the group at large. "I've already sent out half a dozen other scouts to fetch those of us who are on other planets. Take as much time as you need, I don't want anybody to be left behind if they want to come here."

Draco came to stand behind Rayven, and put his arms around her, his hand coming to the place beneath her heart where their child's spirit lay nestled safely. Their small group had come to meet one another in the Gathering Tree, to decide who would go where to fetch their long-absent members home at last. And as much as Draco loved planning and discussing the arrival of their missing brethren, he felt too-long denied the pleasure of his mate's attentions.

He knew he couldn't toss her on the table and ravish her like he so desperately wanted to—for even though his people would think nothing of it, Rayven would have been mortified, and he didn't want her upset in her present condition. So he settled for simply cuddling her closer to him, and sending her waves of love and sexual arousal through their psychic bond.

"Do you have any questions?" Rayven asked the group, trying to ignore the wash of pheromones that traveled from Draco's body to hers long enough to end the impromptu meeting.

Onca, Setiger, Avator and Ursus all shook their heads. After a few more moments of trivial small talk, the group parted, eager to see their assigned tasks done.

When at last they were alone Rayven turned in Draco's arms. He had a small smile playing around his sensual lips, but his eyes were thoughtful. He reached out to toy with the white lock of hair that had fallen over her brow.

"Are you happy, my love? Do your duties as Empress weigh too heavily upon you in your weakened condition?"

Rayven gave an unladylike snort. "Not in the least. Why must I keep telling you that I feel fine? I'm not weak at all, in fact, I've never felt better."

"I still don't understand it. All of our women grow weak and tired during their confinements, and yet you still remain hale and strong as if nothing were different."

"I don't think the normal rules for our people apply to me, Draco, you need to remember that. I keep growing stronger and more powerful in my *Awareness* as the days pass, and my pregnancy isn't doing anything to slow it. I think you'll just have to get over the disappointment of being denied the opportunity to have me at your mercy."

He laughed at her teasing tone and kissed her lightly on the mouth. "It would have been nice, seeing you delicate and fragile during your pregnancy, but I should have expected that you'd be stubborn even in this small way."

Rayven moaned and rubbed against him, climbing up his body as if it were a tree trunk, and kissing his lips hungrily.

"Are you hungry for my body again so soon, *Sudontey*? It's only been a couple of hours." Draco tried not to laugh as he saw his mate's reaction to being saturated anew with his pheromones and lustful telepathic thoughts.

"You devil! You know damn well why I'm so frantic for you. God, I can't remember ever being this hot. Hurry, let's go back to our *Bito*. I have to have you or I'll burst—I don't know how much longer I can wait."

"I like it when you become demanding like this, love. Shall I give you the fucking you're begging for? Shall I fill you with my cock, over and over until you scream?"

"Fates yes! Take me, fuck me, I don't care. Just do it." Rayven squirmed against him in wild, helpless abandon.

"Let me fuck you as we levitate then, for I know how much you enjoyed it last evening. Your cries of fulfillment were loud enough to wake the entire city."

Rayven threw her arms around her mate and went weak with desire at his words.

"Ahh, at last you become delicate and fragile in my arms. I shall have to support us both then," he chuckled wickedly, sending them both shooting into the air.

"Not here! What if someone comes in?"

Draco sent her a mischievous look before he opened a mental pathway and spoke to their people as a whole.

"Please steer clear of the Gathering Tree. Empress Rayven and I are busy learning the wondrous joys of levitation."

Rayven's shocked gasp was swallowed up in Draco's kiss. She heard an echoing laughter from her people along their mental pathway, and her cheeks burned with her embarrassment. She didn't stay vexed with him for long, though, and before too many minutes had passed the Gathering Tree echoed with the sound of their wild passion.

As Empress Rayven clutched Emperor Draco's head to her breast, she sent out a wave of thanks to whatever forces had brought her here, helping her to find happiness and peace after a long life of running and hiding. She was at peace. She was happy.

She was home.

Enjoy this excerpt from

Beyond Illusion

Prologue

"I need you to fly to Vegas this afternoon and catch the opening of Vincent Darque's new touring magic show. Then I'll need the final review from you no later than press time tomorrow."

Ellie Waterhouse looked up from her cluttered desk to meet the eyes of her editor-in-chief. She winced at the look of pure determination written across the older woman's features.

"Lindsey, why don't you send Jon? He's really into the whole magician…thing. I bet he'd love to go."

"That's precisely why I'm not sending him. I've heard that this show of Darque's is going to be one of the best of its kind ever performed before an audience and I want to send my most down-to-earth, jaded and cynical—that would be you—reviewer out there to see it. I want our readers to know exactly whether or not this Vincent Darque is all he's cracked up to be. If he can convince you that his illusions are real, then you'll give him a fair review. Jon would just gush praise all over him and waste our readers' time."

"You sound like you already expect me to give Darque a bad review," she said, while quickly gathering her things. Ellie knew it was hopeless to try to talk her boss out of the trip, when the woman was so clearly bound and determined that she should go.

"I don't expect anything but that you write your review fairly and with your usual panache. Whether you like this show or hate it, it's one of the biggest events this year, and our readers will listen to you before they decide to part with their money to go and see this guy. You're all that stands between our readers and what could be a big waste of their time and money. Their fate is in your hands, my dear." Lindsey wiped away an imaginary tear.

Ellie laughed. "You always get delusions of grandeur when you drink too much coffee, Lindsey. Okay, I'll go. As if I have a choice. But could you please try to keep Jon out of my office while I'm away? The last time you sent me out he came in here looking for—well, he *says* he was looking for some paper clips—and he left my office in such a mess it took me the better part of a week to get it back to normal."

Lindsey looked around the room, at the paper-cluttered desk, the overflowing trash can and the various books and magazines that littered the area. "Yes. I can see how that type of thing could put you off your stride," she said, her voice laden with sarcasm.

"Don't be cute, Lindsey. This is my mess. *Mine*. In this delicately balanced ecosystem, I know where everything is and where everything goes. But when Jon or anyone else comes in and rearranges the ecosystem, it takes a lot of hard work to get it back this way."

"Oh, how my heart bleeds for you," Lindsey quipped cheerily. "Now, here are your tickets for the flight and for the show. Your flight leaves in an hour and forty-five minutes. You'll land in Vegas around eight o'clock. The show is supposed to start at nine, but I suggest you go straight from the airport to the hotel where the show is playing because there's bound to be a line a mile long. I've booked a red-eye flight for you out of Vegas at two in the morning, which, if you sleep on the plane, should afford you just enough rest to come in promptly at nine o'clock tomorrow morning. And don't forget—I want this review on my desk before the magazine goes to press tomorrow afternoon. Got it?"

"I got it, I got it. Sheesh, you'd think I'd know the procedure after working here for four years."

"Enjoy the show."

“Wow, *thanks.*” Sarcasm fairly oozed from her, but she hurried out the door just the same. It was nearly rush hour, and in the middle of Atlanta, Georgia, that could be an adventure all its own.

Chapter One

It was ten after eight when Ellie stepped out of her hired cab, and sure enough, there was practically a mile-long line that led into the Pharaoh's Tomb Hotel and Casino. On the billboard situated above the entrance to the casino, in gigantic neon lettering, the Pharaoh's Tomb proudly announced the opening show of Vincent Darque, Illusionist Extraordinaire and his new show, Darque Dreams.

Though it was well past sunset, Vegas seemed as bright as noon with all of the flashing lights of the strip twinkling down on her. The electric wonderland of Vegas had a magic all its own and Ellie suddenly found it difficult to tamp down on the rising excitement within her. She was about to see one of the most famous magicians in all the world, and even her skeptical heart raced at the thought. In these moments before the show began, all things were possible.

Purse and briefcase in tow, she crossed the busy street and joined the throng of fans that meandered out of the casino lobby. The crowd was like a living, writhing thing, moving to and fro with the shifting of thousands of appendages. After being jostled about for several moments, Ellie was more than eager to make her way into the casino's amphitheater, where the show would begin. There were a few disadvantages to being only five feet three inches tall, and one of them was the surety of being swallowed up in a large crowd of people, bumped and nudged around by those that were lucky enough to be taller than she. She rubbed at the sudden ache in her temples and tried to overcome the urge to snap at the people crowding around her.

It was total chaos as the doors to the indoor amphitheater finally opened and everyone rushed to their seats. Ellie glanced at the ticket in her hand and was relieved to see that the seats were assigned and that she would have a decent view of the stage. It took several long minutes for her to find her way to her seat, and by the time she did she was chagrined to find herself situated behind a much taller woman with very large hair. Luckily, hers was an aisle seat, and by leaning a little to her right she would be able to get a better, if somewhat crooked, view of the performance.

Ellie blew a stray lock of limp hair out of her eye and lamented the fact that she hadn't put her heavy tresses up before the show. The temperature of the monstrous room was a little warm thanks to the thousands of bodies that crowded within it, and not even an army of climate-controlling air-conditioning units was going to change that. She fanned herself with the program flyer she'd been given at the entrance, hoping that she would manage to cool off during the show.

The audience members chanted for their god of the hour, repeating the name *Vincent* over and over again like a mantra. Adults and children alike were anxious for the show to begin, and unashamedly vociferous in their demands. The noise was like thunder, beating its way through the theater. Ellie could feel it in her chest like a giant heartbeat, heady and thrilling.

Then the lights went out, and a deep swell of darkness swallowed the room. The audience quieted and held themselves in a collective state of readiness. The show was about to begin.

The sexy, erotic play of a double violin thrummed into the quiet stillness. The orgasmic release of music made the audience members gasp collectively, and Ellie was no exception. It was a greeting, a welcome into another world. A world where the rules that governed reality need not apply. The violin played for the audience, warning them to leave their skepticisms at the door and open their hearts to the magic that was to be revealed.

Ellie could have listened to the ethereal music all night.

But the show was only just getting started. The music swelled. The stage was flooded with lights and the audience was whipped up into a frenzy of cheering voices. Never before had Ellie seen such a spectacle. She wasn't sure what she had expected to encounter at this performance, but it surely wasn't the mass hysteria one would normally find at a rock concert. The crowd rose from their seats, stomping their feet and clapping their hands, almost drowning out the beautiful, mournful wail of the violin in their excitement.

Suddenly there came murmurs of awe from the crowd and, as one, they raised their faces skyward. Ellie couldn't help it, she too looked up and was shocked to see the figure of a man shoot through the air overhead. He was flying! Ellie tried and failed to see any harness attached to the man, though she knew that it was surely impossible that there wasn't some sort of suspension cable keeping him in the air.

The man flew at the stage, neatly turned a double somersault in midair, and dived toward it. He landed lightly on the balls of his feet as the crowd roared its approval, and bowed gallantly. When he rose, Ellie got her first clear look at his face. She caught her breath. It was Vincent Darque.

His name, Darque, fit him as no other ever could. He was tall, at least six-five, with black hair and black eyes. He was powerfully built, leanly muscled with strong, broad shoulders, a narrow waist and long legs. Dressed all in black, with shining calf-length boots, tight pants and a flowing poet-style shirt, he looked a lot like a pirate. The rakish silver hoop in his ear only added to the effect. His black hair was short, but unruly, and a thick lock fell over his right eye, making Ellie's fingers itch to run through it. She'd seen pictures of him in various magazines and on television specials, of course, so she'd expected him to be an attractive man, but nothing could have prepared her for the powerful presence he commanded on the stage.

Vincent raised his hands and motioned for silence. The audience immediately fell still and took to their seats once more.

"Thank you all for coming tonight. I am Vincent Darque and I've got some special things to share with you. Some of you have been to my shows or seen my television specials, while others of you are here with me for the first time. But I welcome you all equally and ask only that you let yourself enjoy the marvels that I will show you, suspend your disbelief for but a couple of short hours, and prepare to be…*amazed*!" With the last word he clapped his hand and four scantily clad women appeared, seemingly out of thin air, beside him.

For the next hour and a half, Vincent and his montage of beautiful women and burly stagehands created a show that was nothing less than visually stunning. Though she kept the thought firmly in her mind that there was a logical trick to every feat of magic performed, Ellie couldn't help but be amazed at some of the things she saw. The choreography and timing of the show alone made it worth the price of her ticket and she fully intended to give the event a glowing review.

After daring feats involving fire, swords, flight and even motorcycles, it seemed the show was drawing to a close. Vincent bowed on the stage amid roars for more from the audience before he motioned once again for silence.

"Friends, I hope you've enjoyed our show thus far, but rest assured, I've saved the best for last." Suddenly he clapped his hands together and…*disappeared*. There was no dramatic puff of smoke, no flash of light. He just…vanished. Completely and without a trace.

Amid the *ooohs* and *aaahs* of the crowd, Ellie sat grinning in her seat. "Smoke and mirrors," she muttered to herself, while mentally jotting down a checklist of observations for her to write about later in the review. She had to admit that Vincent was a showman unlike any other she'd ever seen, with a decided flair for the dramatic.

A stir through the audience alerted her and she glanced about. She jumped, alarmed, upon finding Vincent standing directly next to her seat.

"Ahh, my favorite part of the show. Audience participation. I find now that I'm sorry I waited so long in the show to do this, as I'm anxious to get to know some of you better." The crowed roared its approval. Ellie had a sudden, sinking feeling of dread in the pit of her stomach. "What's your name, my dear?" Her fears were confirmed as Vincent leaned down to ask her the question.

"Ellie Waterhouse."

"I'm sorry, but it seems I forgot to bring an extra microphone. Could you please lean over a bit and speak into mine?"

Ellie looked at the tiny microphone attached to his collar and pursed her lips. The devilish twinkle in Vincent's jet eyes made her even more uncomfortable. The rogue had planned this on purpose! She couldn't help but feel goaded by his behavior, and she leaned over—trying her best to ignore the strong, bronzed column of his throat and the deliciously masculine fragrance that rolled off of him—and repeated her name.

"Ah lovely, lovely Ellie, would you be so kind as to join me on the stage?"

"I don't think so, no," she answered, careful not to let his microphone pick up her answer.

"Don't be shy. I promise it won't hurt a bit."

About the author:

Sherri L. King lives in the American Deep South with her husband, artist and illustrator Darrell King. Critically acclaimed author of *The Horde Wars* and *Moon Lust* series, her primary interests lie in the world of action packed paranormals, though she's been known to dabble in several other genres as time permits.

Sherri welcomes mail from readers. You can write to her c/o Ellora's Cave Publishing at 1056 Home Avenue, Akron OH 44310-3502.

Why an electronic book?

We live in the Information Age—an exciting time in the history of human civilization in which technology rules supreme and continues to progress in leaps and bounds every minute of every hour of every day. For a multitude of reasons, more and more avid literary fans are opting to purchase e-books instead of paperbacks. The question to those not yet initiated to the world of electronic reading is simply: *why?*

1. *Price.* An electronic title at Ellora's Cave Publishing and Cerridwen Press runs anywhere from 40-75% less than the cover price of the exact same title in paperback format. Why? Cold mathematics. It is less expensive to publish an e-book than it is to publish a paperback, so the savings are passed along to the consumer.
2. *Space.* Running out of room to house your paperback books? That is one worry you will never have with electronic novels. For a low one-time cost, you can purchase a handheld computer designed specifically for e-reading purposes. Many e-readers are larger than the average handheld, giving you plenty of screen room. Better yet, hundreds of titles can be stored within your new library—a single microchip. (Please note that Ellora's Cave and Cerridwen Press does not endorse any specific brands. You can check our website at www.ellorascave.com or

www.cerridwenpress.com for customer recommendations we make available to new consumers.)

3. *Mobility*. Because your new library now consists of only a microchip, your entire cache of books can be taken with you wherever you go.
4. *Personal preferences are accounted for*. Are the words you are currently reading too small? Too large? Too...**ANNOYING**? Paperback books cannot be modified according to personal preferences, but e-books can.
5. *Instant gratification*. Is it the middle of the night and all the bookstores are closed? Are you tired of waiting days—sometimes weeks—for online and offline bookstores to ship the novels you bought? Ellora's Cave Publishing sells instantaneous downloads 24 hours a day, 7 days a week, 365 days a year. Our e-book delivery system is 100% automated, meaning your order is filled as soon as you pay for it.

Those are a few of the top reasons why electronic novels are displacing paperbacks for many an avid reader. As always, Ellora's Cave and Cerridwen Press welcomes your questions and comments. We invite you to email us at service@ellorascave.com, service@cerridwenpress.com or write to us directly at: 1056 Home Ave. Akron OH 44310-3502.

ELLORA'S CAVE
ROMANTICA PUBLISHING